Mark paused b[...] door, his grey e[...] of a sudden.

'You will be all right here by yourself? I hate to leave you like this in a strange place…'

'But you don't have any choice.' Laura smiled, appreciating his consideration when he must have more pressing things on his mind than her or Robbie. 'We'll be fine, Mark. Why shouldn't we be? We have everything we need after all.'

'Have you?' There was a strange note in his voice all of a sudden, an intensity to the look he gave her which made a tremor run down her spine. Laura stared back at him, her greeny-blue eyes the colour of a stormy sea.

He gave her a gentle smile before he suddenly bent and brushed her cheek with a kiss. 'Don't wait up,' he said softly, and then he was gone.

Jennifer Taylor lives in the north-west of England with her husband Bill and children Mark and Vicky. She had been writing Mills & Boon® romances for some years, but when she discovered Medical Romances™, she was so captivated by these heart-warming stories that she set out to write them herself! When she is not writing or doing research for her latest book, Jennifer's hobbies include reading, travel, walking her dog and retail therapy (shopping!). Jennifer claims all that bending and stretching to reach the shelves is the best exercise possible. It definitely beats step aerobics…

Recent titles by the same author:

TENDER LOVING CARE
GREATER THAN RICHES
FOR BEN'S SAKE
A REAL FAMILY CHRISTMAS

A VERY SPECIAL CHILD

BY
JENNIFER TAYLOR

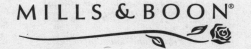

MILLS & BOON®

*All the characters in this book have no existence outside the imagination
of the author, and have no relation whatsoever to anyone bearing the
same name or names. They are not even distantly inspired by any
individual known or unknown to the author, and all the incidents are
pure invention.*

*First published in Great Britain 2001
Harlequin Mills & Boon Limited,
Eton House, 18-24 Paradise Road, Richmond, Surrey TW9 1SR*

© Jennifer Taylor 2001

ISBN 0 263 82289 3

*Set in Times Roman 10 on 10¼ pt.
03-0201-69350*

*Printed and bound in Spain
by Litografía Rosés, S.A., Barcelona*

CHAPTER ONE

'AM I GLAD to see you! Here…catch!'

Nurse Laura Grady deftly caught the plastic apron her colleague, Rachel Hart, tossed towards her. She shot it a quizzical glance, but before she had chance to ask what it was for Rachel had headed out of the office door.

Laura's greeny-blue eyes shimmered with amusement as she fastened the apron over her brand-new uniform dress. Nothing had changed, it seemed. There was still too much work and not enough staff to do it, from the look of things!

She quickly followed Rachel into the ward, realising that it was a relief to know that some things were the same as they had always been. It was her first day back at work after an absence of almost five years and she couldn't deny that she'd spent a sleepless night, worrying about how she would cope.

Would it take her long to slip back into the old routine? Could she cope with the demands of working in a new department? She had been a midwife in the maternity unit before she had left, so the children's ward was a new departure for her, although she'd worked in paediatrics before. Granted, she had taken a refresher course to brush up her skills, but what if she wasn't up to the job?

'It's OK, poppet. Don't cry. We'll soon have you cleaned up.'

Rachel's soothing tones cut through Laura's introspection and she gave herself a mental shake. This was neither the time nor the place to start having doubts!

She joined the ward sister at the side of the bed, her heart aching as she saw the expression on the child's wan little face. The little girl couldn't have been more than six years old and she was looking very sorry for herself.

Rachel turned to Laura and grimaced. 'This is Katie Watson. Admitted with recurrent urinary tract infection. We're going to check for any renal anomalies or scarring. And, as you can see, she's been very, very sick.'

'Too right!' Laura grinned commiseratingly at the little girl. 'Hello, Katie. My name is Laura and I have to say that I think I'd be sick if I had that cover on *my* bed. It's horrible!'

She cast a disparaging look at the bedcover, which was printed with a gaudily coloured jungle scene. Katie gave her a wobbly smile. 'I have a nicer one at home,' the child whispered shyly. 'It's got puppies on it.'

'Oh, wow, I bet that's really great. I love puppies, don't you?' As she was speaking, Laura began to strip the soiled cover off the bed, swiftly rolling it up to put it into a plastic laundry bag. She nodded as Rachel murmured that she'd be back in a moment as the office phone began to ring. Laura turned her attention back to Katie.

'So, do you have a dog at home, then?'

'Yes. But he isn't a puppy. He's three. I miss him.' Katie's lower lip wobbled ominously and Laura hurriedly set about distracting her.

'Three? So he's still only a baby really. I bet he does all sorts of silly things, doesn't he, like chewing your slippers?'

Katie shook her head, her huge blue eyes full of scorn. 'Sandy doesn't do that! He's a good dog. He sleeps in my room when I'm at home, on my bed.' The little girl looked momentarily unsure. 'You won't tell Mummy that, will you? She might make him sleep downstairs if she finds out.'

Laura shook her head so that her reddish-brown curls danced around her pretty heart-shaped face. Her hair was baby fine and the bane of her life, defying all her attempts to keep it neatly styled. She kept it cut short in an effort to tame it, but the soft curls seemed to have a life of their own most of the time.

'No, I won't tell her, sweetheart. It will be our little secret. Now let's get you cleaned up then I can remake your bed and you'll feel a lot better.'

Stowing the last of the soiled linen into the plastic sack, she carried it to the linen chute then filled a basin with warm water. She took it back and drew the curtains around the bed to give them some privacy as she set about stripping off Katie's nightdress. The child looked painfully thin once she was undressed, her arms like sticks and her ribs protruding. Laura sighed softly as she ran the damp washcloth over her emaciated little body.

Anorexia was a frequent symptom of urinary tract infection in children of this age, and a worrying one. She made up her mind to read through Katie's notes the minute she had chance to bring herself up to date with the case. She smiled as she dropped the damp cloth into the basin and reached for a towel. Already she was finding herself getting involved, which was a good sign. Maybe it wouldn't be *that* difficult to pick up the threads of this new job after all.

Once the little girl was dry, she found a fresh nightie in the bedside locker and popped it over her head. 'Right, that's better, isn't it? Now I'll go and find some clean bedding. And I'll make sure it's prettier than the last lot…promise!'

Leaving Katie giggling happily, she hurried off to find the linen cupboard. Rachel was nowhere in sight and the other two nurses on duty were busy with the morning's drugs round. Laura hesitated, wondering if she should ask them to direct her, but it seemed silly to make a fuss. It couldn't be *that* difficult to find where the supplies were kept, for heaven's sake!

After a few false starts she finally located the linen cupboard and hurried inside to hunt through the shelves for something suitable. In common with a lot of hospitals, Dalverston General steered clear of the usual starched white linen for use in its children's ward so that the shelves were stacked with brightly patterned covers and sheets bearing all manner of designs. However, it was on the very top shelf that Laura finally spotted exactly what she wanted—a bed set printed with playful grey kittens and fluffy yellow ducklings, which would be sure to appeal to Katie.

Hefting over the stool, she climbed up to get it, but she was just that bit too short to reach the shelf. She heaved a sigh of annoyance. It wasn't the first time she'd had occasion to rue her diminutive five feet two inches of height, nor would it be the last, but she refused to be beaten!

Standing on tiptoe, she made a grab for the linen then gasped in dismay as she felt the stool skidding from under her. She closed her eyes as she felt herself tumbling backwards, waiting for the inevitable to happen, then found them winging open again as a pair of strong arms fastened around her before she could hit the floor.

'Mmm, so my horoscope was right after all.'

'I…um. Pardon?' Laura took a quick breath as she struggled to make sense of what was happening. One minute she'd been heading straight for disaster and the next she found herself staring into the most beautiful pair of grey eyes she had ever seen. It was little wonder that she was having difficulty following what was going on!

'Uh-huh, in the paper this morning. I always read my horoscope, you see, not that I always believe what it says.' The grey eyes crinkled at the corners as the man chuckled softly. 'I tend to be a *selective* believer, you understand. But it does make me wonder if maybe I should take it more seriously when something like this happens.'

'Something like this…' Laura took another quick breath but it didn't seem to achieve any more than the first had done. The feeling of bewilderment certainly didn't decrease; in fact, it seemed to have grown worse. In desperation she tried a third breath for good measure and was rather pleased with the results when she found that she could manage a simple question at last.

'What do you mean?'

'That my horoscope said not to let *any* opportunity slip through my fingers today.' He chuckled again and she shivered as she felt the vibrations which rippled through her body. It was only then that she realised their position, that this man—this *stranger*—was still cradling her against his chest.

The realisation brought a flood of colour to her cheeks. She opened her mouth to ask him to put her down but he seemed to guess what she'd been about to say. He set her gently on her feet and stepped back, his grey eyes assessing as they skimmed over her.

'Anyway, enough of such nonsense. Are you OK? You haven't hurt yourself?'

There was genuine concern in his deep voice and Laura hastily shook her head. Now that the shock was beginning to wear off she was starting to feel like a fool. Why on earth hadn't she accepted her own limitations, instead of nearly causing an accident like that? A broken arm or leg certainly wouldn't have been a good start to her first day back at work!

'I'm fine. Thank you,' she replied stiffly, carefully avoiding the rather too astute gaze so that he wouldn't see how embar-

rassed she felt. Her averted eyes widened as she suddenly realised what he was wearing, which was very little, quite frankly.

Jogging shorts and a sleeveless vest in well-washed grey marl
weren't the *usual* clothes one expected to see in a hospital corridor, but he wore them well, she had to admit. She knew that
she was staring but she couldn't seem to stop as her eyes feasted
on the perfection of his well-toned physique. His skin was lightly
tanned, gleaming smoothly in the glow from the single bulb
which was all the linen cupboard boasted by way of lighting.
Laura's hands tightened against a sudden urge to run her fingers
over his skin to see if it really did feel as marvellously smooth
as it looked....

She dragged her eyes away from the powerful conformation
of muscles, deeming it wiser to let them home in on other aspects
of his appearance, and immediately noticed how tall he was. He
had to be at least six feet tall, with light brown hair which fell
casually over a wide forehead.

His features were craggy rather than conventionally handsome, she decided thoughtfully, very masculine with that square
jaw, impressive nose and chiselled cheekbones. However, it was
only when he spoke that she became aware of the silence which
had fallen while she'd been taking stock.

'Sure? It must have given you quite a scare....'

'I'm fine. Honestly,' she said quickly, uncomfortable with the
way she was acting. It had been a long time since she'd been
so aware of any man, and that she should be aware of this
stranger now shocked her, made her feel guilty. Surely the fact
that she had loved Ian so much should have made her immune
to any other man's appeal?

She took another of those pitifully ineffectual breaths then
gave him a cool smile, hoping that he would take the hint and
not pursue the subject. She had no idea who he was, but the way
he was dressed could be a clue. A lot of parents stayed in the
hospital with their children so it seemed likely that he was one
of them. The thought that he might be the father of one of her
new charges didn't ease her mind. What caring parent would be
impressed by a nurse who was incapable of getting linen off a
shelf without causing a near-disaster?

The thought made her inwardly groan, although she took care

not to let him see how flustered she felt. 'Anyway, thanks again. You saved me from a nasty tumble.'

'My pleasure.' He returned her smile readily enough but she could tell that he'd sensed her embarrassment. It made her feel more uncomfortable than ever that he should be able to read her mind so easily. However, before she had time to dwell on it, he reached up to lift the bedding off the top shelf and handed it to her.

'I think this was what you were after. Here you go.'

He gave her a last brief smile then left before Laura could thank him, his long legs carrying him swiftly along the corridor in the direction of the lifts. She stared after him for a moment then deliberately turned round and made her way back to the ward.

Katie was as delighted with the bed linen as Laura had hoped she would be, and chatted away non-stop as Laura set to work making the bed. She was glad of the distraction because it meant that she had no time to brood about what had happened. The encounter had disturbed her and not just because of the fright she'd had either. It was very odd.

Once the bed was neatly made again, Laura tucked Katie up then went to find Rachel. She was in the office, going through a stack of papers, and she grinned ruefully as Laura tapped on the door.

'Oh, hi! Sorry to drop you in it like that, Laura, but, as you've probably guessed, we're short-staffed. Anyway, come and sit down while I give you the introductory talk I had planned! Mark's not due for another half-hour yet so we'll have time to get you acquainted with how things are done around here.'

'Mark?' Laura queried as she sat down.

'Mark Dawson, our paediatric reg. You haven't met him?' Rachel frowned as she got up to plug in the kettle.

'No. David White was here the last time I visited the ward,' she explained.

'When Robbie was here as a patient?' Rachel smiled as she spooned instant coffee into two mugs. 'How is he? Up to all sorts of mischief, I'll bet!'

'How did you guess?' Laura laughed softly, her face lighting up as she thought about her son. 'He started school a few months ago and has been leading the teachers a merry dance!'

'He's a real little sweetheart. We were all sorry when it was time for him to leave us, and we don't say that about all our patients, believe me!'

Rachel sat down behind the desk and frowned. 'It's hard to believe that it's only a few months since that train crash you and Robbie were involved in, isn't it?'

'Ten months to be precise.' Laura sighed reminiscently as she thought back. 'I'm just grateful that both of us came through it all right.'

'You must be. It must have been a horrible experience for you, something you never expect to happen,' Rachel suggested with a shudder.

'It was. And yet in a way it had a postive effect because being in hospital afterwards made me realise how much I missed the job. It spurred me on to come back to work.'

'Really?' Rachel smiled. 'Well, it's great to have you back, Laura. I just want to say how pleased I was when I heard that you'd accepted this post. We've been desperate to fill the vacancy, and to get someone with your experience is a real bonus.'

'Thank you. To be honest, I didn't expect to be so lucky as to find a job with such marvellous hours.' Laura took a sip of her coffee. 'Obviously, I need to work but I also need to be there for Robbie. Knowing that I can work nine to five each day makes all the difference.'

'You can thank Mark for that because it was his idea,' Rachel explained. 'He's very keen to encourage women who have left nursing to start a family to come back. His view is that it's not only a waste of valuable training when they leave the workforce but a waste of their experience as well. That's why he suggested we adapt the hours for this post to suit someone with family commitments.'

'Well, I'm really glad he thought of it!' Laura grinned. 'I'm starting to like this Mark Dawson already and I haven't even met him!'

'Oh, give it a couple of days and you'll be like the rest of us…totally besotted with the guy!' Rachel laughed as she saw Laura's expression. 'Honestly! David was great and we were sorry to lose him when he moved to Glasgow, but Mark…well, Mark is something special. We all love him to bits. If I had to sum him up I'd say that he has to be one of the nicest, most caring men I've ever met—'

Rachel broke off and laughed as she looked towards the door. 'I bet your ears are burning. We were just talking about you!'

'Nothing bad, I hope?'

Laura felt a frisson inch its way down her spine at the sound of a familiar voice. Slowly, she turned, her eyes widening as she saw the man who was lounging against the doorjamb. The last time they'd met he had been wearing a lot less than he was wearing now, but the impact he made on her senses was much the same.

She took a quick breath but once again the giddiness was closing in, the same confusion and inability to think straight she'd experienced after he'd saved her from that potentially disastrous fall. As though it were happening in slow motion, she watched him walk towards her. He stopped a few feet away, his grey eyes holding a warmly intimate light which made her feel as though they shared some particularly delicious secret.

'We didn't get chance for introductions before, did we?' He held out his hand and smiled at her. 'I'm Mark Dawson and you must be Laura Grady. I'm very pleased to meet you, Laura. Welcome to the team.'

'So, that brings us to Katie Watson. How has she been today?'

Mark Dawson sat back in his chair and tossed the steel-framed spectacles he'd been wearing onto the desk. He'd spent the past half-hour running through the case histories of all the children in the ward, and Laura had to admit that she was impressed. Although he had their notes in front of him, he'd referred to them only briefly, obviously needing the most minimal reminder to bring each child's details to mind.

She found herself thinking back to what Rachel had said earlier, about him being the most caring man she had met, and silently agreed. It didn't take a genius to see that Mark Dawson was deeply committed to the welfare of his young patients.

She quickly focused her attention on what Rachel was saying, realising that she couldn't afford to let her mind wander. One of the reasons Mark had asked her to sit in on the meeting that morning had been so that she could get an overall view of the patients in the ward, and she had to admit that it had been a great help. She wouldn't like him to think that she wasn't taking full advantage of the opportunity, or that she wasn't as dedicated to the job as he so obviously was…

She frowned, wondering why it seemed so important that he think well of her.

'How was she when you left her, Laura?'

Mark's deep voice cut through her musings and she quickly retuned her mind to the question, not sorry to let that disquieting thought disappear. 'Fine. She was telling me about her dog and that seemed to cheer her up and take her mind off the fact that she'd been so sick, poor little mite.'

Mark smiled, his grey eyes lighting up with an inner warmth which was very attractive. 'Well, that's more than any of us have achieved so far!'

He laughed when he saw her confusion. 'Katie has been extremely withdrawn since she was admitted two days ago. We've all tried to get through to her but without much success. Obviously, you've managed to find something to spark her interest. Well done!'

Laura couldn't help smiling back at the genuine pleasure she heard in his voice. 'It was more luck than anything else, I imagine. I just happened to ask her if she had a dog and that was it.' She frowned. 'Is she worried about being in hospital? Is that why she's been so withdrawn, do you think?'

'That, plus the fact that her mother hasn't been in to visit her as yet.'

Mark's tone was grim as he got up. There was barely concealed impatience in the way he strode to the window then swung round. Laura felt a shiver dance down her spine as she saw the anger that darkened his eyes. Mark would never compromise where a patient's welfare was concerned, she realised.

'Katie's mother, Lisa, has found herself a new boyfriend, it appears. He's taking up most of her time so that she doesn't seem to have any to spare for her daughter.'

'How awful for the poor child!' Laura exclaimed, understanding immediately what had sparked his anger. 'I can't understand how any mother could put her own needs before those of her child.'

'No, I don't imagine you can,' Mark agreed softly. His eyes

held hers for a moment before he turned to Rachel, and Laura forced herself to concentrate once more, although it wasn't easy. There had been something in the way Mark had looked at her which had set every nerve in her body tingling, though she couldn't understand why

'Any luck contacting Katie's father?' he asked the sister.

'No. The number we had on file for him has been disconnected and, with Lisa not having been in to visit, I haven't had chance to see if she knows how to get in touch with him,' Rachel explained.

She turned to Laura with a sigh. 'This isn't the first time Katie has been admitted with UTI. She's been in once before, only her parents were still living together then. Since they split up things seem to have got progressively worse.'

'Worse? In what way?' Laura queried. However, it was Mark who answered. Coming back to the desk, he sat down again and ran his hands through his hair with weary impatience.

'Meaning that Lisa has been very lax about making sure that Katie takes her medication. We put Katie on a daily low dose of trimethoprim after her first admission. She was diagnosed with vesico-ureteric reflux when she was a baby, so we decided prophylactic antibiotics were called for.'

'I see. What grade of reflux was there?' Laura asked in concern.

'Two. Urine was flowing back into one of the ureters and the pelvis, but there was no dilation.'

'I see.' Laura frowned as she thought about what he'd said. It was rare for urine to flow back towards the kidneys but, unfortunately, some children were born with this problem. Instead of urine passing into the bladder and being stored there, it flowed back up the ureters. In Katie's case this meant that urine had actually refluxed into the complex system whereby her blood had been filtered of impurities.

'So how long did this go on for?' she asked in concern. 'And did Katie need surgery to sort out the problem?'

'Fortunately not. By the time Katie was two she'd stopped refluxing so there was no need for surgical intervention. However, she's had several bouts of UTI in the past eighteen months so her GP referred her to us for investigation. We de-

cided that she would fare better on long-term antibiotics to pre-
vent further infections.'

He shrugged but Laura could tell that he was as concerned as
she was. 'There was no problem when her father was around
because he made sure that she took the medication as per instructions. However, since he disappeared off the scene all that
has gone by the board.'

'What a shame! Doesn't Katie have any contact with him at
all now?' Laura asked in dismay.

'Not from what I can gather from her GP. He was so worried
when the mother eventually took Katie to the surgery that he
contacted me direct and asked if we could admit Katie immediately. And I'm glad he did.'

Mark's tone was hard. 'The poor kid has lost a lot of weight
in the couple of months since we saw her last. My main concern
now is that renal scarring may have occurred because of the
renewed bouts of infection. However, there's no way of knowing
until we see the results of the ultrasound scans and X-rays, which
are booked for the end of this week.'

None of them said anything. Laura suspected that they were
all mentally crossing their fingers that the scans wouldn't show
any irreversible damage to Katie's kidneys. It was hard to believe
that any mother could have been so careless as to put her child
at risk the way Katie's mother had done.

The beep of a pager suddenly broke the silence and Mark
grimaced. 'That's for me.'

He picked up the phone to respond to the call while Laura,
taking her cue from Rachel, got up to leave. It was obvious that
the meeting was at an end and suddenly she couldn't wait to get
down to the real nitty-gritty of the job. She had always loved
nursing and her natural enthusiasm had been whetted by Mark's
obvious commitment. Suddenly, she knew that her fears had
been groundless and that she would cope, and couldn't help smiling as the last of her uncertainty melted away.

'Why the smile? Not that I'm objecting, of course. A smile
like that could light up the dullest day.'

There was a teasing note in Mark's voice as he replaced the
receiver, but it didn't conceal the fact that he'd meant what he'd
said. Laura felt a ripple of heat spread from one small point in
the very centre of her being and radiate outwards, filling her

with a pleasure so intense that she was sure it must show. She rushed into speech, afraid that he might ask her what was wrong. Frankly, that was the last thing she wanted to have to explain when she wasn't sure of the answer herself!

'I was just thinking that maybe I would be able to cope with this job after all,' she blurted out. She saw Mark frown and immediately wished she'd stopped to think before saying that. After all, she didn't want him having doubts about her ability to do this job.

'Of course you can cope! Why on earth would you doubt it?' he demanded. He folded his arms across his chest and stared at her, and she shifted uncomfortably.

'Oh, well, I was just worried that I might find it difficult to slot in here,' she mumbled, then jumped as he gave an openly sceptical laugh.

'If I didn't know better then I would swear you were fishing for compliments, Laura Grady.' He suddenly reached out and gave her a gentle shake. 'You're going to fit in here *perfectly*! I can guarantee that.'

'Can you?'

Was that really her voice? Laura wondered shakily as she heard the husky tones which supposedly emerged from her lips. She swallowed then tried again, afraid that Mark would think her a complete ninny, acting this way. 'I mean, thank you. I appreciate your confidence, Dr Dawson.'

'Make that Mark, and there's nothing to thank me for. I knew as soon as I read your CV that you were the right person for this job. I was away on a course when the interviews were held but I'd already made my views clear to the board. I'm only glad that you accepted the post, Laura. Dalverston General needs nurses of your calibre.'

He gave her a last warm smile before he left the office. Laura stood right where she was before she realised that Rachel would be wondering where she'd got to. She squared her shoulders as she headed for the door. Mark's belief in her was something she intended to live up to…starting this very minute!

She left the office and glanced along the corridor just in time to see him stepping into the lift. Perhaps he sensed he was being watched because he looked round. Their eyes met in a look which sent a wave of heat washing through her before he disappeared from view, but the damage had been done already.

Laura went back to the ward, responding automatically as Rachel introduced her to the rest of the team, although a few seconds later she couldn't recall the names of either of the two other nurses on duty that day. Was it any wonder? the voice of her conscience whispered as she hurried off to begin the first task Rachel had set her, getting one of the children ready to go to Theatre.

She bit her lip as she cross-checked Daniel Glover's name tags against the theatre list, struggling to contain the feeling of guilt. Was she really such a shallow person that she could forget who and what she was just because an attractive man was kind to her? Was it really so easy to forget about Ian and the love they'd shared? She hoped not. But maybe she should remind herself of the facts before she made a fool of herself.

She was Laura Grady, a widow with a four-year-old son who suffered from Down's syndrome. No matter how kind Mark Dawson might be to her, it wouldn't change that and neither would she want it to.

All she wanted from life now was the chance to raise her son. She didn't need anything else because she'd had it all already...a wonderful marriage to a man she'd loved. The memory of the love she and Ian had shared was more than enough to see her through the coming years.

Wasn't it?

It was that last thought, which slipped in before she could stop it, that worried her most of all.

CHAPTER TWO

IT WAS a busy day but as the time flew past, Laura knew that she'd been right to accept the job. She enjoyed every minute, finding it easier than she'd dared hope to slip into the routine of caring for her small charges.

Rachel had explained that continuity of care was a key criterion in nursing the children, and that they worked a system whereby each nurse was assigned certain children who would come specifically under her care. Cutting down on the number of people who dealt with each child, helped them form a bond. It also meant that the nurses had far more input into the way each child was cared for, and that they were encouraged to make suggestions.

Laura was delighted when she discovered that Katie had been assigned to her care. Learning what she had about the child's background, had made her more determined than ever to do her best for the little girl. She made a point of stopping to speak to her whenever she got chance throughout the day.

Daniel Glover came back from Theatre and she had a reassuring word with his mother when she saw how anxious Mrs Glover was.

'Everything went extremely well, Mrs Glover,' she assured her, smoothing the sheet over the drowsy child. Although Daniel had come round from the anaesthetic, he was still a bit groggy. 'You'd be surprised how many children have this operation to clear up severe cases of glue ear like Daniel had.'

'That nice Dr Dawson said that but you can't help worrying, can you?' Josephine Glover sighed as she looked at her son. 'I just wish I'd realised sooner that Daniel had a problem with his hearing but, to be honest, he never acted as though he couldn't hear me.'

Laura smiled, determinedly quelling the flutter her heart gave at the mention of Mark's name. She hadn't seen him since that

18

morning as he hadn't been back to the ward. She'd heard Rachel telling one of the parents that he was tied up in a meeting but would be available the following day if they wanted to speak to him. The consultant paediatrician, Simon Martindale, was away on holiday so Mark was having to stand in for him, which must have increased his workload.

Now Laura forced herself to focus on Daniel's worried mother, rather than allowing thoughts of Mark Dawson to intrude. 'A lot of children adapt to the problem of impaired hearing, so you mustn't blame yourself. And, of course, the sticky fluid that collects in the middle ear and interferes with the movement of the eardrum and ossicles and causes the problem tends to build up over a period of time. Each time Daniel had a cold or respiratory infection the situation became worse.'

'I see. But what about these grommets the doctor mentioned—they won't cause Daniel a problem, will they?' Mrs Glover queried uncertainly.

'Not at all. They are just tiny tubes which the surgeon has put into the incisions he's made in Daniel's eardrums. Their job is to equalise the pressure on both sides of the eardrum so that the mucus can drain down the Eustachian tubes into the back of Daniel's throat. They usually fall out of their own accord once the hole in the eardrum closes.'

She smiled encouragingly. 'Quite frankly, Daniel is going to find life a lot easier now that he can hear what's going on!'

Mrs Glover looked a lot happier as she was left to sit with her son. Laura carried on with her work and before she knew it five o'clock had arrived. She went to have a word with Katie before going off duty, smiling when she saw the child's face light up as soon as Katie saw her approaching.

'I'm going home now, poppet. Is there anything you want before I leave—a drink of juice perhaps?' she offered, bending to brush the wispy brown hair back from the little girl's face. There had been a lot of parents in and out of the ward all day, but Katie's mother had been noticeable by her absence. Now Laura felt her heart ache as she saw the child look eagerly toward the doors as they opened to admit two more visitors, and her ensuing disappointment when once again her mother wasn't one of them.

'No, thank you. I'm not thirsty.' Katie managed a wan little smile as she glanced down at the bedspread. 'I really like these kittens, Laura. I wish I could show them to Daddy.'

'Maybe your mummy will phone him and ask him to visit you, then he can see them,' she suggested, mentally crossing her fingers.

Katie shrugged resignedly. 'Mummy and Daddy don't love each other any more. She won't speak to him when he rings up.'

Laura stifled a groan. It seemed so unfair that the poor mite should have to suffer because of her parents' break-up. However, there was little she could say so she gave Katie another warm smile. 'Right, then, sunshine, I'll see you tomorrow. Be good!'

Katie's wistful eyes followed Laura as she made her way down the ward. She paused to wave to the little girl then hurried to the staffroom. The other two nurses, who she'd discovered were called Jane Oliver and Cathy Williams, were already there, putting on their coats. They bade her a cheery goodbye, but didn't wait as they hurried out of the door. They'd disappeared by the time Laura got to the lift. They'd seemed friendly enough but there had been little time to chat as they'd been so busy.

Still, there would be time to get to know one another soon enough, Laura decided, pressing the button for the ground floor. She mustn't be greedy. Considering it had been her first day, it had gone far better than she'd hoped!

An icy wind greeted her as she left the hospital. It was the end of March and the weather still hadn't settled down. There had been a mixture of sunny days interspersed with heavy rain for several weeks. This part of northern Lancashire was very beautiful but the weather certainly wasn't predictable. However, even Laura, well accustomed to the vagaries of the climate, was surprised when it began to snow as she reached the end of the drive. She definitely hadn't expected that!

Drawing the collar of her coat up under her chin, she hurried towards the bus stop then looked round as she heard a car horn. It took her a second before she recognised the driver as Mark. He drew up alongside her and rolled down the window.

'Hop in and I'll give you a lift. Looks as though we're about to have a bit of a storm.'

He glanced at the sky and Laura realised that he was right as she followed his gaze. The sky had turned a funny yellowish-grey colour, indicating that there was a lot of snow on the way.

She hesitated a moment but the thought of the long walk she had once she got off the bus helped her make up her mind.

'Thanks. I appreciate it,' she said, sliding quickly into the seat as Mark thrust open the passenger door.

'No problem.' He gave her a lazy grin before he pulled out into the traffic. Flicking on the windscreen wipers, he focused his attention on the road as he headed towards the centre of the town. The snow was coming down harder now, sticking to the pavements and turning them white. He didn't say anything until he'd cleared the worst of the traffic which always built up at rush hour around the cenotaph. Then he shot Laura a smiling glance.

'Right, where to? I'm afraid I can't remember where you live from your job application.'

'I'm sure you can't,' she replied tartly. 'I wouldn't expect you to.'

'No?' He shrugged lightly, guiding the car expertly around a vehicle that suddenly pulled into the kerb without bothering to signal. He seemed unfazed by the manoeuvre and showed no sign of impatience as he drove past, but Laura suspected that tolerance was an intrinsic part of his nature.

She brushed aside that thought, realising that she was making judgements about him which she wasn't qualified to make.

'No,' she stated firmly. 'I'm sure that you must have read dozens of applications for the job, so why should you recall my details?'

'Hmm, modest, as well as everything else, Laura. Is there no end to your virtues, I ask myself?' He laughed to let her know that he was teasing, although there was the strangest gleam in his grey eyes as he shot her a glance.

'I shall take that with a large pinch of salt, Dr Dawson,' she retorted, struggling to find just the right note of levity and inwardly sighing with relief when he grinned.

'Oh, dear, I can see that I won't be able to soft-soap you, Nurse Grady.' He changed down a gear as they came to a junction, waiting while a lorry trundled past before he pulled out.

He continued in a more sober tone, 'Anyway, as it happens, I *do* remember a lot of what you wrote on your application. Want me to prove it?'

'That's up to you.' She shrugged, determined to let him think that it made no difference to her. However, she would have been lying if she'd tried to deny her surprise when he began to recite from memory.

'Your full name is Laura Anne Grady and you're thirty years of age—not that you look it, I might add.' He gave her another quick grin. 'You look a lot younger than that. It must be your hair.'

Reaching out, he ruffled the red curls at her temple then returned his hand to the wheel. 'All those baby-soft curls make you look more like a teenager than a grown woman.'

He carried on before she could say anything, not that there was much she could think of, Laura realised giddily. The action had been so…so *natural* that it would have been impossible to object. However, that didn't mean it hadn't disturbed her…

'You worked as a midwife on the maternity unit for two years before you left to have your baby.' He shot her a quizzical look and she struggled to concentrate. 'Didn't you think about going back there to work? Good midwives are always in demand.'

'I did. In fact, when I left to have Robbie I intended just to take maternity leave and go back as soon as I could.' She shrugged, unaware of the slightly wistful note in her voice. 'However, circumstances changed and I decided that returning to work wasn't an option.'

'Your son has Down's syndrome, I believe,' Mark said quietly. He must have seen her surprise because he smiled gently. 'Rachel told me all about him. Robbie seems to have won her over all right!'

Laura laughed at that. 'Robbie's a real little heartbreaker! And I'm not saying that because I'm his mother either. He simply loves people of all ages, shapes and sizes, and they seem to respond to him.'

'A very special child indeed, but, then, you so often find that children with handicaps are blessed in other ways.'

Laura felt her eyes fill. It hadn't been all plain sailing since she'd had Robbie—all too often she'd encountered hostility from strangers who had seen the child's handicap and been unwilling to look beyond it. But there had been no hesitation in Mark's assessment and it had touched her deeply.

'Thank you for saying that,' she said quietly. 'Not everyone can understand that.'

'I can imagine. Even in today's more enlightened times there's still a reluctance to accept people with disabilities. However, I imagine that Robbie himself is the best antidote to that kind of thinking.'

Laura laughed at that. 'You're right. Once people get to know him, any prejudices they have soon disappear. Robbie has the gift of making people love him!'

'As I said, a very special little boy indeed, and I can't wait to meet him.'

He looked expectantly at her and Laura took a shaky breath. It had been less a hint than a blatant piece of angling for an invitation, but why? Why would Mark be so...so *interested* in meeting her son?

She had no idea but it was obvious that he was waiting for an answer so she had no choice but to give him one. 'You...you'll see Robbie when you drop me off. He's at my friend's house. Claire offered to fetch him from school each day while I'm working when she collects her son, Ben.'

'Handy. I imagine good child-care arrangements are crucial for any mother who wants to return to work,' Mark observed.

'Exactly. That's one of the reasons this job was so attractive and why I'd decided that returning to the maternity unit wasn't an option. Babies have a nasty habit of wanting to be born at all odd hours of the night!'

Mark laughed. 'The theory being that they arrive *exactly* nine months after they were conceived.'

Laura laughed at that. 'I imagine that's something no one will ever prove! Anyway, knowing that I could work nine to five each day was the incentive for going after this job. I desperately need to work, of course, but Robbie's welfare has to come first.'

'Well, I for one am really glad that you applied for it.' Mark gave her a smile which sent a ripple of heat through her body. There was a slight pause before he cleared his throat. However, Laura wasn't deaf to the roughness in his voice all of a sudden.

'Anyway, you'd better direct me before we end up in Cumbria. In this snowstorm I don't think that would be wise, do you?'

Laura dragged her thoughts into some semblance of order and glanced out of the window. She gasped as she realised how hard it was snowing. 'I never thought it would stick like this!'

She peered through the glass, wishing that she'd been concentrating harder. It wasn't fair to have dragged Mark out of his way and then get them both lost!

She suddenly recognised where they were and sighed in relief. 'Oh, take the next turning on the right. Claire and Sean live in the third house down that road.'

Mark did as she'd asked. He drew up carefully alongside the kerb, although the car still slewed because already the snow was quite deep. 'Stay there and I'll come round to help you,' he ordered, getting out before she could protest.

Laura opened her door but before she could step out Mark was there, his hand fastening firmly around her elbow to steady her. 'Careful!' he warned solicitously. 'It's really slippery underfoot.'

Despite the warning and the steadying hand, Laura felt her feet skid from under her. She made a desperate grab for the nearest solid object and coloured as she found herself clinging to Mark. He grinned down at her, his grey eyes sparkling with amusement and something which made her heart beat faster than it should have been doing.

'Twice in one day? That horoscope was uncannily accurate, wasn't it?'

'Uh… It looks like it.' Laura struggled to hide her confusion as she cautiously straightened. She took a careful step back and held out her hand. 'Thank you very much for the lift, Mark. I do appreciate it.'

'I hope that wasn't intended as a brush-off?'

'I'm sorry?' She stared at him in bewilderment, not sure what he'd meant.

He gave her a lazy grin as his hand fastened around her elbow again and he steered her towards the house. 'You promised that I could meet Robbie, if you remember?'

'Oh, but surely you want to get off home? I mean, it's snowing so hard…' She stopped and took a deep breath then looked him squarely in the eyes. 'Why are you so keen to meet him, Mark? I don't understand.'

He returned her look steadily enough but there was puzzlement in the depths of his eyes. 'Neither do I understand why it's so important, Laura.' He reached up and brushed a snowflake off her cheek; his touch was so gentle that she shivered. 'I just know that it is.'

There wasn't anything she could say to that. Her heart seemed to be beating itself to death as she carried on walking towards the house on legs that weren't quite steady. She was glad of Mark's support because she doubted whether she could have managed the couple of yards which was all it took to reach the front door. Her mind and body seemed to belong to someone else at that moment, to someone she barely remembered from years gone by. It wasn't really *she* who was experiencing this feeling of excitement and anticipation, surely?

It was a relief when the door suddenly opened and a small, familiar figure came hurtling out of the house because once again she knew who she was—Laura Grady, widow and mother!

'Mummy! I's had tea with Ben.'

'Have you? Why, you lucky little boy!'

Laura swept her son up into her arms and hugged him. He planted a kiss on her cheek then promptly turned his attention to the stranger.

'Who's you?' he demanded.

'My name is Mark, Robbie. I'm a friend of your mummy's.'

It was all the cue the child needed. Reaching over, he grabbed hold of the man's neck and transferred his affections to his new friend.

Mark laughed as the little boy kissed him soundly on the cheek. He swung him up into the air, grinning at Laura as Robbie squealed his delight. 'A real little heartbreaker indeed.'

Laura nodded, not sure how to handle the way things were moving so fast. It was a relief when Claire suddenly appeared and started chivvying them indoors. 'Come in before you freeze to death, you idiots!'

Laura stepped inside, realising belatedly that she should explain Mark's presence. 'Mark…Dr Dawson, I mean, very kindly offered me a lift because it was snowing.'

Claire grinned wickedly as she glanced at the tall man with the child clinging around his neck. 'Dr Dawson, is it? Making sure your new staff show you due respect, eh, Mark?'

He grinned back. 'Something like that.'

Laura stared from one to the other, feeling a little like Alice must have felt in Wonderland. 'You two know one another?'

'Of course. Claire and I often ran into one another when she was in A and E. That was before she decided to do her bit for the world population, of course.' He shot a teasing glance at the other woman's very pregnant tummy as Claire laughed.

'One tries one's best! Anyway, it's great to see you again, Mark. Sean will be sorry he missed you. He's working late to-night,' she explained, then turned to Laura. 'You and Mark will have to come round one evening for a meal.'

'Oh, well, I—' Laura began but Mark cut her off.

'Sounds a great idea to me. You sort it out with Laura and I'll bring the wine. Fair enough?' He turned to Laura, ignoring her stunned gasp. 'Do you want to get Robbie ready to go? This snow seems to be sticking so we'd better not leave it too long otherwise Claire might end up with three unexpected guests for the night.'

'I...I'll get his coat.'

Laura hurried to the cupboard to fetch Robbie's blue quilted jacket and matching bobble hat. Mark was talking to Claire and Laura heard her laugh at something he said. She closed her eyes, willing herself to act calmly and rationally, but it wasn't easy to do that. Mark had made it sound as though they were an *item*, and that there could be nothing more *natural* than them accepting a joint dinner invitation!

A ripple of anger ran through her at his audacity and she squared her shoulders before going back to join them. She swiftly scooped Robbie out of Mark's arms and bundled the child into his jacket. Her goodbyes to Claire were no less swift and earned her a startled look, but that couldn't be helped. Claire, more than anyone, should have known how she would feel about going out on...on a date!

The thought was just what she needed to firm her resolve. As soon as Claire had shut the front door, she swung round. 'Look, Mark, I don't know what you—'

'I'm sorry. I sort of got carried away just now, didn't I?' He shrugged but there was no doubting that his apology was sincere. 'I should never have accepted that invitation on behalf of us both. I mean, why should you want to spend an evening in my company?'

Why indeed? Apart from the fact that he was the best-looking, nicest, most fascinating man she had met since…well, since she'd met Ian!

The realisation made her mind go blank so that it was impossible to answer the question, and she saw him grimace. 'Sorry! You don't have to answer that. I've already put you on the spot once tonight and that's one time too many.'

He swung Robbie up into his arms. 'Right, young man, let's get you home!'

He bent to open the car door but Laura hung back. 'We can walk home from here. It isn't far. It was very kind of you to drive me here but I don't want to take up any more of your time.'

He straightened slowly and there was a wariness about him all of a sudden. 'You aren't, but I won't force you to accept my offer if it isn't what you want, Laura.'

'I…I'm not sure if it's a good idea,' she admitted, then wished she hadn't said that because it was too revealing. Surely it wasn't wise to let Mark know how confused she felt?

'Neither am I,' he stated quietly, making her gasp. He suddenly grinned, making an obvious effort to lighten the mood. 'I think that makes us even, don't you? So, come on, let's be brave and take a chance. I'll drive you and Robbie home, you can thank me sweetly, then I'll leave. Sounds safe enough to me— how about you?'

Put like that, it seemed silly to refuse, especially as the snow was falling harder than ever. Laura nodded, waiting while Mark strapped Robbie into the back of the car. He seemed to think it was a huge adventure, going in a strange car, and made excited *vroom-vroom* noises as Mark started the engine.

It took about fifteen minutes to reach her house, thanks to the snow, and as soon as they drew up Laura knew something was wrong. She always left a light to come on in the sitting room, but the house was in darkness when they pulled up.

'Something's wrong,' she explained when Mark shot her a questioning look as she hurriedly undid her seat belt. 'I always leave a lamp on a time switch….'

'Give me the keys and I'll take a look,' he ordered in a tone that brooked no arguments. Taking the keys from her, he opened the car door then paused. 'You and Robbie stay here while I check things out.'

Laura shivered as a blast of icy air flowed into the car before the door was slammed shut. She watched Mark go inside the house, wondering fearfully what he would find. He reappeared a few minutes later, looking very grim.

She got out of the car and her legs felt like jelly as she went to meet him. The wind was whistling along the road, blasting icy flakes of snow into her face, and he exclaimed in concern as he turned her round so that he could shelter her from the onslaught of the storm.

'What's happened?' she demanded, her stomach churning with nerves.

'I'm afraid you've had a burst pipe. There's water pouring down the stairs from the loft,' he explained gently. He put his arms around her when she gave a small cry of dismay. 'I hate to add to the scene of woe but obviously water has got into the wiring, which is why the lights aren't working.'

'How…how bad is it?' she asked in a wobbly voice, and felt him shrug.

'Bad enough that you won't be able to stay there tonight. If you tell me where the stopcock is I can turn off the water, but you're going to need a plumber and an electrician to check things out.'

'That will cost a fortune! And then there's all the carpets… I expect they're ruined.' Laura shook her head but there was no escaping the pictures that were rapidly filling it. It had been hard enough just making ends meet in the eighteen months since Ian had died, so where she would find the money for expensive repairs she had no idea.

Numbly she explained how to turn off the water then went back to the car. Obviously, there was little she could do about the house that night. Instead, she had to concentrate on finding somewhere for her and Robbie to stay. She didn't have enough money for a hotel and she couldn't impose on Claire at such short notice….

'Right, there's nothing else we can do until the morning.' Mark got back in the car and started the engine, shuddering appreciatively as a blast of warm air flowed from the heater. He pulled carefully into the road and headed back the way they'd come.

Laura stared miserably out of the window as her mind raced

this way and that, so that it was a moment before she thought to question what was happening. 'Where are we going?'

'Home. To my house, that is.' He barely spared her a glance as he concentrated on the appalling road conditions. The snow had caught everyone unawares and many drivers had abandoned their cars, making driving even more hazardous for other road users.

'Your house? Oh, but we can't! I mean, it's very kind of you but I really can't impose like that. If you could just take us to…to…' She couldn't continue for the simple reason that there wasn't anywhere she could think of.

'The only place I'm taking you is to my house.' Mark's tone was grim all of a sudden and she shivered as she heard the underlying note of steel it held. It was obvious that once Mark made up his mind he wouldn't be easily swayed. 'In case you haven't noticed, there's a blizzard blowing and I have no intention of driving round this damned town all night long.'

His voice suddenly softened. 'Anyway, you won't be imposing, Laura. I'm happy to have you spend the night with us.' He gave the softest chuckle. 'And Lucy will be delighted to see you, I promise.'

Lucy? Was that the name of his wife or his girlfriend even? For some reason she hadn't given any thought to the fact that Mark might have someone waiting at home for him. Now it seemed to occupy her mind to the exclusion of everything else, even the worry about how she would find the money to pay for the repairs to the house. Yet why should the idea that Mark might be involved in a relationship seem so unpalatable?

Laura had no idea neither did she spend time trying to work it out. She had a feeling that she might find the answer even less to her liking!

CHAPTER THREE

'THIS is Lucy. Isn't she beautiful?'

There was a note in Mark's voice that made Laura suspect that he'd guessed what she'd been thinking on the drive to his home. She shot him a quick look, wondering if he'd deliberately set out to tease her, before it struck her how ridiculous that idea was. It was no business of hers if Mark Dawson kept a whole harem in his flat, and they both knew that!

She bent and ran a gentle hand over the white cat's silky fur as it began to twine around her legs, deeming it wiser to concentrate her thoughts on a safer subject. 'She's lovely. Have you had her long?'

'A couple of years. I found her wandering the streets close to where I used to live in Colchester. She was starving and had obviously been in an accident.' He shrugged. 'The vet said that eight out of ten pure white cats are deaf, like Lucy, and most end up getting run over because they can't hear traffic. I contacted the police but nobody came forward to claim her so I adopted her. She doesn't go out and seems content to be a house cat.'

He drew Robbie forward, crouching down so that he was level with the child. 'Come and say hello to Lucy, Robbie. If you stroke her like this...nice and gently...then she'll be your friend.'

Robbie tentatively ran his hand over the cat's fur then smiled his delight as Lucy began to twine around his legs. 'Pretty pussy-cat,' he said, kneeling down so that he could tickle her tummy as she rolled onto her back.

'She is pretty, isn't she? And she likes you. I can tell.' Mark hunkered down on his heels, gently running his large hand over the animal's fur. 'But Lucy is very special, Robbie. She can't hear, so that means that you must always make sure that she can

see you before you try to stroke her. Otherwise you might scare
her and she could scratch you. OK?'

Robbie nodded gravely. He looked up at Laura, a frown puckering his brow. 'Me special? Like Lucy?'

Laura smiled tenderly at him. Reaching out, she brushed the
cowlick of fair hair back from his forehead, feeling her heart fill
with love. Robbie's handicap was clear to see in his widely
spaced, slanting blue eyes and small features. He was bright
enough to notice the times when people stared at him or made
insensitive remarks. However, Laura had dealt with his bewilderment by explaining to him that he was very special and that
was why sometimes people reacted the way they did. Now, as
she looked at him, she knew that she no longer grieved for what
might have been. He was her child and she loved and accepted
him the way he was.

'Of course you are, darling. You're very special, just like
Lucy.'

'Right, then, young Robbie. If you want to stay here and play
with Lucy then I can show your mum where everything is.' Mark
smiled as he straightened, although it was impossible not to see
the compassion in his eyes as he looked from the child to her.

Had he guessed how hard it was at times, dealing with people's negative reactions, especially since Ian had died and she'd
had nobody to share the heartache with? she wondered
bemusedly.

The realisation stunned her. She had known this man for a
little over eight hours and already he seemed to understand so
much about her life that it scared her, made her feel vulnerable.
It was an effort to act naturally when he turned to her.

'Can I interest you in the grand tour? It won't take long, I
promise. The flat is your typical bachelor pad...bedroom, bathroom, sitting-room and what passes for a kitchen.'

She laughed, her fears melting away as she heard the rueful
amusement in his voice. She was letting her imagination run
away with her, something that happened rarely nowadays. Mark
must have seen through his work the difficulties parents of handicapped children often faced and that explained his perception.
There was nothing more to it than that!

'Why not?' she agreed lightly.

Leaving Robbie sprawled on the floor, she followed Mark into the sitting-room and looked round curiously, immediately liking what she saw. Mark's home had turned out to be the top floor of an old mansion house which had been divided into flats. In keeping with the proportions of the building, the sitting-room was huge, with a high ceiling and intricate plasterwork. It was rather sparsely furnished but it possessed a certain charm which stemmed from the eclectic mix of styles.

Laura's curious gaze skimmed over the claw-footed velvet sofa with its richly patterned throw, the brightly coloured floor cushions, the state-of-the-art CD player, and she smiled. Everything looked as though it were there for a purpose rather than just for show, and the room had a welcoming feel because of that.

'It's very nice,' she pronounced when she realised that Mark was waiting for her to say something. 'Very cosy and inviting.'

'I like it.' He grinned, his eyes reflecting genuine pleasure that she liked what she'd seen. 'I've been here for about five months now and I'm slowly buying bits and pieces to turn the place into a home rather than just somewhere to sleep.'

He put his hand to the back of her waist, guiding her back along the hall to the kitchen. It was as tiny as he'd said it was, little more than a narrow galley with cupboards on both sides and appliances neatly built in under the worktops. They both stood in the doorway and Mark laughed as he shot her a quick look.

'Not the sort of kitchen a dedicated cook would enjoy working in, especially if he or she was claustrophobic! However, as my culinary expertise extends no further than ''something'' on toast, it suits me fine.'

He gave the room a last, satisfied look then led her to the bathroom, which was very high-tech with its corner Jacuzzi and glass-enclosed shower. Laura made appropriately admiring noises but she could feel a little knot of tension bunching her stomach muscles as they made their way to the last room in the flat, Mark's bedroom. She paused in the doorway, unable to explain her reluctance to enter his private domain, although that didn't stop her taking a good look around.

A king-sized bed covered with a navy quilted comforter with navy and white striped sheets proclaimed that the occupant was male. The walls were pristine white with a few, very masculine prints of sailing boats in silver frames scattered here and there. The furniture was heavy, dark oak, from the huge dresser holding a silver-backed hairbrush and a single bottle of aftershave to the enormous wardrobe, the door of which was standing ajar.

Laura caught a glimpse of something light and floral through the opening, maybe a dress or a nightgown, before she hastily averted her eyes. Mark was a hugely attractive and personable man so it couldn't be surprise she felt to discover that he'd had a woman sharing his bedroom. So what did she feel, then? Disappointment? Regret? Jealousy even?

That last thought made her gasp and she hurriedly turned it into a cough as she saw Mark look at her.

'Are you all right?' he asked in concern, bending so that he could study her better.

'I...um. Yes. Just a tickle in my throat, that's all,' she said, quickly turning away. She made her way swiftly back to where Robbie was still playing happily with the cat and stooped down, using the few seconds grace to get herself under control.

What on earth was the matter with her? she wondered sickly, running a trembling hand over the cat's silky fur. How could she be jealous at the thought of the woman in Mark's life? He was a colleague, that was all, someone who'd been kind enough to offer her a lift and then take pity on her when she'd needed a bed for the night. That was the only claim she had on him...the only claim she wanted to have!

'Right, I suppose I'd better rustle up something for us to eat. Or do you want to put Robbie to bed first?'

Laura carefully smoothed her face into a suitable expression as she stood. 'I think it might be better if I settled him down first. He's usually in bed by seven and it must be that now.'

'Almost half past, actually.' Mark grinned as he saw her surprise. 'I know. I hadn't realised how late it was either. It must have taken longer to get here than we thought, thanks to the snow.'

'Then if you don't mind I'll give him his bath....' She stopped and grimaced. 'Drat! I haven't brought anything for him to sleep in.'

'How about a T-shirt of mine—would that do?' Mark immediately offered, bending to ruffle the child's hair.

'If you're sure you don't mind....' she began hesitantly, but he shook his head.

'Of course not. I'll fetch one.'

He headed off to the bedroom, leaving Laura to take Robbie into the bathroom and start filling the bath. Robbie was reluctant to leave the cat at first but, once he'd seen the gleaming corner tub, he soon forgot about her. Laura had the bath filled and was swishing a little of the bubble bath she'd found on a nearby shelf into the warm water when Mark appeared carrying a white T-shirt.

'Will this be OK?' He dropped the T-shirt onto the cork-topped stool then leant over and pressed a switch on the wall beside the bath. The water immediately began to foam as the Jacuzzi jets clicked into action and Robbie clapped his hands in glee.

'Me in! Me in!' he demanded eagerly, holding up his arms to Mark so that he could be lifted into the frothing water.

'Ready... Steady... Go!' Mark swung him up into the air, then with infinite gentleness deposited him in the tub. Hunkering down on his heels, he scooped a handful of sudsy water over the child's tummy. Robbie squealed with delight and promptly retaliated by scooping up two fistfuls of water and dousing Mark with them.

'Robbie!' Laura was horrified when she saw the water soaking into the front of Mark's white shirt, but he just grinned.

'Oh, that calls for reprisals, young man. Just you wait!' He scooped up another massive handful of water, although Laura noticed that he let most of it escape through his fingers before he shot it at Robbie. It was obvious that he was completely unconcerned by the soaking he'd had and that he was enjoying himself almost as much as the little boy was.

Laura felt a lump come to her throat as she watched them playing together. It was so poignant to think back to the times when she'd watched Ian playing in much the same way with his son. It hurt to realise just how much Robbie was going to miss out on now that his father was dead.

'Are you OK?' Mark's gentle voice broke through her reverie and she summoned a smile.

'Yes. I was just thinking...' she began, then stopped, wondering if she should share her thoughts with him. Surely memories like that were too personal to confide to someone who was virtually a stranger? However, it seemed that once again Mark had guessed what had been on her mind.

'About Robbie playing with his daddy?' Mark's tone was so gentle that tears pricked her eyes and she had to blink hard to stop them from falling. She nodded mutely, knowing that it was pointless trying to deny it.

Mark sighed. 'You must miss him a lot, Laura. I knew from your application that you were a widow, and then Rachel told me that your husband died about eighteen months ago. I'm really sorry.'

She took a deep breath, feeling strangely comforted by the quiet words of condolence. She had grown to dread the sympathetic expressions of sorrow in the months after Ian's death, but it was different when Mark said it because she sensed that he really meant it. Odd, but it felt as though some of the cracks which had appeared in her heart after Ian's death had begun to heal all of a sudden...

'Thank you,' she said quickly, refusing to let her mind go any further, because thoughts like that were wrong. She couldn't forget about the man she'd loved just because of a few kind words!

Laura's hands shook as she took a towel from the rack then immediately wondered what to do with it. She stared at the soft blue terry in a daze. Suddenly, she didn't know what to do or say anymore. She had got through the past eighteen months by focusing on the need to take care of Robbie. Now, with Mark temporarily usurping her role, she felt at a loss. It was a relief when he took charge and gave her something positive to do.

'How about we swop? I'll finish bathing this young horror while you make us something to eat?' He grinned up at her, his grey eyes gleaming with laughter, although she wasn't blind to the compassion they held as well.

'There's method in my madness, in case you're wondering. I'm sure you're a much better cook than I am *and* it means that Robbie and I can see who can get the wettest.'

He scooped up another handful of sudsy water, laughing as Robbie crowed with excitement. Laura hesitated but it was obvious that her son was perfectly happy in Mark's care.

'Fine by me,' she declared, doing her best to rise to the occasion. 'But don't blame me if you come off worst!'

The words were hardly out of her mouth when Robbie let loose another deluge of water. She found herself laughing quite freely as Mark splutteringly wiped foam out of his eyes. 'You *were* warned!'

She quickly scooted out of the bathroom as he threatened her with a handful of suds, and was still smiling as she made her way to the kitchen. She opened the fridge and found eggs and bacon, a couple of tomatoes which wouldn't have won any prizes, plus half a dozen shrivelled mushrooms, then set to work to the accompaniment of a lot of excited squealing from the bathroom. However, it was only as she was lifting the bacon out of the pan that she realised how right it felt to be doing this, how very natural.

She put the pan back on the hob and took a deep breath, but her heart was thudding so hard that she couldn't think straight. Maybe that was for the best. Perhaps thinking about why she should feel like this would do more harm than good. For one night at least she should forget about the problems, forget about the rights and wrongs, the yeses and the nos. She would take the next few hours as they came…

'That was delicious! I don't suppose you'd like a career change? I'm in desperate need of a chief cook and bottle-washer….'

Mark sighed comically as Laura smilingly shook her head. The eggs and bacon had been devoured in an appreciative silence which had been like balm to her overwrought nerves. Not only had she been able to eat the meal but she'd actually enjoyed it. She had been right to let events run their own course rather than worrying, she decided as she got up to take their plates to the sink.

'No, you did the cooking so I'll do the washing-up. It's only fair.' Mark got up as well and gently but firmly pressed her back into her seat. Laura shivered as she felt the pressure of his fingers against her flesh. Suddenly she was back to square one. Obviously, it was one thing to decide to let fate dictate what happened and another to carry it through!

She scrambled to her feet, nearly knocking over her stool in her haste. They had eaten at the breakfast bar, a neat little contraption which pulled out from the wall and provided seating

facilities in the tiny kitchen. However, with two of them standing, one of them being exceptionally large, the room seemed to
shrink even more.

She bit her lip as she tried to edge past Mark to plug in the
kettle. 'Excuse me,' she muttered, turning bright pink as she felt
her breasts rub against the solid wall of his chest. He had dis-
carded his wet shirt in favour of a T-shirt in a washed-out shade
of blue which made his eyes look like grey velvet in contrast. It
was obvious that the garment was an old favourite because the
cloth had that worn-thin softness about it that provided little
barrier between their two bodies.

Laura felt the flush on her cheeks deepen as her nipples
peaked in response to his nearness. She quickly slid past him,
keeping her face averted as she filled the kettle and plugged it
in. Mark didn't say anything as he carried on clearing the table,
but there was less comfort in the silence than there might have
been.

Had he noticed her response just now? she wondered miserably. And had he been as shocked by it as she was? After all,
they were little more than strangers so surely anyone would have
been shocked to witness such blatant evidence of her...her
arousal!

Her hands shook so hard as she took two cups out of the
cupboard that one of them slipped through her fingers and shat-
tered as it hit the tiled floor. Laura gasped in dismay, her eyes
filling with tears as she saw what she'd done.

'I'm sorry! I don't know how that happened. Oh, I don't know
what to say...' She knelt down to gather up the shards of china,
wincing as she inadvertently knelt on a jagged piece.

'Leave it! It's only a cup, Laura. It doesn't matter.' Mark was
beside her in an instant, his face full of concern as he saw the
blood welling through her tights.

'Hell's teeth, you've cut your knee!' he declared, drawing her
upright with a firm hand under her elbow. Pulling over one of
the kitchen stools, he urged her to sit down. 'Sit there while I
get the first-aid kit from the bathroom.'

'There's no need...' she began, but he was already hurrying
from the room. She rested her head against a cupboard and
closed her eyes, overwhelmed by misery and shame. How *could*

she have felt like that just now? How could she have responded that way to any man apart from Ian?

'Here we go.'

Mark came back with a green plastic box and placed it on the worktop close to where she sat. He opened the lid then turned to her. 'Can you take those tights off so that I can check there's nothing in that cut?'

Laura's face flamed at the thought of undressing in front of him, but before she could assure him that the injury was too minor to require any attention he added smoothly, 'I'll just get some water to clean it with while you do that.'

Deliberately, he turned his back on her as he went to the sink and ran water into a basin. It was obvious that he'd sensed her reluctance to comply with his request and was giving her some privacy.

Laura got up and quickly wriggled the ruined hose over her hips then tossed the small bundle into the waste bin. 'I...I'm ready,' she said in a quiet little voice, studiously avoiding Mark's gaze as he looked round.

'Good.' He came back with the basin and knelt in front of her. Lifting her foot onto his bent knee, he carefully examined the cut. Laura bit her lip, trying not to think about how it felt to have his cool fingers skating so gently over her warm flesh, but it was impossible not to be aware of the sensations they aroused. Flashes of heat and cold raced under her skin, making her alternately shiver and burn as if with fever. When he looked up it was an effort to feign indifference as she saw the concern in his eyes.

'It really hurts, doesn't it? Damn!'

He seemed to blame himself for her injury, which was so unfair that she hastened to reassure him. 'It isn't too bad. And it was my own fault for being so clumsy. I'm not usually so careless, Mark. I'm sorry.'

'It doesn't matter...honestly!' He shook his head to emphasise the point so that a swathe of light brown hair fell across his forehead. Laura was instantly transported back to that morning when they'd met. In a flash she recalled how he had looked dressed in those shorts and vest, his skin gleaming with health and vitality over those perfectly toned muscles.

Her breath caught so that she had to make a conscious effort to exhale, and missed what he said. Why was she so aware of him? she wondered sickly. Why did he arouse feelings in her which no man apart from Ian had been able to do?

'Laura?'

He touched her lightly on the hand and she flinched. He'd obviously noticed her abstraction but he made no mention of it as he quietly repeated the question. 'Are you allergic to adhesive dressings?'

She shook her head so that the red-brown curls danced around her face. 'I...I don't think so,' she muttered, barely able to think straight in her confusion.

'Hmm, a very professional answer, Nurse Grady.' His mocking tone was the best antidote in the world and she tried harder to concentrate.

'Then, no, I'm not allergic to adhesive dressings or anything else, apart from strawberries,' she declared firmly.

'Strawberries, eh? I shall have to bear that in mind.' He took a square of adhesive dressing out of the box and peeled off the backing then pressed it over the wound.

Laura bit her lip, refusing to let the question slip out. Asking *why* Mark should need to remember her allergy was a definite step in the wrong direction! After all, what difference could it make to him what she could and couldn't eat?

She curbed that thought, climbing down from the stool as fast as she could after he'd finished. 'Thank you,' she said stiffly, fixing a polite smile to her lips.

'My pleasure...if that's really the right way to phrase it in the circumstances.'

His rueful expression made her laugh, and suddenly it was easier to shuffle her thoughts into some sort of logical sequence again. Maybe she was reading too much into the way she'd responded to his nearness just now. It was a well-known fact that certain stimuli produced predictable physical responses. It had been less a question of her reacting to *Mark* as a person than the natural response of her body.

It was an explanation that made far more sense than any other so that she was able to relax as Mark made coffee and suggested they drink it in the sitting-room. Laura led the way, opting for one of the floor cushions in front of the fireplace rather than the sofa. Mark had lit the fire while she'd been tucking Robbie up in bed, and it gave off a welcoming heat. Although the flat had central heating, the room was so lofty that the air still felt chilly and she held her hands out appreciatively to the blaze.

'Here you go.' Mark put one of the cups on the floor beside her then curled his long legs beneath him, Indian fashion, as he sank onto a cushion. He took a tentative sip of his coffee then set the cup aside when he found it was too hot to drink. The glow from the fire lit his face as he bent forward, lending the very masculine lines an unaccustomed softness.

Laura looked away, uncomfortably aware that her heart was beating faster than normal. Suddenly, the explanation for her odd behaviour seemed less than watertight. It was a relief when Mark spoke in a purely practical tone and she could focus on something other than her own whirling thoughts.

'Right, I suppose we'd better get organised now that we're fed and watered. You're due in work at nine, I know, but what time do you need to drop Robbie off at school?'

'Eight-thirty. But I have to pick up Ben on the way. I offered to take both boys to school, seeing as Claire is collecting them. Much to Robbie's delight.'

She smiled, finding it easier once she was concentrating on her son. 'Robbie adores Ben—it's a real case of hero-worship. Mind you, he's crazy about Claire and Sean and just about everyone else he regards as a friend!'

'He's a very outgoing child from what I've seen, which is a real bonus.' Mark smiled back. 'It's thanks to you that he has such confidence, Laura. You're doing a great job with him.'

'Thank you,' she replied, deeply touched. She shrugged, not wanting him to guess how much it had meant to hear him say that. 'But I can't take all the credit. Robbie is naturally gregarious, it's part of his nature.'

'So many Down's children are like that, you find. They have this wonderfully *accepting* attitude towards other people and seem to blossom with the right kind of attention.' He frowned thoughtfully. 'I take it from what you just said that Robbie goes to the local infants school?'

'Yes. They've been marvellous with him. Ian and I were worried about what would happen with his schooling. We went to see the headmaster and explained the situation to him, and he immediately offered Robbie a place.' She smiled with real pleasure. 'Mr Brook, the headmaster, says that the other children are learning a lot by having Robbie in the school.'

'That's great! You don't often get that kind of enlightened thinking, even today. Far too often schools focus on the problems of teaching a handicapped child alongside his peers.' Mark reached over and squeezed her hand, his delight obvious in the warm smile he gave her.

'With this kind of support, Robbie is going to have the best start possible in life, isn't he, Laura?'

'Except that he no longer has a father.' The words came out before she could stop them and she saw Mark's eyes darken with pain.

'I'm sorry,' he said contritely. 'That was incredibly crass of me. I didn't mean to hurt you, Laura.'

His hand briefly tightened around hers before he abruptly stood up. Walking to the window, he pushed back the velvet curtains and stared out into the night. It was obvious from the slump of his shoulders that he was berating himself for the remark, and Laura knew that she had to say something.

'I know you didn't, Mark. Please, don't go blaming yourself when there's no need,' she said quietly.

He turned to look at her. 'Are you sure about that?' He shrugged when he saw her puzzlement. 'It's obvious that you aren't over your husband's death yet.'

It was said very flatly and without inflection, yet she felt there was more to the statement than first appeared. However, before she could decide if it was wise to question him further the phone rang.

Mark grimaced as he strode towards the hall. 'I hope that isn't what I think it is!'

He came back a few minutes later, shrugging on his coat. 'It was the hospital. There's been an accident on the outskirts of town. A minibus ferrying a dozen kids home from a trip to the theatre has skidded and overturned.'

'How dreadful! Are any of them badly hurt?' she asked in concern, immediately getting up.

'Nobody seems to know for sure as the ambulances haven't got to the scene yet.' Mark's tone was grim. 'God knows what they're going to find in conditions like these.'

Laura shivered. 'It's such a dreadful night. I take it you're needed?'

'Yes.' Mark grimaced. 'Second night on the run, too. I got dragged out of bed in the early hours of this morning as well. With Simon being away, we're a bit pushed at present. Still, I managed to snatch an hour's sleep in the doctors' lounge, before going out for a run to get rid of the cobwebs, so I can't complain.'

An hour's sleep didn't seem very much, bearing in mind that he'd been on the go all day long as well, Laura thought. She followed him out to the hall, waiting while he collected his keys and mobile phone from the table. He paused before opening the door, his grey eyes concerned all of a sudden.

'You will be all right here by yourself? I hate to leave you like this in a strange place....'

'But you don't have any choice.' She smiled, appreciating his consideration when he must have more pressing things on his mind than her and Robbie. 'We'll be fine, Mark. Why shouldn't we be? We have everything we need after all.'

'Have you?' There was a strange note in his voice all of a sudden, an intensity to the look he gave her which made a tremor run down her spine. Laura stared back at him, her greeny-blue eyes the colour of a stormy sea.

He gave her a gentle smile before he suddenly bent and brushed her cheek with a kiss. 'Don't wait up,' he said softly, and then he was gone.

'Take care...' The words floated after him but she wasn't sure if he'd heard them as he disappeared at a run down the stairs. Laura closed the door then made her way to the sitting-room window in time to watch him driving away. The snow was still falling, a thick curtain of white that veiled the countryside and made it look strangely unfamiliar. Maybe that was why she felt disorientated all of a sudden, as though she'd stepped out her own safe little world into another.

She let the curtain fall into place, shivering as she went back to the fire. The flames were blazing up the chimney and sending out a comforting heat, but she couldn't seem to get warm. She didn't want her world to change in any way! She had Robbie and her memories and now a job that she knew she was going to love. She should be content... No, she *was* content!

Laura turned away from the fire in sudden impatience and caught a glimpse of herself in the mirror over the mantelpiece. For a moment she didn't recognise herself. Was that wild-eyed stranger really her?

She closed her eyes then immediately knew that had been a mistake as an image began to form in her mind's eye. Giving a murmur of dismay, she struggled to erase it, but it refused to go. Suddenly, she could see in perfect detail the expression on Mark's face as he'd bent to kiss her just now....

She opened her eyes abruptly, refusing to let her mind go any further. Switching off the lights, she made her way to the bedroom. Robbie was fast asleep, his small form no more than a bump in the huge bed. Laura stared down at him, letting all the love she felt for this very special child fill each and every corner of her heart. So long as she had that to fill the emptiness then she had more than enough. Mark had been wrong. There was nothing she needed—or wanted—to make her life complete!

CHAPTER FOUR

THE sound of the phone ringing woke Laura the next morning. She glanced at her watch as she scrambled out of bed and was surprised to discover that it had gone seven. She hadn't expected to sleep so well in a strange bed but she'd dropped off the moment her head had touched the pillow.

She hurried into the hall, shivering as she picked up the receiver. Although the central heating was switched on, there was a chilly draft flowing around her bare legs.

'Hello?' she answered, tugging the hem of the T-shirt down as far as it would go. She'd had no choice but to help herself to one of Mark's T-shirts to sleep in, and hoped he wouldn't mind. She made a note to take it home with her to wash before it hit her that she might not be going home that day if her house was in such a bad state. The thought of what she and Robbie would do if it turned out to be uninhabitable filled her with panic. Accepting Mark's hospitality for one night, that was all well and good, but she really couldn't put upon him for any longer!

'Laura, it's me. Are you all right?' Mark's voice brought her back to the present with a rush and she took a steadying breath. Once she had time to think things through she would come up with a solution, she told herself firmly.

'Fine, thanks. How are things at the hospital?'

'Pretty grim. It's been a rough night, as you can imagine. We've got three of the children in Intensive Care and four others on the ward. The rest were able to be taken home by their parents.'

'But no fatalities?' she queried hopefully.

'The teacher who was driving the minibus, I'm afraid. She didn't make it.' Mark's tone was filled with regret. 'It was Rachel Hart's sister, too.'

'No! Oh, poor Rachel. How awful for her. Is she there at the hospital?' Laura exclaimed in dismay.

'We finally persuaded her to go home about an hour ago. Tom Hartley, the surgical reg, took her.' Mark sighed heavily. 'Her niece, Bethany, is one of the injured children. She's had the lower part of her right leg amputated.'

'I don't know what to say.' Laura felt her eyes fill with tears at the thought of what her colleague must be going through. It put her own problems very much into perspective. 'Poor Rachel. She's going to find it very hard to come to terms with what's happened.'

'She is. The fact that Rachel's sister was divorced and has had no contact with her ex-husband for several years means that Rachel is going to have to find the strength to help Bethany through all this as well. It isn't going to be easy either.'

Mark paused reflectively, before getting down to the reason he was phoning. 'Look, I'm afraid I'm not going to be able to get back to drive you into work. One of the kids is still causing us some concern and I need to be here.'

'That's all right,' Laura hurriedly assured him, although she couldn't help wondering how she was going to get Robbie to school and herself to the hospital. Not for the first time she wished she had a car, but the cost of running one was just too much for her limited budget.

'We can catch the bus if you tell me where it stops—' she began, but Mark interrupted.

'There's no need. I've booked a taxi to pick you up at a quarter to eight. You'll probably need to collect some stuff from your house so just tell the driver where to take you. He can drop you off at the hospital after you've taken Robbie and Ben to school.'

Laura's heart quailed at the thought of how much it would cost to make such a lengthy trip by taxi. However, before she could tell Mark that she preferred to go by public transport someone called him.

'I have to go,' he said quickly. 'I'll see you later.'

The line went dead. Laura slowly replaced the receiver, trying not to think how the pounds were going to add up as the taxi's meter ticked away. It had been kind of Mark to think about ordering her a cab, especially as he must have been rushed off his feet all night long. She couldn't ignore the warm feeling it gave her to know that he'd been thinking about her...

She made her way swiftly back to the bedroom, refusing to let that thought take root. Robbie was awake and happily bouncing up and down on the bed as though it were a trampoline. He gave a cry of delight as he saw Laura and hurled himself towards her.

'Me jump, Mummy!'

She kissed his sleep-flushed cheek. 'I can see that! But I don't think Mark would appreciate you bouncing all over his bed, young man. Come on, down you get.'

She swung him down onto the floor, taking hold of his hand as he went to scramble back on the bed. 'No, Robbie. That's enough,' she said firmly. 'We are guests in Mark's house and we have to treat his things carefully.'

Robbie eyed her consideringly, obviously trying to decide how far he could push her, but in the end he accepted that she was serious and nodded gravely. 'Carefully,' he parroted.

'That's right. So come along, let's go and have some breakfast then we can get ready for school.' She led the child out of the room and soon had him happily settled with a bowl of cereal. The cat came in as she was putting the milk away in the fridge and began curling hopefully around her ankles, making odd little mewing noises.

'Do you want some milk, too, Lucy?' she asked, then grinned at her own foolishness. However, it was obvious that the cat had a very good idea what was being offered. She ran to where her dish and water bowl were kept and waited patiently while Laura poured a little milk into the dish. Robbie crowed with delight as he watched the cat lapping up the milk.

'Clever pussy-cat,' he declared, scrambling down from the stool to go to her. Laura just managed to stop him as he reached out to stroke the animal.

'Remember what Mark told you last night? You must make sure that Lucy can see you before you stroke her. If you scare her she might scratch you,' she warned.

'Uh-huh.' Robbie crouched down, waiting patiently until the cat looked up and saw him. Only then did he gently run his hand over her fur, earning himself another odd little murmur, which was what obviously passed for a purr.

Leaving them playing together, Laura went and had a quick shower, wishing that she could spend longer under the powerful jets. Mark's bathroom was a vast improvement on her own. She and Ian hadn't got round to updating the antiquated fitments before his death, and since then she hadn't had the money to spend on any improvements.

She sighed as she turned off the water and picked up a towel. It seemed unlikely that she would be able to afford them now in view of the damage the burst pipe had caused!

By a quarter to nine that morning, Laura was in the staffroom, taking off her coat. The taxi had arrived promptly and had ferried her around, making what would otherwise have been a very stressful journey relatively straightforward. The snow was several inches thick in most areas of the town, and buses were running only along selected routes.

Laura had no idea how she would have managed if Mark hadn't ordered the taxi for her, and was grateful for his thoughtfulness. However, the fact that he'd apparently paid for it himself in advance was something she intended to sort out with him. She didn't want to be in his debt any more than she already was!

Conditions at her house had been no better or worse than she'd expected. The carpets were ruined and it was going to take a lot of work to get the place straight. Given the choice, she would have loved to have moved out while someone else sorted out the mess but that just wasn't possible.

Claire had immediately offered to have Robbie to stay when Laura had explained what had happened. She'd urged Laura to stay as well, but she'd refused. Someone had to do the clearing-up, although she quailed at the thought of setting to after a hard day at work. Still, at least she had some of the problem solved, which was a relief. So long as Robbie was taken care of then she would manage well enough herself.

The night staff were still on duty when she went into the ward, which was strange. Madge Bickerstaffe, the night sister, greeted her with relief. 'Thank heavens! I had this horrible feeling that we might end up having to stay all day if you lot couldn't get into work! Jane only made it a few minutes ago. She had to walk because there were no buses along her route. And Cathy phoned to say that she'll be here as soon as she can dig her car out of her driveway.'

Laura smiled at the fervent welcome. 'Nice to be needed!' She looked round the ward, immediately noticing how crowded it was with the addition of extra beds. 'How are things here, anyway?'

'A lot less hectic than they were at ten o'clock last night, I can tell you.' Madge grimaced, her pleasant face shadowed with sorrow. 'You heard about Rachel's sister, did you?'

'Yes, Mark told me this morning,' Laura confirmed, without stopping to think. She coloured as she saw the quizzical look Madge gave her, although the older woman didn't question her further.

'Such a tragedy. She taught both my two lads and they thought the world of her. A wonderful teacher and a devoted mother, too, from all accounts.' Madge looked down the ward, her eyes alighting on a bed close to the door. 'That poor kid is going to have a lot to come to terms with in the next few months.'

'I believe she lost part of her right leg,' Laura murmured softly.

'There wasn't anything anyone could do. Tom Hartley went out with the ambulance crew and he had to amputate at the scene of the accident. He was really shaken up about it. Thank God Mark was here to talk some sense into him. If I had to choose anyone to be with in times of crisis, it's Mark Dawson. He's just great!'

It was obvious that Madge held the same high opinion of Mark as everyone else did. Laura glowed with pride before she realised how silly it was. Just because Mark had been kind to her last night, that didn't mean she had any right to feel so *possessive*. It was a little disconcerting when Mark suddenly appeared while she was still berating herself.

'Hi, you got here all right, I see,' he said, smiling at her in a way that didn't help. Was it her imagination or was he looking at her as though she were more than just a very new colleague and unexpected house-guest?

She took a deep breath, conscious of Madge's interested gaze moving from Mark to her. Maybe it wasn't imagination after all, a small voice whispered insidiously. Not if Madge had noticed as well!

She buried that thought as deep as she could, determined not to let it surface again. 'Yes, thank you,' she replied, as polite as a guest at a vicarage tea party.

Mark's eyes gleamed with amusement as he heard the formal note in her voice. His own tone was almost too bland in contrast. 'Good.'

He turned to Madge, sounding far more purposeful as he brought her up to date on the condition of one of the children who was in Intensive Care. Laura edged away, making her way to Katie's bed to give herself a bit of breathing space. She was bound to feel a little...well, *edgy* around Mark after last night, but it would be silly to go reading too much into it. After all, she simply wasn't used to being in anyone's debt this way.

'So, how's my best patient today?' Laura asked, noticing how despondent Katie looked. She gave the child a warm smile as she picked up a hairbrush from the locker. 'Want me to brush your hair for you, poppet?'

Katie nodded as she wriggled herself up against the pillows. She sat very still as Laura gently ran the bristles through her wispy hair. 'My mummy doesn't brush my hair anymore,' she said in a dull little voice. 'She says that I'm not a baby now and that I have to do things myself 'cos she's tired of doing everything for me. Do you think that's why she hasn't been to see me, Laura? 'Cos she's tired?'

Laura put down the brush, wondering how best to answer the innocent question. How could any mother stay away from her child like this?

'I'm not sure, sweetheart. Maybe your mummy is a bit tired and is finding it difficult to get here,' she replied, not wanting to give the woman even that much of an excuse but feeling that she had to rather than hurt Katie's feelings any more.

Katie nodded sagely. 'Uh-huh. Mummy said that she needed a holiday 'cos she was tired. Do you think that she's gone to the seaside? She had her swimming costume on the bed.'

Laura just managed to contain her shock. 'Did she? When was that, Katie? Can you remember?'

'Course! It was the day I came here,' Katie explained importantly.

'I see. What a clever girl you are to remember!' Laura smiled at the child, although it was hard to hide her dismay. Maybe she was way off track but she had a nasty suspicion that she might know what had happened to Katie's errant mother!

She found the little girl a colouring book and some crayons and left her colouring in a picture while she went to have a word with Mark. He was in the office, slumped behind the desk with his eyes closed, when she tracked him down. She paused in the doorway, wondering if she should disturb him. He had been up all night and the effects of the long hours were clear to see in the deep lines etched either side of his mouth. She was just turning to leave when he opened his eyes and grinned at her.

'I'm not really asleep. Just catnapping.' He stretched his arms above his head and yawned luxuriantly. Laura hastily looked away as muscles rippled beneath his thin T-shirt. He hadn't stopped to change before rushing out the previous night and was still wearing the same outfit he'd put on after bathing Robbie. She couldn't help thinking back to what had happened in the kitchen as she'd brushed past him...

She cleared her throat, forcing herself to concentrate, although it wasn't the easiest thing she'd had to do. Mark Dawson seemed to have an alarming effect on her equilibrium, making her mind spin off at tangents whenever it got chance!

'It's about Katie. I have a nasty feeling about where her mother might have got to.'

'Really?' Mark's brows drew together.

'It was something Katie just said, about her mother being tired and needing a holiday...' she began, but Mark was ahead of her.

He shot to his feet, his face darkening with anger. 'You mean that you think she's gone away somewhere?'

She shrugged. 'I might be wrong, of course, but yes. You said that you were unable to contact her at home and that she hasn't been in to see Katie. It just seems to add up, doesn't it? Her mother has gone off with the new boyfriend, leaving Katie if not at home alone, then in *hospital* alone.'

'I think you could be right. In fact, I'm going to have a word with Gill Marsh, the social worker, right away. I had asked her to see if she could get in touch with Katie's mother—maybe she needs to get onto the police to see if your suspicions are correct.'

'I might be wrong,' she warned.

'And, there again, you might not.' Mark came round the desk and smiled at her. His grey eyes were so warm that Laura felt her breath catch. It was an effort not to show how she felt as he added softly, 'Thanks, Laura. I knew you were going to be worth your weight in gold as a member of this team, and I was right.'

The teasing softness of his tone didn't disguise the fact that he meant every word, and Laura's heart kicked into overdrive. It was a relief when Fiona Watts, Director of Nursing, suddenly appeared to check how they were faring for staff.

Laura left them discussing the problem and went back to the ward. Cathy Oliver, the staff nurse on duty, had taken charge, and she asked Laura to see if she could persuade Bethany to eat something.

Laura went to the girl's bed, her heart aching at the expression of despair on the teenager's face. The double blow of losing her mother and part of her leg was going to be very difficult for the youngster to get over.

'Hi, Bethany, I'm Laura. I'm going to be your nurse while you're here.'

She paused but Bethany didn't say anything. She was lying on her back, a cage holding the bedclothes away from her injured leg. Her pretty face was covered with scrapes and her left arm was bandaged from wrist to elbow. Laura took the chart off the end of the bed and scanned through it, relieved to find that Bethany's arm wasn't broken but just badly bruised.

Putting the chart back in its place, she picked up the bowl of cereal from the breakfast tray. 'Can I help you with this, love? It must be difficult managing by yourself with your injured arm.'

Bethany's dull blue eyes glanced her way before she deliberately turned her face into the pillow. Laura sighed as she put the bowl back on the tray then took it back to the kitchen. Bethany needed time to come to terms with what had happened, but it wasn't going to be easy to help her, from the look of it.

The day seemed even more hectic than the previous one, thanks to the influx of new patients and being a member of staff down. Fiona Watts managed to find temporary cover over lunchtime from the surgical wards. They were slightly less busy because all elective surgery due to take place that day had been cancelled because of the bad weather. The snow had caused havoc in the town and there was a lot of grumbling in the canteen when Laura went for her lunch about the trouble people had had getting into work.

She selected her food then looked round for a seat, hesitating as Mark waved to her from the far side of the room. However, there were very few spare places left so it would have been silly to refuse his invitation. He stood and pulled out her chair with old world courtesy as she put her tray down.

'Thanks.' Laura took her seat, feeling a little frisson dance down her spine as he smiled at her with such warmth that she would have needed to have been blind not to notice it. Did he always smile at people that way? she wondered giddily as she began unloading her plate of shepherd's pie from the tray. As though they were very special?

She had no idea what the answer was so decided it was wiser not to think about it. Picking up the bottle of mineral water she'd bought to drink with her meal, she struggled to undo the cap.

'Here, let me do that.'

Mark took the bottle from her, swiftly dealing with the recalcitrant metal cap. He filled her glass with the sparkling water then set the bottle beside her plate.

'Thank you. You have the devil's own job getting the tops off some of these things, don't you?' she said for something to say then inwardly winced. Talk about witty repartee!

'You do. I can't decide if the manufacturers are paranoid about people contaminating their products or merely sadistic and enjoy watching everyone struggle!' He grinned at her, instantly turning her inane remark into a point worthy of discussion.

Laura picked up her knife and fork, realising with a glow of pleasure how typical it was of him. Mark would *never* hurt anyone's feelings by making them feel embarrassed if he could help it.

'So, how has it been this morning? I bet it's been hectic in the ward,' he observed, leaning back in his chair with a frown on his face. It was obvious that he really was interested to hear how they'd been managing so Laura gave him a run-down between mouthfuls of food.

'And what about Bethany? How has she been?' he asked finally.

Laura sighed as she took a sip of mineral water. 'She hasn't spoken all morning. I've been to see her several times but she refuses to look at me most of the time, let alone say anything.

Rachel was just arriving as I left for lunch so maybe she can get through to her.'

'Let's hope so. Poor kid. She's only fourteen and I can just imagine how she feels as though her whole world has come to an end,' Mark said sadly.

'Then it's up to us to make her see that it hasn't,' Laura replied with quiet determination.

He smiled at that, his grey eyes warm as they lingered on the determined set of her mouth. 'Well, if anyone can achieve that you can. Which is why I asked Cathy to assign Bethany to you.'

'Thank you.' There was no doubting that it had been meant as a compliment, and her heart warmed at the thought that Mark regarded her so favourably. She glanced down at her plate, toying with the last forkful of mashed potato. It was hard to disguise her pleasure but she had to try. Letting Mark see how much it had meant to her could be putting unwarranted pressure on him. He wasn't responsible for her happiness and she wouldn't let him think that he was because he would take it to heart. Mark was too nice a person to willingly hurt anyone...

She put down her fork with a clatter, fixing a smile to her mouth as she found him watching her. The thought that Mark might view her the same as everyone else was strangely unpalatable. 'Have you managed to speak to the social worker about Katie, by the way?'

'Yes. Gill's promised to get onto it right away. She agreed that the best solution would be to contact the police so we'll just have to wait and see what they come up with.' Mark's tone was grim. 'If that wretched woman really has gone off on holiday and abandoned Katie...!'

He suddenly sighed, making an obvious effort to collect himself. 'Still, maybe we should wait and see what Gill turns up. It could be that there's another explanation for Lisa Watson's absence. How were things at your house this morning, by the way? It was hard to see how bad the damage was last night.'

Laura grimaced. 'Bad enough! The hall carpet is ruined and part of the ceiling has fallen in.' She sighed, thinking about how much it was going to cost to repair everything. 'I can't really tell until I've cleared up some of the mess, but it's going to be costly getting things straight.'

'Surely your insurance should cover it?' Mark frowned as she looked away. 'Laura?'

'I…I'll have to get onto them,' she muttered, not wanting to admit that she didn't have any insurance. There had been just a couple of hundred pounds in their savings account when Ian had died and she'd needed that to pay the bills. She'd been able to claim state benefits but there had never seemed enough to spare for non-essentials. Keeping Robbie fed and warm had been her main priorities. Insurance premiums had had to go by the board.

Now she pushed back her chair, not wanting Mark's pity if he realised how difficult things were. She would manage somehow. She always did! 'I'd better get back to the ward. Jane will be waiting to go for her lunch.'

'If you need a hand, clearing up, Laura—' he began but she cut him off.

'Thanks, but I'll be fine, Mark. You've done enough already.'

She knew he was going to say something else but she didn't give him a chance. With a last brief smile she turned on her heel and fled. Too much sympathy and she might find herself having a good old cry, and that was something she certainly couldn't do! She had to be strong, for herself and, more importantly, for Robbie.

She put her dirty dishes in the rack and sighed. But wouldn't it be lovely to have someone to lean on at times like this, to have someone to share the bad times with and make them seem not half so bad?

Unwillingly, her gaze drifted back across the room and came to rest on Mark's downbent head for a second before she turned away. Mark Dawson might be a lovely, caring man but he most definitely wouldn't want to get landed with either her or her problems!

'We were able to tidy everything up in Theatre once we got back here. The leg was amputated below the knee, as you know, and I took care to ensure that the stump will eventually heal smoothly and, hopefully, cause as few problems as possible.'

There was a small crowd gathered in the office late that afternoon. Laura had been asked to join the group as her input into Bethany Jones's recovery would be considerable over the coming weeks. Now she couldn't help feeling sorry for Tom Hartley, the surgical registrar, as he took them through every detail of the operation he'd performed to save the teenager's life.

Bethany had been trapped in the minibus for several hours and there had been no choice but to amputate to get her out as she'd been in danger of bleeding to death. However, it was obvious to all of them that Tom blamed himself for not being able to have done more, despite the fact that the surgical consultant, Morgan Gray, had assured him that he would have made the same decision. Evidently, Bethany's injuries had been so severe that the leg would have been amputated even if she'd been transferred immediately to hospital.

'You did the right thing, Tom. We're all agreed on that, so stop blaming yourself.' Mark clapped the other man on the shoulder as everyone murmured their agreement. Nevertheless, Tom still looked drawn when he excused himself a few minutes later.

Mark sighed as he looked around the room. Cathy was there, as well as Penny Carmichael, the physiotherapist, who would be co-ordinating Bethany's exercise regime. Normally, Rachel would have been involved as well, but it was too soon for her to be consulted in the circumstances.

'Right, we need to work out Bethany's care plan. All of us are going to work closely together on this so everyone should feel free to put forward suggestions or raise any concerns. OK?'

They all nodded before Mark continued, 'As you all know, it will be at least six weeks before the swelling reduces enough for a permanent prosthesis to be fitted. In the meantime, the bandages and plaster cast will help mould the stump into a suitable shape to accept the artificial limb. Tom has done a damn fine job to ensure that any pressure pain from the prosthesis will be minimal, by severing the nerves well above the stump, so that will help.'

Mark sighed as they all nodded. 'However, we all know that it isn't going to be easy. Bethany's willingness to co-operate will be the determining factor in her long-term recovery, and that's where you come in, Laura.'

He smiled at her. 'I want you to work your magic on the poor kid, make her see that it isn't the end of the world even though it probably feels like it at the moment.'

Laura flushed, conscious of the speculative looks the others were giving her. However, she appreciated Mark's confidence and only hoped that she wasn't going to let him down.

'I'll do my best,' she assured him, earning herself another warm smile. They ran through the rest of Bethany's care plan, with everyone adding their comments before Mark wound up the meeting. Penny stayed behind to have a word with him about one of the other children as Laura and Cathy returned to the ward.

'You and Mark seem to have really hit it off, don't you?'

Laura paused in front of the swing doors, wondering if she'd imagined the edge in Cathy's voice. 'He seems very nice,' she observed quietly, looking at the other nurse uncertainly. Cathy gave her a wide smile but her pale blue eyes held a warning gleam.

'He is. Too nice for his own good at times. He's always picking up lame ducks and getting saddled with them.'

The younger woman didn't say anything more before she pushed open the doors. Laura followed her into the ward, her mind whirling. Had Mark mentioned something about helping *her* last night, implied that she was one of those so-called *lame ducks*?

Her temper rose a good few degrees as she made her way down the ward to see what Daniel Glover was up to. She wasn't a charity case! She didn't need anyone's help, and that included Mark Dawson's! The idea that she might have become the object of his pity stuck in her throat so that she found it impossible to forget about it for the rest of the afternoon. It didn't help one little bit to leave work at the end of her shift and find him waiting for her.

If he thought he could play the good Samaritan again then he was in for a shock!

CHAPTER FIVE

'Hop in and I'll give you a lift.'

Mark opened the car door, his brows rising as Laura made no attempt to get into the car. 'Laura? What's wrong?'

'Nothing.' She gave him a tight smile, anger making her greeny-blue eyes sparkle. 'Thanks for the offer, Mark, but I wouldn't dream of putting on you again tonight. I'll see you tomorrow.'

She walked past him, striding purposefully down the drive towards the gates. However, she'd gone no more than a couple of yards when he caught up with her. Taking hold of her arm, he drew her to a halt, his face holding an expression of bewilderment tinged with the first stirrings of anger.

'What's got into you?' He shook his head when she opened her mouth. 'And don't tell me that nothing is wrong because it's patently obvious that something has upset you.'

'I am not upset!' she declared rather too fervently. She looked away, determined not to let him see how hurt she felt. Maybe it was her own fault for being so gullible but it hurt to realise that he made a habit of helping those less fortunate than himself. She was nobody's *lame duck*, despite what he thought!

The thought was just what she needed to steady her. 'Look, Mark, I don't know why you went out of your way to help me last night, but I can assure you that your involvement in my problems has come to an end. I appreciate what you did but that's it. I'm not a charity case and I can stand on my own two feet. Understand?'

'No. Quite frankly, I have no idea what this is all about.' He bent towards her and his expression was unaccustomedly harsh. 'I most certainly don't view you as a charity case, Laura!'

'No?' She gave a tinkly laugh which echoed with hurt. 'Then how do you see me, Mark? As a lame duck perhaps? I have it on good authority that you make a habit of collecting them. But don't worry, you aren't going to get landed with me!'

She tried to remove her arm from his grasp but he refused to let her go. His grey eyes were the colour of a winter sky as he glared at her from under lowering brows. 'I don't know who's been putting such nonsense into your head but you're wrong, Laura. I *don't* see you as a lame duck! In fact, I—'

He stopped abruptly as a car hooted to warn them that they were standing in the middle of the drive and that people were trying to get past. Waving an apologetic hand towards the driver, he took a firmer grip on Laura's arm and drew her out of the way. As soon as the car had passed, he started down the drive.

'Where are you taking me?' she protested, struggling to keep up with him. He slowed as he realised the difficulty she was having—taking two steps to his one—and set a more sedate pace as they reached the street.

'Somewhere where we can talk and get this sorted out.' He held up his free hand when she opened her mouth. 'No. Somebody has been filling your head with rubbish and I don't intend to leave things like this.'

He suddenly grinned. 'Humour me, Laura. It's been one heck of a day, not to mention night, and I feel too fragile to put up much of a fight. Can't you find it in that caring heart of yours to take pity on a poor overworked doctor?'

It was hard to resist when he turned on the charm like that. Laura tried her best but she could feel her resolve melting. She gave a quick nod, refusing to let him think she was *too* much of a pushover, and earned herself a smile which made her head whirl.

In a daze she let Mark lead her to a small café further along the road. It was almost empty at that time of the day and he chose a table in the corner well out of earshot of the only other occupant. Pulling out a chair for her, he waited until she was seated before sitting down himself.

'I come here quite often,' he explained as he picked up the laminated menu. 'The food's quite good and it saves me cooking.'

He handed Laura the menu but she didn't even glance at it. 'Nothing for me,' she stated firmly. 'Look, Mark, I really can't see—'

'Any point in us having this discussion?' He shook his head. 'That's where you're wrong. Of course there's a point. I want to know how you've managed to get it into your beautiful head that I'm treating you like a charity case.'

'Well, aren't you?' She picked up the salt shaker then set it down again with a thud. Did Mark really think she was beautiful? she couldn't help wondering before she could stop herself. 'It's obvious how you see me, Mark!'

'Obvious to whom?' He paused as the waitress came to take their order. He ordered cod and chips, shrugging when Laura reiterated that she didn't want anything. As soon as the waitress had gone, he repeated the question. 'Obvious to whom, Laura?'

She looked away, not wanting to mention Cathy by name. 'Everyone. Look, Mark, I know you only want to be kind. Everyone says what a nice person you are, so…'

He swore softly under his breath. His eyes were filled with exasperation when she looked at him in surprise. 'To hell with *everyone*! It's you I'm interested in, Laura—it's your opinion that counts! And if I've done something to offend you I apologise.'

This was starting to get out of hand, she realised with a sinking heart as she heard the regret in his voice. The last thing she wanted was to…to *hurt* Mark by refusing his help!

She took a deep breath and tried to muster her thoughts into some sort of order. 'I just hate the idea that you feel obliged to help me because I'm some pitiful person who can't manage by herself,' she admitted in a voice that hinted at how hurt she felt.

Mark reached across the table and took her hand. 'I don't feel like that about you, Laura, believe me.' His fingers tightened around hers, warm and strong and so infinitely reassuring that she almost sighed in pleasure.

'I admire and respect you for the way you've coped since your husband died. I don't see you as a charity case but as a beautiful and capable woman whom I want to help any way I can.'

'But you hardly know me,' she protested, while her heart filled with joy at what he'd said.

'Because we only met yesterday?' He shrugged. 'Time is irrelevant. You can know people for years and never feel close to them. And then you can meet someone and feel that you've known them all your life after only a few hours '

'Is…is that how you feel about me, Mark?' she asked, without pausing to think. She bit her lip, afraid to hear the answer because she wasn't sure it was wise. This wasn't what she wanted! her conscience shouted. There was Ian to think about, how much she'd loved him and how she still missed him. She didn't want to get involved this way!

'Yes, if you want the truth.' He gave her hand a gentle squeeze then released it. His voice was suddenly flat. 'But I don't think the truth is what you want to hear just yet so maybe we should forget about it for now. Just accept that the reason I want to help you isn't because I'm trying to notch up brownie points against the day I meet my Maker!'

He turned it into a joke, saving her from the need to answer. Laura let out a sigh of relief, realising belatedly that she was trembling. Guilt and anger were potent forces and she'd been beset by both in such a short space of time that it was little wonder she'd been affected this way. When the waitress returned with Mark's meal and he asked her if she would have a cup of tea, she accepted gratefully.

Mark kept up an easy conversation as he ate, restricting it mainly to what had happened at work that day. It was neutral ground and Laura guessed that was why he'd chosen it. However, it was obvious that he was interested to hear what she had to say about the new cases who'd been admitted the previous night.

She suspected that he found it difficult to switch off his role as a doctor. Not for Mark an end to the working day as soon as he walked through the hospital gates. It brought it home to her once more how much she admired him.

They left the café a short time later and walked back to the hospital. Nothing had been said, but by tacit agreement Laura had accepted his offer to drive her to Claire's. Maybe it was silly but she couldn't bear the thought of hurting him by her refusal.

The snow had started to fall again and Mark urged her into the car then quickly slid behind the wheel. Starting the engine, he shot a grimace at the sky. 'Looks like it could be even worse than last night.'

Laura nodded as she fastened her seat belt. 'It does. Let's hope that it doesn't cause as much chaos.'

It was a vain hope, she soon realised as they reached the centre of Dalverston. Traffic was at a standstill around the cenotaph, thanks to a lorry which had skidded in the fresh snow. Mark wound down his window and frowned as he spotted a crowd clustered around the cab.

'I think I'll just go and take a look in case they need help,' he said, easing the car into the side of the road and cutting the engine.

'Give me a shout if you need me,' Laura offered immediately, earning herself a smile.

'Will do.'

He quickly slammed the door to stop the snow blowing inside the car. Laura huddled in her seat and watched as he made his way to the lorry. He conferred briefly with some of the bystanders then beckoned her over.

Laura immediately got out of the car and went to join him, shivering as snow blasted into her face. 'What is it?' she demanded, her stomach sinking as she saw the look on Mark's face.

'I think we have a bit of a problem.' He drew her into the lee of the vehicle to shelter them. 'The driver has his wife with him and she's in labour. Evidently, he was driving her to hospital when he skidded. Someone's called an ambulance but no one seems to know how long it will take to get here because of the snow and all this traffic.

'I don't think the driver's too badly hurt. The main problem seems to be that his foot is trapped under one of the pedals, but the woman definitely needs assistance. Can you see what you can do, Laura?'

'Of course. Is she still in the cab?'

When Mark nodded she hurriedly climbed onto the running board so that she could see inside the cab. The driver was slumped against the door, holding a piece of rag to his head. Laura could see that it was bleeding from a cut on his temple but, as Mark had said, he didn't appear badly hurt. She turned her attention to his wife, a woman of about her own age who was obviously in pain and scared to death.

'Can we get this door open?' she demanded, jumping down to the ground. 'I need to take a proper look at her.'

The door had jammed as the lorry had hit one of the bollards surrounding the cenotaph. It took Mark, plus a couple of bystanders, several minutes to force it open. Laura climbed back up to the cab and introduced herself to the terrified mother-to-be.

'My name is Laura and I'm a trained midwife. Can you tell me your name and how far apart your contractions are?'

'Sally...Sally Middleton. They're coming about every two minutes, I think...' The woman gasped as another contraction began. Laura placed her hand on the woman's distended abdomen then glanced back at Mark.

'We need to get her out of here as fast as possible,' she told him quietly. 'This baby isn't going to wait much longer to be born.'

Mark didn't question her assessment. Jumping down from the cab, he went to the rear of the lorry and Laura heard him opening the doors. He came back a few seconds later. 'If we can get her into the back of the lorry at least she'll have some privacy and shelter.'

'Fine.' Laura moved aside so that Mark could lift the terrified woman out of the cab. It was a difficult manoeuvre but he made it appear effortless as he cradled her in his arms.

'Jim...!' The woman shot a frightened glance at her husband who managed a groggy smile.

'You go with the doctor, Sal. I'll be fine, love. Once they get me out of here I'll be right with you,' he replied encouragingly.

Mark carried the woman to the back of the lorry. One of the bystanders had found some flattened cardboard boxes in the back and had had the presence of mind to fashion a makeshift bed out of them. It wasn't ideal but it was some protection from the coldness of the metal floor.

Mark gently laid Sally down as Laura climbed in beside him. 'I'm just going to check on the driver,' he informed her *sotto voce*. 'I'm a bit concerned about his foot—I want to check that the blood supply to it hasn't been cut off. Give me a shout if you need me.'

'Will do, but I'm sure we're going to be fine, aren't we,

Sally?' Laura said, smiling encouragingly at the frightened woman.

'I hope so....' Sally bit her lip as her eyes filled with tears. 'We've waited so long for this baby. You won't let anything happen to it, will you?'

'Nothing is going to happen to your baby, Sally.' Mark knelt down and took her hand. His grey eyes were so warm as they rose to encompass Laura that she immediately forgot how cold it was in the back of the lorry. 'Laura is a trained midwife and she's delivered more babies than you and I have had hot dinners. Although, I admit, she might not have worked in these conditions before. This could be a first!'

Sally laughed as he'd intended her to then groaned as another contraction began. Laura knelt beside her, focusing her attention firmly on helping the poor woman through the next few difficult minutes.

'I'll be back as soon as I can.' Mark touched her lightly on the shoulder then disappeared back out into the snow. Laura could hear a lot of thumping and banging coming from the cab but she tried to block it out of her mind. One of the motorists had produced a torch and she smiled ruefully as she examined Sally by its light. Mark had been right about this being a first. She certainly hadn't delivered a baby by torchlight in the back of a lorry before!

Sally was fully dilated and the baby's head was crowning. After checking that the cord wasn't wrapped around the child's neck, Laura concentrated on the delivery. With no possibility of pain relief, the mother's breathing became all-important.

Fortunately, Sally had attended classes at the antenatal clinic and responded well to Laura's calm instructions so that it was all over in a surprisingly short time. Laura lifted the squalling infant onto its mother's stomach and smiled at her. 'You have a lovely little girl, Sally. Well done!'

'A girl?' Tears streamed down the exhausted woman's face as she laid a gentle hand on her daughter's sticky head. 'And she's all right? You're sure about that?'

'Positive. But don't just take my word for it—ask the doctor and he can tell you.' Laura smiled as Mark came to join them. 'Isn't she gorgeous, Mark?'

'She is...every single tiny finger and toe.' He grinned as he looked at the anxious mother. 'Your baby is perfectly fine, Sally. There's no need to worry.'

'And Jim?' Sally asked, suddenly remembering her husband's plight. She struggled to sit up then smiled in relief as Jim appeared. 'Oh, Jim, it's a girl… We've got our baby at last!'

Mark helped Laura up as Jim hobbled into the back of the lorry and knelt down beside his wife. 'Let's give them a few minutes, shall we?' he said softly.

He helped Laura down from the lorry, smiling as a cheer went up from the crowd once they heard the news about the baby's safe delivery. Everyone seemed delighted by the happy outcome and there was little sign of impatience from the drivers who'd found themselves caught up in the drama.

Laura smiled as she looked round at the smiling faces. 'Funny how the birth of a child has such a positive effect on everyone. Normally people would complain bitterly if they were delayed on a night like this, wouldn't they?'

'They would. But a baby is special, isn't it? I defy anyone not to feel moved when they witness the birth of a child,' he agreed quietly. 'It's always given me a tremendous buzz whenever I've been fortunate enough to deliver a healthy child.'

There was a note in his voice that made her frown. She looked at him curiously. 'Why do I have a feeling there was more to that statement than first appears?'

He smiled down at her. 'You're too perceptive, Laura!' He sighed. 'But you're right. I did five years with the WHO after I qualified. I worked all over the place. Africa, India, Rumania…which was possibly the worst of all. I saw far too many babies die because their mothers hadn't received adequate medical care. It made me value what we have in this country— a health service that does its best to ensure that every baby born has the best start possible in life.'

'But there are never guarantees,' she said sadly. 'Even with the best care available you can't cover every eventuality.'

His eyes darkened. 'You mean Robbie, don't you? But could you really imagine your life without him, Laura?'

She smiled, her sadness lifting in an instant. 'No. Neither do I want to try!'

She looked round as the sound of sirens warned them that the ambulance was on its way. There was a scramble as people hurried back to their cars to make room for it to get through. It drew up beside the lorry and Laura laughed as she recognised the crew.

'Hi, there. I see you two have drawn the short straw tonight,' she teased as Jenny Partridge and Joe Henderson came to join them.

'Who else?' Jenny replied ruefully. 'Joe and I were looking forward to a nice night in the bay with our feet up, too. So, what have we got? Control said something about a woman in labour—'

She broke off as a wail issued from the rear of the lorry. 'Seems we're too late!' she declared ruefully, rolling her eyes.

Laura quickly filled her in on the details. 'Everything seemed to be perfectly straightforward so I can't imagine there'll be any problems,' she concluded.

'Well, you're the expert,' Joe observed laconically, 'although I hear you've deserted Maternity in favour of Children's Med.'

'Their loss is our gain,' Mark stated, looping an arm around Laura's shoulders.

Laura coloured as she saw Jenny share a smiling glance with Joe. It was obvious what was going through the other woman's mind, and once again Laura experienced that same feeling of guilt. She moved away, avoiding Mark's eyes as she felt him look at her. It was a relief when Jenny climbed into the lorry to get the mother and baby ready to be transferred to the ambulance.

'Thank you, both of you.' Sally blinked back tears as she cradled her daughter to her as they were lifted down on the stretcher. Snugly wrapped in blankets, the tiny child blinked as a snowflake landed on her cheek. She opened her mouth and let out a squall of annoyance, and everyone laughed.

'It was our pleasure. You just take care of that gorgeous little girl.' Mark smiled at Sally then shook Jim's hand. Jim's foot had turned out to be badly bruised but that was all. He was able to hobble after his wife as the stretcher was loaded on board the waiting ambulance.

Mark sighed as it drove away. 'Right, now that's over, let's get on our way.'

His voice sounded unusually flat and Laura shot him a curious look, wondering what was wrong. Unless it was just that he was tired after working such long hours. Two sleepless nights on the run would wear anyone out, she thought worriedly as they made their way back to the car.

It took some time to clear the backlog of vehicles and get on their way. Mark didn't speak, seemingly preferring to concentrate on driving. The snow had stopped but the roads were slick with the new layer of snow lying on top of the old, so she could appreciate how difficult conditions were. When he drew up in front of Claire's house, he didn't switch off the engine.

'Right, here we are, then. Mind how you go, Laura. The pavement will be slippy, I imagine.'

Although it was said pleasantly, there was no doubt in her mind that he didn't want to linger any longer than necessary. She hurriedly opened the car door, pausing only long enough to thank him. 'I appreciate the lift, Mark. Thank you.'

He inclined his head but he didn't say anything. As soon as she'd closed the car door, he drove away. Laura walked up the path and rang the bell, feeling ridiculously hurt by the abrupt dismissal. Mark was tired so he must be longing to get home, she tried telling herself, but it didn't work. It still felt as though he couldn't wait to be rid of her!

Robbie's excitement at spending the night with Ben eased Laura's mind. She spent half an hour listening to what he'd done at school that day. Robbie's lessons were adapted to his capabilities as he couldn't always cope with what the rest of the children in his class were doing.

Laura was hoping that he might eventually be able to read, as some Down's children could, but she was realistic in her expectations. The fact that Robbie gained such pleasure from mixing with children his own age, and learned vital social skills, was more than enough for now.

Claire urged her to stay and eat with them but Laura refused. She had to make a start on clearing up the mess at her house, and the sooner she set about it the better. She kissed Robbie goodbye then left, huddling into her coat as she set off to walk the short distance home. There was a gas camping lantern stored in the shed so she found that first then went inside to survey the damage.

Everywhere smelt cold and damp and the hall carpet squelched as she walked on it. Her heart sank at the enormity of the task she had set herself, but there was nothing she could do so she set to work. Rolling up the carpet was difficult enough, but it was impossible for her to carry it outside. The water had made it too heavy for her to lift no matter how hard she tried. Panting for breath, she looked for an alternative, and decided that it might be easier if she tried *rolling* it out of the front door and around into the back garden.

Running a grimy hand over her brow to push back her hair, she opened the door then cried out as she was confronted by the tall figure of a man standing on her step. It was only when he spoke that she realised it was Mark, although her heart sank as she heard the anger in his voice.

'What the hell do you think you're doing, you crazy woman?'

'I…Um…' Completely disconcerted by his sudden appearance, Laura struggled to answer the question. He swore softly as he came inside and slammed the door with enough force to make the whole house shake. In the glow from the lantern she saw that his face was set in uncompromising lines, and she felt a ripple of unease run down her spine.

'Why didn't you tell me what you were planning on doing?' he demanded in that same hard-edged tone which was so out of character.

Laura blinked, feeling foolish tears stinging her eyes. Crazy though it sounded, it hurt to know that Mark was angry with her.

'I never thought about it,' she muttered in a choked little voice, turning away so that he couldn't see that she was upset. He caught her arm and swung her round, his eyes darkening as he saw the tears on her lashes.

'Hey, what's all this? What are you crying for?' he asked more gently.

'Because…because I'm tired and I'm cold and I can't lift this rotten carpet and you're shouting at me!'

It all came out in a rush, as though a cork had popped out of a bottle and released all her pent-up emotions. Tears streamed down her face and she heard Mark groan. He drew her to him, cradling her against him as he rocked her gently to and fro as though comforting a child.

'I'm sorry. Really, I am. I didn't mean to shout at you.' He drew back and looked into her tear-drenched eyes. 'I was just worried, you see.'

'Worried,' she repeated blankly. Nervously, she wet her lips, feeling heat lick along her veins when she saw his eyes darken as they followed the movement of her tongue. There was a roughness about his voice all of a sudden which could no longer be attributed wholly to anger and her heart rate increased.

'Yes. I rang Claire's house to apologise for the way I acted earlier by driving off so abruptly, and she told me that you'd gone home to start clearing up. I'd assumed that you would be staying with her, but obviously I was wrong. I don't think she has any idea what a state this place is in, but I had.'

His arms tightened, drawing her even closer so that she could feel the power of his body even through the thick layers of clothing he was wearing, and her heart raced even more. 'I drove here as fast as I could, terrified that I'd find you lying on the floor, having electrocuted yourself or something!'

He tried to inject a teasing note into his voice but it didn't quite work. Laura's heart was racing almost out of control now. The thought that Mark cared so much was like a light coming on inside her, dispelling the darkness that had filled her for so long.

The thought made her gasp and he bent to look at her, his eyes narrowing as he saw the expression on her face. 'Laura…?' he murmured questioningly, then he gave a soft groan.

She knew that he was going to kiss her before his head began to lower but there was no thought in her mind of resisting. She felt the first light contact of his lips as they settled over hers, and the one thought which ran through her mind was that they felt *familiar*. It was as though part of her had known Mark's touch all her life so that responding to it was as natural as breathing.

She stretched up on tiptoe to meet him, and heard the sigh he gave. There was a note of relief and pleasure in it, along with surprise. Hadn't he expected her to welcome his kiss? she wondered in the moment before his mouth settled more firmly over hers and the ability to think deserted her.

His lips were warm and eager, so filled with passion and yet so tender, that it was like a cocktail of emotions all shaken up together. Laura responded blindly, delightedly, letting her lips mimic the movements of his. It was the sweetest, most seductive dance imaginable, and when it was over they were both shaken and breathing heavily.

He cupped her face between his big warm hands, looking at her with an expression in his eyes that made her very bones seem to melt. 'I could very easily fall in love with you, Laura Grady.'

Maybe it was the use of her full name and not just what he said that brought her back to earth with a sickening jolt. Laura felt herself go cold as she realised what she'd done.

How could she have kissed Mark in the very house where she'd lived with Ian?

It felt like the worst kind of betrayal, made her feel sick as she wondered what kind of a woman she must be to forget about her husband like that!

She pulled free from his arms, refusing to look at him because she felt so ashamed. She didn't want to look at him and remember how she'd felt, how he'd *made* her feel!

'I'd like you to leave,' she said woodenly.

'Leave?' There was raw astonishment in the word and on his face when she chanced a glance at him. The lantern light seemed to have leached all the colour from his face so that he looked like a stranger as he stood there, staring at her.

'You want me to go after what just—'

'Yes!' She couldn't let him finish the sentence, didn't want to hear it, didn't need to. She knew what she'd done and would never forget it. 'I want you to go now, please, Mark.'

'I see. I'd ask you why but I already know the answer so there doesn't seem any point.' He gave a bitter laugh and his mouth twisted with pain. 'Your husband must have been quite a guy, Laura. Obviously, no one is ever going to match up to him. But don't go blaming yourself for what just happened. You made it clear before how you feel, but I didn't take the hint. No, it was all my fault and I apologise for it. Frankly, it's something I shall regret for a long time to come.'

He left the house, closing the door so quietly behind him that it seemed somehow worse. If he'd betrayed even a trace of anger then it would have helped. But to hear that flatness in his voice and to know that she was responsible for it, that made everything worse.

Mark had realised that she'd felt uncomfortable when he'd put his arm around her earlier that night, which was probably why he'd driven off so quickly after dropping her at Claire's. But she had made no attempt to stop him kissing her just now because it hadn't even crossed her mind! If anyone was to blame it was her, not him. Mark would have stopped the very instant he'd felt her withdrawal, but it simply hadn't happened.

Now she knew that she wasn't just guilty of betraying Ian but of hurting Mark as well. It was hard to decide which crime was worse.

CHAPTER SIX

'WHO spilled all this cereal on the floor? Daniel Glover, you come back here this minute!'

Laura placed both hands on her hips as she waited for the little boy to obey the command. He came back down the ward, his slippered feet dragging on the floor. He looked the picture of contrition but she knew that would last no longer than the few minutes it took to chastise him about his latest escapade. Daniel was feeling a lot better and they were all paying for it!

'Did you empty these Rice Crispies all over the floor by Tim's bed?' she demanded, determined not to soften as Daniel looked up at her with puppy-dog appealing brown eyes. At the tender age of eight, Daniel had learned how to manipulate the female of the species, as she knew to her cost!

Laura's heart flipped as another very appealing male face sprang to mind. It had been two days since the episode at her house and she'd had no chance to speak to Mark about anything other than work. He'd been polite but impersonal whenever they'd come into contact so there had never been an opportunity to mention it. But what could she expect? She'd made it clear how she'd felt that night, and Mark was simply following her lead, but she couldn't deny that she missed the warmth he'd shown her previously.

Now she deliberately chased all thoughts of Mark from her mind as she focused on making Daniel see that he couldn't keep getting up to mischief. 'Did you pour this cereal on the floor, Daniel?' she said in her sternest voice.

'Uh-huh.' He gave her a guileless smile. 'But I didn't do it on purpose. It was an experiment, you see.'

'Experiment? What kind of experiment?'

Laura turned to look at Tim, who flushed uncomfortably. Although Tim Matthews was several years older than Daniel, the two boys had struck up a friendship. Tim was one of the pupils

71

injured in the minibus crash. He had an unstable fracture of his left tibia, which had been repaired using pins inserted through the bone and locked into place by an external metal frame. Tim had fractured the radius in his left arm as well, although as the break was in the centre of the shaft it had been possible to manipulate the bone back into position and hold it in place with a plaster cast.

Now Laura repeated her question for his benefit. 'What sort of experiment?'

'We—Daniel and me—well, we just wanted to see if we could get a Rice Crispie to sort of…well, sort of roll down my cast from one end to the other,' Tim mumbled.

'Roll down your cast?' Laura raised her eyes to the heavens. 'I don't believe it! All this mess because you two were trying to do such a crazy thing?'

She went over to the bed and lifted up the boy's injured arm, sighing as a couple of Rice Crispies fell out of the top of his cast.

'I won't ask whose idea it was because I can guess!'

She treated Daniel to a stern look and he looked suitably chastened. 'But I warn you both that if I find you doing anything like this again then I'll…' She searched for a suitable punishment to threaten them with then grimaced. 'Well, I'll think of something!'

She tilted Tim's arm towards the light and tried to peer inside the cast. 'I hope none of those Crispies are stuck in there otherwise we might need to replaster your arm.'

'Problems, Nurse Grady?'

The quiet question made her heart respond out of all proportion to how it should have done. Laura struggled to fix a suitable expression to her face as she turned to find Mark standing behind her. She cleared her throat, wishing her heart would stop thumping the way it was doing.

'Just a very minor one, Dr Dawson,' she replied evenly, lowering Tim's arm to the bed. 'This pair have been conducting an experiment to see if a Rice Crispie can travel from one end of Tim's cast to the other.'

'I see. And did it work?' Mark asked blandly, although she could see the laughter in his eyes. Seeing it made the way he'd been acting towards her all the more marked. Suddenly she wished with all her heart that they could go back to the way they'd been before he'd kissed her!

'Laura?' he prompted, and she quickly gathered her thoughts.

'No. And I've forbidden them to try it again. No more experiments until you leave here. Understand?'

Both boys nodded, but the expression on Daniel's face as they moved away from the bed told her that he was already planning something else. She sighed as she looked back over her shoulder. 'I wonder what that little imp is going to get up to next?'

Mark laughed softly. 'It's a good sign when a child gets up to mischief.'

'I know. But it's a lot easier when they're confined to their beds and you know exactly what they're up to,' she retorted dryly. 'Daniel's going to turn my hair grey soon!'

'Then you'll be pleased to know that he'll be leaving us tomorrow.' Mark led the way down the ward, glancing back when Laura hesitated. 'I wonder if I could have a word with you in the office? It won't take long.'

Her heart leapt as she wondered what he wanted to speak to her about, although she didn't question him. Cathy was helping Jane change one of the children's drips and she gave Laura a hard look as she passed the bed.

'Have you remembered to order a gluten-free meal for Jessica Collins, the new admission we're expecting?' she asked sharply. 'You need to get the order in before ten otherwise the kitchen staff will complain.'

'Yes. I phoned it through earlier,' Laura replied blandly, refusing to rise to the challenge in the other woman's voice. Cathy had been filling in for Rachel for the past few days and Laura had wondered several times if the staff nurse found it difficult, coping with the extra responsibility. On several occasions Laura had fallen foul of the other woman's acerbic tongue over some minor misdemeanour. However, there was no sign of irritation as Cathy turned to Mark with a charming smile.

'I won't be long now if you need me, Mark,' she informed him sweetly. 'Jane and I just have this to finish and then I'm free.'

'Actually, it was Laura I wanted a word with.' Mark returned her smile but Laura was aware of a certain reserve about the way he spoke to the other woman. 'I know how busy you are so I won't drag you away from what you're doing. Laura can fill you in later as it's nothing urgent.'

It was obvious that Cathy was less than pleased by that but there was little she could say. However, Laura suspected that she would make her feelings only too clear later! She followed Mark to the office and stood just inside the door, waiting to hear what he had to say. He went straight to the desk, picked up a slip of paper and handed it to her.

'Gill Marsh has confirmed your suspicions about Katie Watson's mother. The police have been to the house and a neighbour told them that Lisa Watson is away on holiday.'

'Really? Do they know where she is?' Laura asked in horror, looking down at the note which simply repeated what Mark had told her.

'The neighbour thought it was the Canaries, but wasn't sure. The police are making enquiries.'

'It's incredible, isn't it? You wouldn't believe that she would go off like that.'

'You wouldn't. But I don't think Lisa cares about anything apart from herself.' He sighed as he sat on the edge of the desk. 'Remember you mentioning Katie's dog? Evidently, Lisa turned it out of the house before she went away. It's been wandering the estate ever since, and people have been feeding it scraps. A woman reported it to the police when she saw them at the Watsons' house. Fortunately, they managed to catch it and have taken it to the RSPCA kennels.'

'Oh, how could she do such a thing? Katie simply adores that dog. Her face lights up as soon as you mention it.' Laura shook her head in dismay. 'So what happens now? Any luck contacting her father?'

'The police have been in touch with the firm where he used to work but he left there a few weeks ago. They're seeing if they can trace him, but it won't be easy if he's moved out of the area.' Mark sighed. 'I thought you should know in case Katie starts asking questions. We need to decide what to tell her.'

'The truth,' Laura said firmly. 'We tell her that her mother is on holiday and we're trying to find her father. I think she already has a good idea what's going on so it would be wrong to lie to her…although perhaps we shouldn't mention anything about the dog, apart from the fact that he's safe. He is, isn't he? The RSPCA will keep him?'

'For a while. But we can work something out, I'm sure.' Mark stood up. 'Right, that's what we'll do, then. I wanted to see what you thought as you're the one who seems to have had the most success with Katie. Thanks, Laura.'

It was obvious the meeting was at an end but she hesitated. Suddenly the desire to clear the air between them was too strong to resist.

'Look, Mark, about what happened the other night—' she began, but he cut her off.

'I can't see any point in rehashing past events. Forget it, Laura. I have.'

'Have you?' The question came out before she could stop it, and she saw him stiffen. He didn't say anything, however, leaving it up to her to continue.

She took a deep breath, struggling to find the courage to make him understand how she felt. 'If you've forgotten about it then why have you been acting so…well, so distantly around me?'

'I shouldn't have thought you'd have noticed let alone cared,' he said in an offhand tone that stung.

'Of course I noticed! And I care,' she replied vehemently. 'I want us to be friends, Mark.'

'And what if I wanted more than that? What then, Laura? Are you ready to move on yet, to put your loss behind you and start living again?' He shook his head. 'I don't think so, not from what—'

He stopped abruptly as he looked past her. 'Do you want me, Cathy?'

'I just thought that you could take a look at Bethany Jones while you're here. She's been experiencing quite a lot of pain this morning.' Cathy turned to Laura and her tone sharpened. 'I hope you remembered to note it down on her chart when you did her obs?'

'Of course.' Laura replied, struggling not to let her annoyance show. Cathy had made it sound as though she was too inept to know one of the basic rules of nursing!

'That makes a change!' Cathy shot Mark a laughing look but Laura wasn't deaf to the malice in her voice. 'Laura tends to overlook little details like that. Still, I suppose it's hard to slot back into the routine after such a prolonged absence from work.'

It was so blatantly untrue that Laura only just managed to bite her tongue. It wouldn't have been ethical to argue with her superior in front of Mark, although she would have it out with Cathy later. However, she had a sudden misgiving as she saw Mark frown and wondered if it might have been better to challenge the staff nurse there and then.

'Any change in a patient's condition, no matter how insignificant it may seem, should be noted,' he stated flatly.

'I know that,' Laura replied as evenly as she could, but before she could add anything, let alone explain that the accusation was totally unfounded, the younger woman butted in.

'Now that you're free, Laura, will you take Katie for her bath? I told her not to be so impatient and that you'd be there as soon as you could.'

Cathy sighed as she turned to Mark. 'It's difficult keeping on top of the work at present, with us being one down. You need to be on your toes all the time and a lot of staff find it hard to keep up in a busy department like this.'

Once again there was the innuendo that she wasn't coping as well as she should. Laura's pretty mouth compressed as she followed Mark and Cathy back to the ward. Did Cathy always act this way? Or had the staff nurse singled her out for these snide remarks for some particular reason?

The questions nagged at her while she was giving Katie her bath. The little girl was due to go for her scan the following day and was obviously nervous. Laura put aside her own worries while she tried to convince the child that there was nothing to be scared of.

'It really won't hurt, poppet. All that happens is that a lot of sound waves pass through your body and make pictures on a screen, a bit like when you watch television. You won't be able to feel anything.'

She gave Katie an encouraging smile. 'Anyway, I thought you'd had a scan before so you must remember that it didn't hurt?'

'Yes, but Daddy was there. And he said a special magic word to make sure that it wouldn't hurt, and held my hand.' Katie's huge blue eyes filled with tears. 'I wish Daddy was going to be there tomorrow. I miss him!'

'I know you do, love.' Laura wrapped the child in a thick towel and hugged her. It broke her heart to imagine how confused poor Katie must be that both her parents were absent. Setting the little girl away from her, she lifted Katie's chin so that she could look straight into her eyes.

'Would you like me to stay with you while you have your scan? I could hold your hand if you want me to.'

'Please.' Tears shimmered on Katie's lashes. 'Promise, Laura?'

'Of course I do!' She gave the child another hug then set about drying her hair. Once it was done, she fastened the wispy brown curls back with a bright yellow scrunchie then smiled at the little girl.

'That's better. Now that you're all pretty again, how about helping me do some jobs? I need someone to arrange some flowers for me.'

'Yes!' Katie brightened up immediately. She took hold of Laura's hand and skipped along beside her as they returned to the ward. Mark was just coming out and he paused to hold the door open for them, smiling as he saw the child's happy face.

'Two sunny smiles for the price of one,' he teased. 'It makes it worth coming to work to see my two best girls looking so happy.'

Laura's heart tumbled around in her chest. She was at a loss to know what to say, but Katie had none of her reservations.

'Is Laura your best girl as well as me, Dr Mark?' she asked seriously.

'She certainly is. I would say that Laura is my favourite nurse.' His tone was teasing but Laura heard the undercurrent it held and her heart bumped a bit more. It was an effort to retain an outward show of calm.

'She's mine, too!' Katie suddenly turned and hugged Laura tightly around her waist. 'I love her!'

Laura tried to stop herself but she couldn't help it as her eyes flew to Mark. He gave her a slow smile and the expression in his grey eyes almost made her melt. 'I don't blame you, sweetheart. I'd say it would be only too easy to love Laura.'

He gave them both a last smile then went on his way. Did he

have any idea of the turmoil he'd left behind him? Laura wondered giddily as she took Katie into the kitchen and sat her at the table with the bouquet of flowers that needed arranging.

Her hands shook as she filled a vase with water. Probably! Mark must know very well how confused she would feel, how disturbed, yet he'd said what he'd felt anyway. It scared her because she wasn't sure that she could ever give him what he seemed to want. The thought of letting Mark down, of hurting him, was almost more than she could bear.

The day whizzed past once again. Laura had worked in paediatrics before she'd decided to go into midwifery. She'd chosen children's nursing as her branch programme after her initial foundation course and had always loved the daily contact with the children. However, she realised that working in Dalverston General was better even than her previous experiences.

The holistic attitude that prevailed in caring for the children made the job even more satisfying. Although priority was given to caring for their physical needs, emphasis was placed on their overall well-being. It was good to know that it was considered as important to talk to a child as it was to replace a soiled dressing! If the children had problems that could affect their recovery, it was imperative that something be done. However, it was proving extremely difficult to help Bethany Jones when the teenager still refused to talk to anyone.

Laura was escorting Tim Matthews back to bed after a visit to the bathroom when she spotted Rachel leaving the ward. It was obvious that Rachel was upset, despite the fact that she did her best to hide it.

'Are you OK?' Laura asked solicitously, stopping the wheelchair. With one arm injured as well as his leg, it would be some time before Tim was able to use crutches to get around, something that caused him a great deal of embarrassment. At thirteen he hated the fact that he had to be accompanied to and from the bathroom!

Laura had tried to afford him as much privacy as possible, but the fear that he might slip and undo everyone's hard work had forced her to stay close at hand, much to the boy's dismay. Now it was obvious that he couldn't wait to get back to the ward and forget his ordeal.

'Yes, of course,' Rachel replied automatically, then sighed. 'Not really.' She glanced at the impatient boy in the wheelchair. 'But you don't want to hear my woes when you're so busy.'

Laura checked her watch. 'I'm due to go for my break in five minutes. Why don't you meet me in the canteen and we can have a chat?'

'Well…' Rachel hesitated briefly, then smiled. 'I'd like that, Laura. I could do with someone to talk to, to tell the truth.'

'Then I'll see you up there just as soon as I can,' Laura assured her. She pushed Tim back into the ward and helped him into a chair beside his bed. Daniel came hurrying over and the two boys soon had their heads together, no doubt plotting some new bit of mischief. The only consolation, Laura decided as she went for her break, was that it would take Tim's mind off the indignity of having someone with him when he went to the loo!

Rachel was seated at a table near the window, nursing a cooling cup of coffee, when Laura arrived at the canteen. She put her own cup on the table and sat opposite her.

'So how's things?' she asked gently, stirring sugar into her tea.

'Oh, you know…' Rachel shrugged.

'Yes, I do.' Laura replied quietly. 'Losing someone you love is so hard. Nothing anyone can say makes the pain go away, but it does get easier, Rachel, believe me.'

'I just keep thinking what a waste it was! Suzy was only thirty-six…far too young to die!' Tears welled from Rachel's eyes and she quickly brushed them away with the back of her hand.

Laura didn't say anything, knowing that it was best to let her talk. Bottling up the grief Rachel felt at the death of her sister would only make the healing process that much more difficult. Yet wasn't that what *she* had been doing since Ian had died? Hadn't she bottled up *her* emotions for Robbie's sake?

'I know all about it. We do courses on bereavement but it still hits you hard.'

Laura dragged her thoughts back to the present situation as she realised that Rachel was speaking, but she had to admit to feeling shaken by what she had discovered about herself. 'Of course it does. It's one thing to learn how to help others but quite another to apply that knowledge to yourself.'

She deliberately tried to be encouraging, knowing that it wouldn't help to let Rachel get too dejected. 'What you've learned should help when dealing with Bethany, though.'

'If only!' Rachel ran a weary hand through her hair. 'She won't even speak to me. I keep trying to get her to talk about what's happened, but she just turns away whenever I bring up the subject of her mother. And as for her leg... Well! How would any fourteen-year-old feel about that? It must seem like the end of the world to poor Bethany, losing part of her leg at her age!'

Rachel's voice had risen and Laura saw a few heads turn their way. Tom Hartley was sitting at a table close to where they were and he got up abruptly. His face was pale and set as he left the canteen.

Rachel must have noticed his abrupt departure because her face contorted with sudden pain. 'Tom heard me say that, didn't he? Oh, I didn't mean to upset him! He's taken it so hard, you see. Blames himself, although there's no need. Everyone agrees that if he hadn't amputated Bethany's leg at the crash site she would have died.'

There was real regret on Rachel's face as she stared at the door. Laura found herself wondering if Rachel and Tom were involved in some way. She hadn't heard any rumours but she hadn't been back at work all that long. No wonder Tom blamed himself for not being able to do more to help Rachel's niece, though, if that were the case.

'It was a dreadful thing to have happened to poor Bethany,' she said quietly. 'But we have to focus on making her see that it *isn't* the end of the world, even though it may feel like it. We shall all just have to keep trying that bit harder to get through to her.'

Rachel smiled sadly. 'Well, I'm only thankful that you're responsible for her day-to-day care, Laura. Mark told me that he'd decided you were the best suited to handle this situation, and I agree with him.'

'Thank you. It's nice that somebody has confidence in me,' she replied, unaware of the wry note which had crept into her voice.

'Of course we do!' Rachel frowned. 'Is something wrong?'

Laura shrugged, not sure if she should mention it. 'Cathy seems to have a bit of a downer on me, that's all.'

'And she's making your life difficult?' Rachel grimaced as she saw Laura's surprise. 'I'm afraid Staff Nurse Williams isn't the easiest of people to get along with. We've had a few run-ins since I took charge of the ward. Cathy applied for the post of Sister, you see, but didn't get it, mainly because of her attitude.'

'I see. It must have made things awkward for you. But I can't understand what she has against me.' Laura sighed. 'Maybe she just doesn't like me.'

'Or maybe she's jealous of you and Mark?' Rachel suggested quietly.

Laura coloured. 'There is no *me and Mark*!'

'No? Then I must have got it wrong.' Rachel laughed as she got up. 'Although I have to say that I don't think so. Mark Dawson's conversation is peppered with your name, Laura. Whatever is going on, he certainly seems to be very aware of you! Anyway, thanks for sparing me the time for this chat. It has helped and I appreciate it.'

She gave Laura a warm smile before she quickly left the canteen. Laura got up as well, not wanting to be late back and earn herself another reprimand. She quickened her pace, deciding to question Rachel further about her name cropping up in Mark's conversation. However, when she reached the corridor she could see Rachel talking to Tom Hartley and decided not to interrupt them.

She squared her shoulders as she went back to the ward. What was there to discuss anyway? No matter how Mark felt it didn't change things. She still loved Ian and didn't need another man in her life...except as a friend, of course. So long as she and Mark could be friends then she would be content.

'It really isn't as difficult as you imagine, Mrs Collins. The hospital dietician will be round to see you in the next few days to explain what Jessica can and cannot eat, but basically she'll have to avoid anything which contains gluten.'

Mark smiled at the anxious parents, giving the appearance that he had all the time in the world to spare. Laura knew just how busy he was, with their consultant being away, but nothing would make Mark rush.

'I just don't know where she's got it from, that's all I can say.' Les Collins turned and glared at his wife. 'There's never been anything like this in my family, Barbara!'

'You're right that coeliac disease can be hereditary, Mr Collins.' Mark put in smoothly, neatly avoiding another sparring match between the couple. Les and Barbara Collins had seemed on edge ever since seven-year-old Jessica had been admitted, and several times there had been a sharp exchange of words between them.

'However, from what you and your wife have told us, there doesn't seem to be any history of it in either family in this instance. Our main concern now must be to ensure that Jessica receives the right treatment. Basically, that means making adjustments to her diet to eliminate any food that contains gluten.'

'I still don't really understand it,' Barbara Collins admitted. 'This *gluten* has given Jessica this disease—is that what you're saying, Doctor?'

'In a way. Perhaps it would help if I went through it with you again from the beginning?' Mark offered. He glanced at Jessica and smiled as he picked up the toy rabbit she'd brought into hospital with her. The toy had a bandage neatly wrapped around its middle. 'Poor old Bunny looks as though he's been in the wars. What's wrong with him?'

'He's got a poorly tummy like me,' Jessica whispered shyly. 'Nurse Laura put a bandage on him to make him better.'

'Oh, I see. Well, with Nurse Laura to look after him he'll soon be up and hopping about, just like you will, sweetheart.'

He gave Laura a smile that brought the colour to her cheeks. The situation seemed to have improved since the talk they'd had that morning and she couldn't deny how good it felt to know they were friends again. Maybe she *had* known Mark only a few days but he seemed to have earned himself an important place in her life and she'd missed this feeling of closeness....

She pushed that thought to the back of her mind as Mark explained to Jessica that he needed to talk to her mummy and daddy for a few minutes. Laura set about tidying the bed as the parents moved away then looked round as Mark called to her.

'Would you mind coming, too, Laura, please? You'll be responsible for Jessica's care so I'd like your input, if you don't mind.' He shot a wry look over his shoulder at the couple and lowered his voice. 'Not to mention that another referee wouldn't go amiss!'

She chuckled at that, her face alight with laughter as she went to join him. 'Surely a big man like you isn't scared?'

'I'm an abject coward, didn't you know?' His grey eyes were teasing as they met hers. 'I can face many things, but getting between a man and wife who are each determined to blame the other… Well!'

He rolled his eyes, making her splutter with laughter. However, her amusement soon dried up as she happened to catch Cathy's stony stare as she accompanied Mark from the ward. Belatedly, Laura realised that maybe she should have asked permission, but it was too late to go back now.

Anyway, she reasoned, it wasn't long before she was due to finish for the day. The night staff were already arriving and Cathy would be busy giving the night sister her report.

Mark took Mr and Mrs Collins to one of the relatives' suites. There were two of them attached to the ward, fitted out with money raised by the hospital's League of Friends. Each suite comprised a bed-sitting room, with tea-and coffee-making facilities and *en suite* bathroom. A lot of parents made use of them but it just so happened that one was vacant at the present time. Mark waved the couple towards the settee which opened out to form a double bed when the room was in use.

'Please, sit down. I've asked Nurse Grady to join us as she'll be responsible for Jessica's care on a daily basis.' Mark waited until Laura had taken one of the straight-backed chairs before seating himself. 'Hopefully, I'll be able to introduce you to the nurse who'll be in charge of your daughter during the night before you leave, but the nursing staff are just in the process of changing over at the moment.'

He looked at the couple. 'Right, let me explain exactly what's wrong with Jessica. Your GP suspected that she might be suffering from coeliac disease. That is why he arranged for her to come into hospital to have a jejunal biopsy, which confirmed his diagnosis.'

He paused, but as neither of the parents seemed inclined to

question what he'd said he carried on. Laura was struck by his consideration as he carefully explained what was wrong with the child in the simplest of terms.

'Jessica is hypersensitive to the protein, gluten, which is found mainly in wheat, rye and barley. Oats may also cause a problem but that's something we'll have to determine at a later date. This sensitivity has resulted in damage to the lining of her small intestine. The damage in turn has made it difficult for her to absorb necessary nutrients and minerals, which is why Jessica has been losing weight and is very anaemic. Are you with me so far?'

He smiled encouragingly and Barbara Collins nodded. 'Yes, thank you. I'm beginning to understand it a bit better now.' She shot a look at her husband. 'So it has nothing to do with my cooking, then?'

Laura had to bite her lip. Surely Les Collins hadn't accused his wife of that! She could hear the amusement in Mark's voice but oddly the Collinses didn't appear to be aware of it. It made her wonder if it was just that she was particularly receptive to Mark's moods which made her notice things other people missed....

'Nothing at all, I assure you.'

She dragged her thoughts back as Mark continued, wishing that it weren't so difficult to stop them wandering all the time.

'We'll completely exclude gluten from Jessica's diet,' he explained. 'And over the next couple of weeks we expect to see a marked improvement in her health. The swelling around her tummy should subside very quickly as there won't be undigested food in the large bowel causing fermentation. However, it will take several months before everything settles down, and you must realise that Jessica will need to avoid gluten for the rest of her life.'

'Well, I still don't know how she got it,' Les Collins said belligerently. 'It's going to make things right awkward. I mean, if she can't have wheat that means she can't eat bread, doesn't it?'

'There are substitutes,' Laura put in quickly. 'The dietician will explain all that to you, but you can buy gluten-free bread, flour and pasta. And there are no restrictions on Jessica eating meat, fish, eggs, fruit and a whole lot more. It's simply a case of adapting her diet.'

'Doesn't sound too bad, I suppose.' Barbara sounded relieved. 'I thought it was going to be worse than that, didn't you, Les?'

'It's bad enough,' Les replied. 'I bet this gluten-free stuff costs a packet!'

'It's available on prescription in cases like this,' Mark assured him. He turned to Laura, obviously not intending to let the man grumble on. 'As I said, Laura will be taking care of Jessica while she's with us. We like to involve parents as much as possible so maybe she would be kind enough to take over from here?'

Laura nodded. 'Of course. First of all there are no restrictions on visiting times in the children's ward. You're welcome to come in at any time and we're keen that you take as active a role as you want in looking after Jessica.'

'How do you mean?' Barbara Collins frowned as she considered that.

'I mean that you can help wash and dress Jessica, play with her, even help when we perform simple treatments like taking blood samples.' Laura smiled as she saw Barbara shudder. 'You don't have to do anything you don't feel comfortable with. There are no hard and fast rules, but most children find it reassuring to have their primary carer, usually their mother, around—'

She broke off as Jane popped her head round the door. 'Sorry to interrupt but there's a phone call for you, Laura. It's urgent.'

Laura's heart turned over at the thought that something might have happened to Robbie. She looked at Mark, who nodded. His face mirrored her concern as she hurried from the room. She ran straight to the office and picked up the receiver, but the line was dead.

Thinking that perhaps Claire had got cut off, she quickly dialled her friend's number. It was Sean who answered and he was obviously surprised to hear her. When Laura explained what had happened, he quickly assured her that the call hadn't come from them and that Robbie was fine.

'Thanks, Sean. I'll see you later…well, fairly soon now,' Laura said in relief, although it was a puzzle to know who had wanted to speak to her so urgently.

'How about staying for a meal?' he offered. 'Go on, why not? It's ages since we had time to chat. Claire was just saying that all you seem to do at the moment is race in and out of the door!'

Laura laughed at that. 'Trying to make me feel guilty, are

you? All right then I'd love to have dinner with you. See you later.'

She hung up and turned to find Mark standing just inside the room. There was the oddest expression on his face, a mixture of pain and disappointment, which disappeared so fast that she found herself wondering if she'd imagined it. However, there was no way that she could have imagined the chill in his voice.

'In future, Nurse Grady, would you ask your friends not to phone you at work unless it really *is* an emergency. The children in this ward have to come before your social life during working hours.'

It was so unfair and uncalled for that she opened her mouth to protest, but just at that moment she caught a glimpse of Cathy in the corridor behind him. The look on the other woman's face made Laura feel sick. She refused to argue and give Cathy even more to gloat about!

'I apologise, Dr Dawson,' she said stiffly, walking towards the door. He stepped aside to let her past without uttering another word but that didn't mean Laura wasn't smarting. Who did he think he was, speaking to her that way? She put one hundred per cent commitment into her work—she always had—and to be accused of being lax in any way stuck in her throat.

She hurried to the staffroom to collect her coat as it was time to leave. Jane was already there and she looked round as Laura slammed the door.

'Uh-oh! Don't tell me that Cathy has taken another pot shot at you,' she exclaimed sympathetically.

'What do you mean?' Laura frowned.

'Oh, just that she really seems to have it in for you. Understandable, I suppose. She's been lusting after Mark Dawson ever since he set foot in this place so I don't suppose she likes the idea that he has his sights set on someone else.'

Jane shut her locker and grinned. 'Not that Mark has ever shown the least bit of interest in her, I might add. But that isn't going to stop our Cathy. She intends to get him by fair means or foul!'

Laura's head was whirling. It wasn't the first time someone had said that—Rachel had said much the same thing earlier. Not that either of them were right about Mark being interested in *her*, of course! The way he blew hot and cold was proof of that!

'See you tomorrow!'

Jane was almost out of the door when Laura gathered her addled wits. 'By the way, who phoned me earlier? Did they leave a name? They'd rung off by the time I got to the phone,' she explained as Jane paused.

Jane shook her head. 'Sorry. I've no idea who it was. Cathy just said there was a call for you and it was urgent. I told her that you were in a meeting but she said to fetch you.'

'And she didn't mention what it was about?'

Jane shrugged. 'No. In fact, I never even heard the phone ringing. It was Cathy who heard it.'

'I see. Well, thanks anyway.' Laura managed a smile as the other nurse left, but her thoughts were nothing to smile about. Had there really been a phone call for her or had Cathy invented the whole thing to make her look bad in Mark's eyes?

She sighed as she opened her locker. If it had been a trick then it had worked! The question now was what she should do about it. Or should she do anything? After all, she didn't owe Mark Dawson any explanations, not when he'd been so quick to jump to conclusions! It was her business what she did and with whom she did it....

She gave a bitter laugh as the stupidity of that thought hit her. She didn't *do* anything, neither was there a *whom* to do it with! Since Ian had died she'd done nothing but look after Robbie and struggle to make ends meet. Suddenly it struck her how empty her life was. Yet what was the alternative? To forget about Ian? To make a new life for herself with someone else?

She closed her eyes as Mark's face sprang to mind. Pain welled up inside her as she realised how futile it was. It would be the ultimate betrayal of the man she'd loved, and she couldn't do it! No matter how she felt about Mark Dawson, he couldn't replace Ian. As long as she had Robbie, she had something to live for. She didn't need anything more!

CHAPTER SEVEN

'THAT was delicious! I've been eating out of tins for the past couple of days so you can't imagine just how good that tasted.'

Laura realised what she'd said the moment she saw her friend pause. She steeled herself as Claire gave her a frowning look.

'What do you mean, you've been eating out of tins?' Claire put their dirty plates on the table and glared at her. 'I had a feeling that you were hiding something, Laura Grady! Just how bad *is* your house?'

'Well…' Laura sighed as she looked down at the pretty floral place-mat. When she'd arrived at her friends' house it had been to discover that the two boys had eaten their tea. She'd been glad that she'd taken the time to go home first and change when she had seen the effort Claire had made.

They'd eaten in the dining-room, a lovely room that looked out over the back garden, where Robbie and Ben were happily building a snowman. Claire had laid the table with her best china and linen so that the simple roast chicken she'd served had seemed all the more special.

Laura appreciated all the trouble her friend had gone to on her behalf. It made it that more difficult to avoid a truthful answer by glossing over the facts, as she had been doing for the past few days.

'Pretty bad,' she admitted at last. 'I've managed to get the place clean but that's about all.'

'Have you had someone in to check the wiring?' Sean asked quietly. He sighed when she shook her head, his handsome face filled with concern. 'Why not, Laura?'

'Why do you think?' She shrugged, trying to make light of the situation. 'Money is a bit tight at the moment. I've scraped together enough to get a plumber in to repair the broken pipe but the rest will have to wait till I get paid.'

'I hadn't realised things were so grim!' Claire sounded upset as she sank onto a chair. 'I wish you'd told us, Laura. I'm sure that Sean and I can lend you some money….'

'No, really.' Laura fixed a smile into place. 'Everything will work out so there's no need to worry.'

'I suppose you'll be able to claim on your insurance eventually, but it does tend to take time to get things sorted,' Sean said thoughtfully.

'Mmm.' Not for the world would she admit that there was no insurance. Laura hurriedly changed the subject, not wanting her friends to guess just how dire her circumstances were. Claire and Sean needed all the money they had with a new baby on the way, although she appreciated their generosity.

'Anyway, how's junior doing? How long is it now, Claire?'

'Six weeks.' Successfully distracted, Claire smiled happily. 'I went for a check-up this morning and everything is fine. The Blimp is coming along nicely.'

'The Blimp?' Laura laughed. 'I hope you've got a few other names in mind aside from that!'

'We're still arguing about them.' Claire stood and dropped a kiss on her husband's head. 'But Sean will come round to my way of thinking by the time he or she is born.'

Laura felt a lump come to her throat as she saw the loving look that passed between the couple. Their happiness was almost palpable, making her own life seem even emptier in contrast. It seemed such a long time since she'd had anyone to share the joys and sadness with, to turn to at a time of crisis like at the present.

Unbidden, Mark's face sprang to mind before she swiftly blocked it out because there was no point thinking along those lines. Turning to Sean, she asked him how his job was going, listening with genuine interest as he regaled her with stories about his work in Dalverston General's busy A and E department. He was halfway through a tale about an elderly man he'd treated that morning when the doorbell rang.

'I wonder who that can be.' He stood up as Claire appeared, carrying a delicious looking apple pie. 'I'll get it, darling. You sit down.'

He hurried from the room and the sound of voices drifted back into the room as Claire set about slicing the pie. Laura barely heard what her friend was saying as she recognised an all too familiar laugh coming from the hall. Her heart was pounding even before the door opened and Sean ushered Mark into the room.

'Mark! How lovely!' Claire exclaimed, jumping up to welcome him.

'Hello, Claire. Sorry if I'm interrupting your supper.' He came further into the room and Laura knew the exact second he saw her. His smile wavered before he collected himself, but not fast enough to hide the fact that he was surprised to see her.

'Hello, Laura. I didn't know that you were here.'

Laura smiled grimly, knowing just how true that was. If Mark had known she was here she doubted whether he would have turned up! It hurt to realise it so that her tone was chilly. 'So I gathered. Hello, Mark.'

His eyes darkened as he heard the lack of welcome in her voice, but surprisingly it wasn't annoyance that caused the change in them. Laura took a much-needed breath as she turned to reply to something Sean had said, struggling to control the turmoil she felt. Why had Mark looked at her with such *relief*? It was very odd.

'You must have a slice of this pie… No, I insist!' Claire turned to her husband, effectively cutting short Mark's protests. 'Can you fetch another plate for Mark, please, darling?'

'Of course. Sit yourself down, Mark. Believe me, you'll be glad you let Claire bully you when you taste that pie. She has a way with pastry…and a lot of other things we won't mention!'

'Sean Fitzgerald!' Claire's cheeks were bright pink as she picked up a napkin and hurled it after her husband. She rolled her eyes when he merely laughed as he left the room. 'That man will drive me insane one of these days!'

It was obvious that she meant it in the nicest possible way and Mark laughed deeply. 'Mmm, you don't look too bad on it, Claire.' He looked at Laura, making an obvious effort to be polite. 'Does she?'

'Indeed not.'

Laura groaned inwardly as she heard the stilted note in her voice. She stared down at her place-mat as she felt Claire look at her curiously. However, her friend obviously decided not to say anything as she steered the conversation towards more impersonal topics, like the weather.

'It's started freezing again,' Mark said in reply to Claire's question. 'It's going to make the roads very dangerous unless the gritters get out soon.'

'Did you drive over here?' Sean asked, coming back with an extra plate.

'No, I walked.' Mark accepted the slice of pie with a smile of thanks.

'Walked? But it's an awful long way from where you live to here,' Laura observed in surprise before she could think better of it.

Mark turned to her and once again she could see that same strange expression in his eyes when he looked at her. 'I needed to clear my head so I hardly noticed how far it was.' He took a deep breath and it seemed as though a weight suddenly lifted from his shoulders even as she watched. 'And I'm certainly glad I came now!'

Sean laughed. 'I told you Claire's pie was something special, didn't I?'

Everyone laughed, Laura included, yet she knew in her heart that Mark hadn't been referring to her friend's skill at baking. Her hand shook as she lifted a small piece of pie to her mouth but she barely tasted the warm tangy apple, richly spiced with cinnamon. Mark had meant that it had been worth the long walk in the cold to see *her*, but why should he feel like that after what had happened earlier?

It was a puzzle that eluded her attempts to solve it as they ate their dessert then had coffee. When Mark pushed back his chair with a groan she was still no closer to understanding.

'That was great. Thanks, Claire. I wouldn't mind, but I'd eaten before I set out so I'm absolutely stuffed now!'

'What you need, my friend, is a little exercise to work off all that food.' Sean shot a glance out of the window at the two children, who were still happily building their snowman. 'How about we challenge that pair to a snowball fight? Are you game?'

'On one condition. That the girls come as well.' Mark grimaced. 'Of course, they won't be much use because women are such lousy shots, but at least they can make the snowballs for us.'

'Why, you chauvinist, Mark Dawson!' Claire declared, glaring at him. She turned to Laura with a grin. 'Shall we show them just who's the best shot around here?'

'Why not?' Suddenly Laura could think of nothing more fun than taking part in the childish challenge. She winked at her friend. 'It's going to be a nightmare, you realise that, don't you? Men are such *babies* when they lose....'

She ducked as Mark aimed a playful cuff at her ear. His grey eyes were alight with laughter as he caught hold of her hand to haul her to her feet. 'We'll soon see who cries for mercy first, young lady!'

'Oh, thank you for the *young*, kind sir!' She grinned up at him, her heart rolling over as he treated her to one of his wonderfully warm smiles. She quickly looked away as Claire announced that she was going to fetch her coat, but she couldn't deny that it felt good to know they were friends once more.

Laura went with her, gratefully accepting the woolly hat and scarf her friend offered her. She was glad she had when they stepped out into the garden because the night was bitterly cold. The sky was like a huge sheet of black velvet dotted with silver star spangles, the curl of a new moon hazy with frost. Laura drank in a deep lungful of crisp night air, simply enjoying the sheer beauty all around her, then spluttered as a massive snowball exploded against her neck.

She swung round, trying not to laugh as she saw Mark pick up Robbie and try to hide behind him. 'Coward!' she teased. 'Hide behind a poor defenceless child, would you?'

She scooped up a handful of snow and started towards them then gasped as Robbie let loose a shot that caught her squarely in the face. He was giggling like mad, obviously revelling in the fun.

'Defenceless? I don't think so!' Mark set the little boy on his feet and crouched down beside him. 'OK, partner. Let 'em have it!'

It was all the excuse everyone needed. Snowballs whizzed across the garden from every direction. Laura wasn't sure who was on which team so simply bombarded anyone and everyone who happened to come into her line of fire. She caught Ben squarely in the back as the child bent to gather up more snow then shrieked as he promptly retaliated. Both boys were having a great time, squealing with excitement every time they scored a hit.

Mark was helping Robbie, very much to his own detriment, she realised, seeing the amount of snow caked on his clothing. Maybe it was unfair to take advantage but she did so anyway, seeing that he couldn't defend himself as well as he might normally have done. She let loose at least a dozen snowballs, one after the other, until he held up his hands in defeat.

'Pax! I submit. If I had a white flag I'd wave it,' he declared.

'So long as you admit that you were beaten fairly and squarely,' she declared loftily.

He grinned that lazy grin which always turned her insides to water as he shook the snow out of his tousled hair. 'I don't know about fairly….'

He backed away, trying his best to look suitably scared and failing miserably as she promptly scooped up another handful of snow. 'I take it back. You and Claire are the superior shots, Laura. Sean and I shall accept defeat gracefully.'

He turned to the others then frowned as he caught sight of the expression on Claire's face. 'Hey, are you all right?'

'Just a bit of a twinge—Oh!' Claire gasped and clutched Sean's arm.

'That looks like more than a twinge.' Mark declared, hurrying towards her. He helped Sean get Claire back inside the house, where they took her straight into the sitting-room, but she refused to sit down.

'I don't think I can. My back is aching so much—' She broke off, turning fearful eyes on her husband. 'It's the Blimp! I…I think I might be in labour!'

'Well, I don't think you need worry too much. With two doctors and a fully qualified midwife, you couldn't be in better hands,' Mark declared, obviously trying to reassure her. However, Laura could see the concern in his eyes when he turned to her.

'Why don't you check her over while I call an ambulance, Laura? Best to err on the side of caution, wouldn't you say?'

'I most certainly would.' She helped Claire off with her coat then urged her to lie down on the sofa as Mark hurried away to make the call. Sean sat beside his wife, his face white with strain, although Claire didn't seem to be in any real discomfort after those first few twinges.

Placing a hand on her friend's abdomen, Laura checked the baby's position, which was what she would have expected at thirty-four weeks. 'Everything seems to be fine from what I can tell. How do you feel now?'

'Fine. There was just that sharp twinge and now I can't feel anything.' Claire smiled ruefully. 'I bet it was a Braxton-Hicks' contraction and my back is aching from bending over making snowballs!'

'Could very well be.' Laura looked round as Mark reappeared. 'We think it could have been a false alarm. Claire is fine now and I can't feel anything going on. The baby's head doesn't feel as though it's engaged—it's far too active!'

Sean laughed, looking relieved. 'I think he's going to be another footballer like his big brother.' He looked round. 'Where are the kids, by the way?'

'In the kitchen,' Mark informed him. 'Ben is making them both some hot chocolate.' He smiled at Claire. 'He's going to be very disappointed if it was a false alarm. He was almost beside himself with excitement at the thought that his new brother or sister was about to make its appearance.'

Claire smiled lovingly as she took Sean's hand. 'Ben has been thrilled about this baby from the moment we told him. I was a bit worried at first that he might be jealous, but there's been no sign of it.'

'He's a great kid. You and Sean are very lucky.' Mark turned to Laura and smiled warmly. 'And so are you. It makes me feel a bit left out being the only one here who doesn't have a child of his own.'

'Oh, your time will come, Mark.' There was a twinkle in Claire's eyes as she looked pointedly at Laura.

Laura cleared her throat but she could feel the heat warming her cheeks. Claire was matchmaking again, and it wasn't very subtle either! 'So, what about the ambulance—did you ring for one?'

'I did. But there's a backlog of calls at the moment because of the appalling road conditions. They're doing their best but they aren't miracle-workers and they're having to prioritise. If you don't think that it really is an emergency, maybe I should phone back and cancel.'

Sean glanced at his wife. 'What do you think, darling? Was it a false alarm?'

Claire shrugged. 'I think so...' She suddenly laughed. 'If I, a fully qualified nurse, can't decide if it was or wasn't a *real* contraction then what hope do our poor patients have?'

'I think it's entirely different when you're dealing with a situation like this,' Mark assured her, laughing. 'The tendency for medical personnel is to play things down. However, I wouldn't like to think that we're being too relaxed about this.'

'Neither would I.' Sean stood up. 'I know it's six weeks until the Blimp is due but I'm not taking any chances. If you could cancel that ambulance, Mark, I'll drive Claire to hospital myself just to be on the safe side.'

'And he says he isn't going to be a fussing new father....' Claire sighed as she accepted Sean's hand and let him haul her to her feet.

'It isn't fussing at all. It's just being sensible,' Laura assured her. She followed the couple from the room. 'I'll stay here and look after Ben so you don't need to worry about him.'

'Would you? Thanks, Laura.' Claire hugged her then turned resignedly towards the door. She was still mumbling about it being an awful lot of fuss about nothing as the two men helped her to the car.

Laura watched Sean back carefully out of the drive and set off down the road at a snail's pace as Mark came hurrying back inside, rubbing his cold hands together to warm them.

'I hope they'll be all right,' she said quietly as she closed the door. 'The roads are so bad tonight.'

'Sean will take care. And the main road should be clear by now.' Mark gave her shoulder a reassuring squeeze before he went to the phone. 'I'll just make that call to the ambulance station and tell them what's happened.'

'And could you give Maternity a ring to let them know that Claire's on her way?' Laura smiled as he glanced round. 'Nothing like being prepared, and if I remember anything at all about working in the unit it's that babies just *love* to choose the most difficult night of the year to make their appearance. I bet the place is snowed under with deliveries...if you'll excuse the pun!'

Mark groaned exaggeratedly. 'I don't believe anyone would come out with something like that!' He shook his head as he picked up the receiver. 'I see that you do have *some* faults after all, Laura Grady! You aren't quite as perfect as I imagined you to be.'

She didn't say anything, mainly because she couldn't think of anything suitable. But that didn't stop her pulse racing. Did Mark think she was perfect, then?

She pushed that ridiculous notion to the back of her mind as she went to tell Ben where his parents had gone. The boy seemed disappointed when she explained that she didn't think the baby would be born that night. However, he cheered up when he discovered that Robbie was going to spend another night with him. Considering the age difference between them, with Ben being almost eight and Robbie approaching five, they got on extremely well. Ben was a naturally thoughtful child, who made allowances for Robbie's handicap, and Robbie obviously hero-worshipped Ben, trailing after him as the older boy led the way upstairs.

Laura watched them go, thinking how wonderful it would be if Robbie had a brother to play with, someone like Ben who would accept him as he was and love him unconditionally. She and Ian had spoken about having another child, but at the back of her mind had been the lingering fear that something might go wrong again. It was another reason she could never get involved in another relationship. It simply wouldn't be fair to any man to deny him a family and yet she couldn't take the risk of having another handicapped child.

'Why so sad?'

Mark had come up behind her and Laura deliberately tried to shake off the feeling of melancholy which had beset her before she turned. There was no chance of her ever finding herself in the position of having another child, so there was no point worrying about it! Even so, she couldn't deny the ache that filled one small corner of her heart as she wondered about the woman who would one day give Mark the children he obviously longed for.

Would she be young and pretty, full of fun or serious? Maybe he'd met her already and those clothes she'd seen in his wardrobe belonged to her.

'Laura?' His tone was gentle as he prompted her to answer so she couldn't blame that for the way she jumped. Colour flooded her face as she realised where her thoughts had been wandering. She swiftly walked to the kettle and picked it up.

'I was miles away. Sorry. How about another cup of coffee to warm us up?' she suggested with an over-bright smile.

'Sounds good to me. But let me make it.' His brows rose when she held on tightly to the kettle as he tried to take it from her. 'Don't you want to take off your coat?' he asked, almost too blandly.

'Oh!' She gasped as she realised that she was still wearing her coat, as well as the hat and scarf Claire had lent her. 'Well, yes, of course. How silly of me. I didn't realise I still had them on.'

'No wonder, with all the excitement that's been going on around here.'

He offered her the perfect excuse yet she could see something in his eyes as he took the kettle from her which told her that he understood. How much, though? Had Mark managed to lock into her thoughts just now? Had he somehow worked out what she'd been thinking—about him and the unknown woman who had left her clothes in his flat?

The thought made her feel hot and bothered, angry and yet ashamed of feeling like that, because it really wasn't anything to do with her. The truth was that Mark Dawson could have a string of lovers a mile long and it would be none of *her* business!

She swung round on her heel before her wayward thoughts got the better of her common sense. 'I'll just go and hang up my coat. Oh, and I may as well settle the boys down as it's getting late.'

'Fine. Take your time. I'll make us a pot of proper coffee, not instant, as a treat.'

Mark's tone was warm and held a nuance that did little to settle her nerves. Her legs felt like two wooden sticks as she marched stiffly down the hall. Crazy though it sounded, she couldn't shake off the feeling that he *had* guessed what she'd been thinking…

She sighed as she hung her coat on a peg and put her damp scarf to dry on the radiator. Mark Dawson might be many things but he wasn't a mind-reader. Thank heavens!

* * *

It took a good half-hour before Robbie and Ben settled down for the night. Robbie always had a story before he went to sleep, but he wanted Ben to read it to him. Laura's heart filled with tenderness as she watched the two of them snuggled up beneath the duvet in one of the twin beds in Ben's brightly painted bedroom.

Ben was patience itself as Robbie interrupted him to ask questions all the time, wanting to know what the characters in the story were eating for their tea and where their mummies were, points the author had chosen not to include! When they came to the last page, Robbie gave a deep sigh.

'Nice story, Mummy.'

'It was. And Ben read it beautifully. Say thank you to him.'

'Thank 'ou, Ben,' Robbie said dutifully, then planted a huge kiss on his friend's cheek.

''S' OK.' Ben mumbled, looking both embarrassed and pleased by the show of affection. He went and got into his own bed, snuggling down beneath the quilt while Laura kissed Robbie and tucked him in. However, there was a trace of concern on Ben's face when she went to turn off his bedside lamp.

'Mum will be all right, won't she?' he asked quietly.

'Of course she will. Don't you worry about her, love. I expect she'll be back before too long,' Laura said encouragingly. The boy smiled in relief and closed his eyes as she switched off the lamp. She turned to leave then stopped as she found Mark lounging against the doorjamb.

He backed out onto the landing so that she could pass, waiting while she pulled the door to. 'I was wondering what was taking you so long,' he explained softly, so as not to disturb the children.

'Robbie wanted a story and he wanted Ben to read it to him,' she explained equally quietly, although her heart was making enough racket to deafen her.

Did it really have to behave so shamelessly? she wondered. So what if Mark *did* look particularly attractive in the dim light, his light brown hair glistening like a new penny, his grey eyes as smooth and sensuous as silk—was that really an excuse?

She firmed her lips and tried to do the same to her resolve, but it wasn't easy when all her senses seemed to be suddenly hyperactive. Why had she never noticed just how delicious the spicy scent of his aftershave was? Or how warm his skin felt when he put a guiding hand on her back as they walked towards the stairs? Little bands of heat seemed to be imprinting themselves onto her spine where each of his fingers touched, and she shivered delicately.

'Are you cold?' Mark sounded concerned as he felt the tremor that passed through her. 'Here, let's go into the sitting-room again. The fire is lit so it will be lovely and warm in there.'

He opened the door and Laura gulped as she looked inside the room which was lit only by a single lamp and the flickering glow from the fire. She'd been completely unaware of her surroundings while she'd been concentrating on Claire, but now she couldn't help thinking that it looked like the perfect setting for a seduction! Suddenly she wasn't sure she would be able to resist if that was what Mark had in mind.

'Sugar?'

'Er...pardon?'

She looked around helplessly, defeated by that simplest of questions. Mark smiled at her, a slow, sexy smile that made those separate bands of heat melt together to form a red-hot current which flowed right down her spine and ended up at the tips of her toes.

'Do you take sugar in your coffee?' he explained like a perfect host, but the twinkle in his eyes told her that he had a very good idea what was wrong with her!

'No... Yes... I mean, I do if it's proper coffee but not if it's instant,' she babbled, inwardly wincing as she saw his brows rise.

'Really? You must explain the logic behind that. But seeing as it is *proper* coffee then I think that's a yes.' He gave her a gentle push. 'Make yourself comfortable. It won't take long.'

On leaden legs, Laura walked into the room as he disappeared towards the kitchen. One part of her mind—the rational bit— was crying out that this was a mistake, while the other part— the flighty bit—was telling her not to listen.

After all, what harm could there be in them having a cup of coffee together? the beguiling little voice insisted, taking advantage of her weakened state to get its point across. She was no closer to resolving the dilemma when Mark reappeared, carefully balancing two brimming cups on what looked suspiciously like a biscuit-tin lid.

'I couldn't find a tray,' he explained, setting the cups on the table in front of the sofa. 'That's the trouble with being in someone else's house—you don't like rooting around to find things.'

'No.' Laura took a quick breath then bent to pick up one of the cups, jumping as Mark's hand shot out to cover hers.

'It's scalding hot so I'd let it cool down for a minute or two,' he advised. He let her go and sat on the sofa, patting the cushion beside him. 'Come on, sit yourself down. There's nothing else you can do at present. Claire will be fine.'

If *only* it was concern for her friend that was troubling her, Laura thought desperately. Sitting next to Mark came into the category of *Big Mistake*, but she couldn't for the life of her think of a way to avoid it apart from making a fuss, which would only make matters worse!

She took her seat, prudently leaving as much space as possible between them, which wasn't nearly enough to ensure against a further assault on her vulnerable senses.

She bit her lip as tautly honed muscles rippled beneath his grey chambray shirt as Mark reached for his cup. He took a sip of coffee and she stifled a moan as she watched his throat work as he swallowed. How could something so...so *normal* as drinking be so sexy?

She made a grab for her own cup then flushed with embarrassment as coffee slopped over the side. 'How stupid of me!'

Putting the cup back on its saucer, she licked the drops of coffee off her fingers then stilled as she happened to glimpse the expression on Mark's face. To describe it as lustful didn't do it justice because there was such a mixture of emotions there at that moment that it was impossible to separate one from another. However, it was only when he suddenly got up that she realised she'd been staring at him.

'I'm sorry.'

The harsh grating of his voice ran through her like a shock wave. In contrast, her own voice sounded almost too weak to carry to where he stood staring into the fire.

'What for?'

'Because I'm going to commit a cardinal sin and I'm afraid you'll hate me for it.'

He turned and her pulse began to race when she saw the desire in his eyes as he reached for her hands and drew her to her feet. There was a note of agony in his voice as he bent towards her but it couldn't disguise the hunger she heard in it as well.

'I know you don't want what I do, Laura, but I need this!'

His mouth suddenly found hers and the rest of the sentence was swallowed up in the blaze of passion that ignited between them. Laura was stunned by how quickly she went from bewilderment to desire in one great leap. There was that first gentle touch of Mark's mouth on hers and then a fierce surge of passion which swept them both away. Suddenly she couldn't seem to get enough of him, couldn't absorb sufficient sustenance from the gentle blending of lips.

She gave a low moan as she wound her arms around his neck and drew his head down so that he would deepen the kiss, heard the groan he gave as he realised what she wanted. Hearing it set loose the last of her inhibitions. She made no attempt to stifle the desire that surged through her as his tongue met hers in a ritual as old as time.

They were both trembling when finally they broke apart, Mark as well as her, both wrung out by the ferocity of the passion they'd shared. Mark lifted her face and she could see the glimmer of tears in his eyes as he looked at her as though she were the most precious thing in the world.

'I never imagined it could feel like this, Laura.'

She didn't ask him what he meant, what *it* was, because she knew. She didn't ask because then she would have to deal with the answer and she couldn't do that—not here, not now. Maybe it was cowardly, but she simply couldn't cope with the repercussions it would cause if Mark said the words, *told* her that he loved her. It was enough to know it in the secret depths of her heart.

When he kissed her again it was with a tenderness that brought tears to her own eyes. Maybe Mark wouldn't say the words because he knew that she wasn't ready to hear them, but he was telling her in his own sweet way how he felt. She would have needed a heart of stone not to have felt something in return, although she shied away from discovering what it was. She wasn't ready to do that just yet either.

'Laura…Laura!' His tone was as rough as sandpaper, as dark

as a dream as he said her name over and over as though he loved the very sound of it.

Laura murmured in response, soft little sounds that weren't really words at all but which somehow managed to convey their own special kind of sense. When he drew her closer she returned the compliment, wrapping her arms tightly around his trim waist, letting their hips come into even closer contact so that she could feel his hunger for her. Feeling it awoke an answering hunger inside her, a need that yearned to be satisfied. It had been so long since a man had held her, loved her, made her feel the magic only two people could create.

When Mark's hands went to the hem of her sweater and slid beneath it she didn't stop him. Why should she when she wanted what was happening as much as he did?

Slowly, delicately, his fingers ran over the warm skin over her ribs, making her tremble with anticipation as they moved ever closer to their goal. Laura knew that she was holding her breath but Mark was holding his as well so it didn't seem to matter. Both of them seemed to be held in thrall, drawing out the moment when his hands would find her breasts and caress them for the very first time, so that the waiting seemed even sweeter.

There was just another inch to go, then half an inch, then a distance too small to measure. His hands were just cupping her delicately, reverently, when the telephone rang. The shrill sound was an ugly intrusion which made them both jump.

Mark stared at her, his eyes faintly glazed, his breathing rapid and shallow. 'I...I'd better get that.'

'Yes.' Her voice sounded whispery thin and she felt Mark tense. Lifting her chin, he stared into her eyes as though willing her to believe him.

'What we did just now wasn't wrong, Laura. You know that, don't you?'

'I...' She closed her eyes, unable to agree or disagree, unable to give him the answer he needed or the one he didn't want to hear. She didn't know if what had happened had been right or wrong, that was the trouble!

Had it been right to let Mark kiss her, to kiss him back, to long for more than that? Had it been wrong to forget she was a widow and remember that she was a woman? How could there be an answer to any of those questions without delving into the past? But that was something she was afraid to do. She wanted to put what had happened into a capsule, separate it from everything which had gone before or might come later. Then there would be no need to answer Mark or her own conscience!

He swore softly, painfully, before he let her go and strode from the room. Laura heard the phone go quiet then the rumble of Mark's voice as he spoke to the caller. She closed her eyes, feeling tears welling behind her lids. She might not have said anything but Mark obviously thought he knew what her answer was, and maybe it was for the best. Whatever he wanted from her, she couldn't give it to him...for so many reasons.

Mark was a very special man, too special for her to break his heart by making promises she couldn't keep.

CHAPTER EIGHT

'THAT was Sean. Seems as though it was a false alarm after all. Niall Gillespie, the consultant, was in the maternity unit and he checked Claire over himself. He's happy to let her come home.'

Mark had come back to tell her what was happening. Laura quickly smoothed all expression from her face before she turned.

'Well, if Niall says it's OK then there's definitely no need to worry.' She summoned a smile, praying that he wouldn't guess how much effort it cost her to act naturally....

Laura felt her stomach sink as it hit her how impossible that was going to be. How could they act *naturally* with each other after that kiss?

She rushed on, not wanting to think about it. 'I must say that I'm glad it was a false alarm. Although the baby is viable at thirty-four weeks, it's not ideal for it to be born so early, is it?'

'No. The longer Claire can hold on, the better,' Mark agreed evenly, taking his cue from her. Obviously he'd sensed that she didn't want to talk about what had happened because he made no reference to it as he checked his watch. 'Anyway, you don't need me here, so I'll get off home now that I know everything is all right. Sean said to tell you that they should be back in about half an hour.'

'Fine.' She followed him out to the hall, waiting while he took his coat off a peg. He hunted his gloves out of his pocket, grimacing as he dropped one on the floor.

'Here.' Laura bent to pick it up, fixing a determined smile to her mouth as she handed it to him. 'Now, don't say thank you. It's bad luck!'

'I don't believe in all that superstitious nonsense,' he replied flatly. 'I think we make our own luck, be it good or bad.' He drew his gloves on then looked at her, and it was impossible not to see the sadness in his eyes. 'We make our lives what they are by the decisions we take. You can't blame it on luck or anything else.'

She knew what he meant, of course, and her heart wept. Mark was telling her that it was up to her what the future held, that it was *her* decisions that would affect the rest of her life. Maybe she could have lived with that thought if she hadn't known that any decision she made would affect him too.

He opened the front door then stopped, a frown drawing his brows together. 'You aren't thinking of going back home tonight, I hope?'

'I'm not sure…' She sighed as she saw his expression darken. 'I suppose I could stay here. Claire certainly won't mind.'

'Good. It's far too late to be trekking off home at this time of the night, especially as I doubt if you've had a chance to get things properly sorted out yet. I can imagine the state the place is in after the electricians have been at work,' he added wryly.

'Mmm.' She looked away but not fast enough to allay his suspicions.

'You *have* had the wiring checked, haven't you, Laura?' His tone sharpened with concern. 'You must realise how dangerous it is if water has got into the electrical circuit?'

'Of course I do.' She answered the last question because that was the easy one. And it wasn't really lying, she assured herself, just *fibbing* by omission!

He stared at her for a moment then shrugged. 'Good. I wouldn't have a moment's peace, thinking about you in that house on your own with faulty electrics.'

'There's no need to worry,' she assured him firmly because it was the truth. She hadn't *attempted* to turn on a light since the pipe had burst so she'd been in no danger! However, she knew that Mark would take a very dim view of the fact that she'd been managing by gaslight for the past few days and cooking on a camping stove when he obviously believed that she'd had workmen in to put things to rights.

If only! she thought ruefully. Although she had worked hard these past few days, the house was still a mess and would remain that way until she could save enough money to pay for the repairs. Still, it really wasn't his problem so there was no need to tell him just how bad things were.

'Right, I'll see you tomorrow, then.'

Mark gave her a last smile then carefully made his way up the ice-slick path. He paused by the gate to wave and for a moment he was silhouetted by the glow from one of the streetlights.

Laura felt her heart give a funny kind of bump, like the jolt an engine gave when it was jump-started after breaking down. She took a deep breath and quickly closed the door as Mark headed down the road. Going to the kitchen, she set about washing the dishes, refusing to think about what had happened. She didn't want to think about it because there was no point. She was Ian's widow and she was luckier than a lot of women because she'd known what it was to be loved. Yet as she stacked the clean dishes in the rack her traitorous mind was whispering that it must be a very special feeling to be loved by a man like Mark Dawson.

'I just want to check that dressing on your leg, Bethany. OK?'

Laura drew the curtains around the girl's bed then sighed as she turned round. Bethany had picked up her personal stereo and was in the process of putting on the headphones, making it clear that she had no intention of carrying on a conversation.

Bethany had been in the ward for four days now and in all that time she'd refused to say anything more than the odd yes or no. Laura knew that if they were going to help her they had to find some way to break through the barrier she'd erected between herself and the world.

'Who are you listening to?' she asked as she began removing the dressings from Bethany's leg. The wound was healing well, thanks to Tom Hartley's skilled surgery, and everyone agreed that Bethany should have little difficulty when the time came for her to be fitted with a prosthesis. However, the girl's attitude would be the determining factor as to how well she would cope with the artificial limb, and so far it hadn't been encouraging.

There was no reply, so Laura continued determinedly, refusing to be put off by her silence. 'My little boy absolutely loves that new band that was on television last Saturday. I can't remember what they're called but I'm sure you must know who I mean. They sing that song about—'

'The ship?' Bethany shrugged nonchalantly when Laura glanced at her. 'I saw them at a gig a couple of weeks ago.'

'Did you? Why, you lucky thing!' Laura felt her spirits lift. At long last she'd managed to break through the wall of silence. 'Were they playing here in Dalverston?'

'No, in Preston. Mum took me in the car.' The teenager bit her lip and Laura could see tears in her eyes as she added in a choked voice, 'She bought tickets for me and some of my friends as a birthday treat.'

'That was a lovely idea. I bet you all enjoyed it. But, then, mums usually know the sort of presents their children like,' Laura observed quietly, mentally crossing her fingers. Rachel had said that her niece hadn't spoken about her mother since the accident so this was a real breakthrough.

She chose her next words with care, knowing how important it was that the girl deal with her grief rather than bottling it up. 'You must be very sad about what has happened, love. Losing your mum like that is hard, but everyone wants to help—'

She broke off as the curtain was brusquely swished aside and Cathy appeared.

'Haven't you finished that yet, Laura?' the staff nurse demanded rudely. 'For heaven's sake, get a move on. We couldn't keep this ward running if we all worked at your speed!'

Laura was furious both about the reprimand and the interruption, which couldn't have come at a worse moment. However, it wouldn't have been ethical to take the other woman to task with Bethany listening.

'I won't be long now,' she said coldly, letting Cathy know by the tone of her voice how she felt.

'Well, just make sure you're not!' Cathy twitched the curtains back into place and disappeared.

Laura counted to ten then carried on with what she'd been doing, but no matter how hard she tried she couldn't get Bethany to respond again. She left the girl reading a magazine, rueing the lost opportunity. It had been a real step forward to have Bethany talk about her mother like that. If only Cathy hadn't interrupted they might have made some more progress....

'Good morning, Laura. How are you today?'

She felt her heart jolt as she recognised Mark's deep tones. She spun round, unable to hide her pleasure at seeing him. Despite the fact that she'd spent a restless night, trying not to think about what had happened between them, she couldn't deny that her heart lifted as she saw him.

In a fast sweep her eyes took appreciative stock of the crisp white shirt and deep blue tie he was wearing with well-pressed grey trousers. He rarely wore a suit when he came into the ward, preferring to present a more relaxed front when dealing with the children. However, the sight of his muscular body in the casually formal clothing was enough to make her pulse race. It was an effort to respond to the greeting with suitable composure.

'I'm very well, thank you. How are you?'

'Oh, so-so.' He grinned as he saw her frown. He lowered his voice and she felt goose-bumps break out all over her body as he explained softly, 'I had a bit of a restless night and didn't get much sleep. I seemed to have rather a lot on my mind.'

'Oh!' It was impossible to control the heat that rushed up her face. It was almost a relief when Cathy came bustling over just then because she wasn't sure that she could have thought of anything to say. It made her feel all shivery inside to imagine Mark lying awake, thinking about those kisses they'd shared….

'Come straight back after you've delivered Katie to the radiology unit. I want you to give Tim a bed-bath.'

Laura dragged her thoughts back into line as she realised that Cathy was speaking to her. 'Oh, but I promised Katie that I would stay with her while she has her scan,' she said quickly. 'She's really scared, and—'

'It's out of the question. I need you here,' Cathy said curtly, cutting her off in mid-sentence. She rolled her eyes as she turned to Mark. 'Honestly, it doesn't take a genius to see how pushed we are at the moment, without staff taking it upon themselves to go AWOL!'

She was obviously inviting his sympathy but it backfired. He frowned as he looked down the ward to where Katie was sitting by her bed. 'I know that you're under a great deal of pressure, Staff. However, allowing Katie to become distressed won't help either the radiologists to do their job or her recovery. Katie is already upset because her mother has seen fit to absent herself so it would seem sensible to me that Laura should stay with her if it will help.'

Cathy's mouth pursed, making it clear that she was furious that Mark should have disagreed with her. 'It is my responsibility to ensure that the running of this ward isn't compromised in any way.'

'I understand that. I also appreciate that it's a difficult task, balancing all aspects of the job.' Mark smiled but there was no doubting his authority. 'Perhaps it would help if I had a word with Fiona Watts to see if she can find someone else to cover for Sister Hart while she's absent from duty?'

'That won't be necessary, thank you.' Cathy's tone was clipped. She turned to Laura and it was impossible to ignore the hatred in her eyes. 'You may stay with Katie while she has her scan but I want you back here straight afterwards. Understand?'

Mark sighed as the staff nurse strode away. 'Maybe I was a little hard on her. It can't be easy stepping into Rachel's shoes. She does such a fine job of running this ward that you don't realise how difficult it really is, balancing everyone's needs.'

Laura didn't say anything because it was hardly her place to comment. However, she couldn't deny a certain trepidation as she thought about the repercussions this was going to have. Cathy had been difficult enough to work with before, and now she would be even worse after Mark's intervention, even though he'd been right to do so.

'Right, I'd better get going now that I've stirred up a hornet's nest here!' Mark's tone was so rueful that it made her smile despite her qualms.

'I bet you were born with a wooden spoon in your mouth,' she teased.

'So that I could stir things up?' He laughed. 'I didn't do it on purpose, honestly!'

'But you still manage to have that kind of effect!' she retorted without thinking.

'Do I?' His tone was warm and as smooth as honey. Suddenly Laura knew that they were no longer talking about the disturbance he had caused by siding with her. Her mind winged its way back to what had happened at Claire's house the previous night, and she bit her lip.

Mark had had a devastating effect on her then, made her feel things she'd thought she would never feel again. She felt both guilty and oddly elated that she was able to feel like that when she'd believed that part of her had been dead.

'I'll pick you up tonight after you finish work.' His tone was slightly rough around the edges. It made a tremor work its way down her spine so that it was difficult to think clearly, but she had to try. There was no point allowing things to progress any further when there was no future for them.

'I don't think that would be—'

'Sensible?' He smiled, his eyes warm and tender as he saw the worry on her face. 'Neither do I. But sometimes you have to take risks, Laura, and I'm willing to take one now.'

He gave her a last reassuring smile, but it did little to settle her mind as she went to fetch Katie and take her down to the radiology unit. Maybe Mark was willing to take a chance but was she willing to risk hurting him? Having that on her conscience would be too hard to live with, more painful even than the guilt she felt about being attracted to him. Hurting Mark wasn't an option, but that was what she would end up doing if she didn't make him understand that she hadn't anything to offer him.

The worry nagged away at her so that she was glad to be distracted by the need to soothe Katie's fears when they arrived at the radiology unit. Katie was to have an X-ray, as well as a renal ultrasound scan, so Laura helped to get the little girl ready, keeping up a stream of bright conversation to take the child's mind off what was happening. However, it was obvious that Katie was very nervous.

'Right, poppet. Laura and I just have to go behind that screen while I take the pictures.' Karen Price, the radiologist, smiled at the little girl. She was a pleasant, motherly sort of woman in her late thirties who, surprisingly, had never married and lived with her widowed mother. Laura had always found her extremely kind and was glad that Karen was on duty that day.

'Will it hurt when you take the pictures?' Katie's bottom lip quivered ominously. 'Daniel said that all my bones would light up and burn.'

Laura sighed, wishing to heaven that Daniel didn't have such a vivid imagination! The little boy had been due to go home that morning but he'd complained of earache so Mark had decided to keep him in for another day. 'No, of course it won't hurt, sweetheart. I promise. You won't feel anything at all. Karen will just press a button and, abracadabra, she'll have a picture of your tummy.'

'That's the magic word! The one my daddy said last time.' Katie's face lit up. 'He said that it wouldn't hurt if he said that and it didn't and now you've said it too, Laura!'

'So now you *know* it won't hurt, don't you?' Laura laughed as she kissed the little girl's cheek then followed Karen out of the room while the X-ray was taken. After that, there were no more problems. Katie lay perfectly still while Karen did the renal ultrasound.

The radiologist smiled when she'd finished. 'What a good little girl you've been! I think you deserve one of my special badges.' She dug in the pocket of her lab coat and produced a black enamel badge.

Laura laughed when she saw the hologram of a skeleton that was painted on it appear to move as Karen tilted it from side to side. 'That's great, isn't it, Katie? Everyone will be really envious because they haven't got one.'

'I bet Daniel will wish he had one,' Katie said importantly as she let Karen pin the badge to her nightdress before they set off back to the ward. As soon as they got back she went rushing over to Daniel's bed to show him her new treasure.

The rest of the day passed much as Laura had expected. Cathy was sharp to the point of rudeness whenever she spoke to her. They had been sent a relief nurse from the surgical ward, Meg Andrews, and she rolled her eyes after one particularly nasty exchange, which had centred on how fast Laura had handed out the afternoon drinks of juice—not fast enough for the staff nurse's liking.

'What have you done to rattle her cage? She's never given you a minute's peace all afternoon long! I wouldn't put up with it if I were you. You want to have a word with Fiona Watts and explain what's going on.'

Laura shrugged uncomfortably as she wheeled the trolley back to the ward kitchen. 'I'm sure she doesn't realise just how nasty she's being.'

'No?' Meg laughed. 'Come on, Laura, anyone can tell that she has it in for you! What have you done? Stolen her boyfriend by any chance?'

Laura couldn't stop the sudden colour that flooded her face. She quickly turned towards the sink, busying herself washing the dirty glasses. 'I've no idea. We just don't seem to have hit it off, that's all.'

'Well, I'd do something about it if I were you,' Meg said, giving her an odd look as she picked up a teatowel. 'Cathy has a reputation as a troublemaker. She got a nurse suspended from Orthopaedics when she was there, said that she'd done something or other.'

She shrugged when Laura looked at her in alarm. 'Louise was a friend of mine as it happens, and I know for a fact that it was a pack of lies but she couldn't prove it. In the end she decided to resign as she couldn't face working with Cathy again, but be warned. Don't let the same thing happen to you.'

'I certainly won't!' Laura exclaimed in horror. 'I need this job and I certainly don't want to be put in the position of having to resign from it when I'd never be able to find anything as suitable.'

'Then watch your back, kiddo. Our Cathy fights dirty so be careful.'

Meg went back to the ward, leaving Laura to mull over what she had learned. It occupied her thoughts to the extent that she gave little thought to what Mark had said earlier. When she found him waiting in the foyer for her at the end of her shift she stopped dead.

He raised his brows but there was no denying the faint uncertainty in his voice. 'I did mention that I'd give you a lift home, didn't I?'

'I...um, yes.' She took a quick breath as she wondered what to do, but suddenly the thought of the long journey in the cold was less than appealing. Although the buses were running to schedule along most routes, services to the part of town where she lived were sketchy at the best of times. It could be ages before one came along and then she still had to stop off at Claire's to collect Robbie as she'd decided that it wasn't fair to impose on her friend for another night.

'Hmm, if I were a sensitive soul I'd be wounded by your obvious lack of enthusiasm.' Mark grinned as he tucked her hand into the crook of his arm. 'But I have the hide of a rhino so I'll ignore it. Let's go.'

Laura laughed because it was impossible not to. Mark had a way of making seemingly awkward situations *easy*. 'Lead on, kind sir,' she teased. 'Or perhaps that should be Sir Rhino?'

'Getting cheeky now, are we? We'll soon sort you out, young

woman.' He bent and scooped up a handful of snow then threatened her with it.

'Oh, no—not the snow torture…please!' She could hardly speak for laughing because it was so ridiculous. Here they were, two adults acting like a pair of teenagers!

Mark let the snow dribble through his fingers and sighed theatrically. 'All right, you win. I'll leave the snow torture until another day, but only on one condition.'

'And that is?' She stopped as they reached his car, smiling up at him.

'That you let me take you and Robbie out for a meal tonight.'

'Well…'

'You'd be doing me a favour,' he hurried on persuasively when she hesitated. 'My favourite café down the road is shut for the next week while it's being renovated. The thought of trying to find somewhere else to eat all on my own…'

He shuddered, trying to look suitably overwhelmed by the idea and failing miserably. It was obvious, though, that he really did want her to go with him and suddenly Laura could think of no reason to refuse. What harm could there be in accepting his invitation when it would be a treat both for her and Robbie? It could hardly be classed as a *date* with the little boy in tow!

'Then yes, thank you. I'd love to come.'

'Great!' He kissed her lightly on the lips then unlocked the car door before she had time to draw breath. Laura slid into the seat, trying to stifle her qualms as she wondered if Mark had got the wrong idea. But what was the right one? That she'd agreed to go with him out of pity? Or because it would be a free meal?

She took a deep breath as he swung the car onto the main road. Neither of those were true. She had agreed to go with him because she'd wanted to. Never had something so simple been so complicated!

'I can't believe this! I really and truly don't know what to say…'

Mark put both hands on his hips as he stood in the middle of her hall and surveyed the damage. Laura gulped. Why, oh, why, hadn't she given any thought to what would happen when he saw the state her home was in still? Now she fixed a determinedly cheerful smile to her face.

'It isn't that bad. Once I've freshened up the walls with a bit of paint and cleaned the carpet—' she began.

'It will be perfectly fine?' He glared at her, his handsome face set into such stern lines that she took a step back. 'Come on, Laura, the place is a mess! It's going to take a team of workmen to get everywhere straight. Why on earth haven't you had someone in to help you?'

'Because I haven't got the money for a team of workmen so I'll just have to do the best I can, won't I?'

She turned to Robbie, forcing herself to smile when she saw his anxious little face. 'It's all right, darling. You go upstairs and find your blue jumper then I'll come and help you get changed. Mark is taking us out for our tea—won't that be nice?'

'Mummy naughty?' he asked, looking uncertainly from her to Mark.

Mark sighed as he hunkered down beside the child. 'Mummy is very naughty for not telling me that she needs help to clear up the house, but I'm not really angry with her.' He glanced wryly at Laura then turned to the child once more. 'Now go and find your jumper then we can go and have something to eat. OK?'

Robbie nodded, obviously reassured that everything was all right again. How Laura wished she had his confidence! However, much to her surprise, Mark didn't make any further comment about the state of the house.

'Right, you go and get yourself ready. While you're doing that, do you mind if I use your phone?'

'Of course not. It's in the sitting-room.' Laura showed him the way then hurried upstairs to get changed, rather surprised by his acceptance of the situation.

She shrugged as she delved into her wardrobe for something to wear. Perhaps Mark had decided that it wasn't his business. It seemed rather out of character, but it was the only explanation she could come up with so it would have to do.

As quickly as possible she changed out of her work clothes into a long-sleeved, emerald green dress in a smooth jersey fabric. She'd had it for years but it suited her—the colour brought out the red in her hair while the slim-fitting style made the most of her petite figure.

Low-heeled black leather boots seemed the best choice in view of the weather, although she would have preferred the extra height afforded by her best pair of court shoes. Still, she didn't look *too* bad, she decided as she finished outlining her mouth with raspberry lip gloss, and at least Mark shouldn't be ashamed to be seen with her.

He was coming out of the sitting-room when she arrived downstairs with Robbie five minutes later. He paused to watch her descend the last few steps and she'd have needed to have been blind not to have seen the appreciation in his eyes as he took note of what she was wearing.

'You look lovely, Laura,' he said simply but she knew in her heart that she'd never heard a more sincere compliment.

'And me!' Robbie claimed their attention, making them both laugh as he pointed to his jumper. 'Me lovely?'

'You certainly are, sunshine.' Mark swung the child up onto his shoulders, making Robbie chortle with glee as he suddenly found himself perched six feet up in the air.

Laura laughed as she watched him wrap his arms tightly around Mark's neck. 'Mind he doesn't choke you!'

Mark grinned. 'I think he's going to be a wrestler with a grip like that! So, are we ready, then? Who's hungry?'

'Me!' Robbie shouted, almost deafening them. Mark put him down so that Laura could put his coat on, then helped her into hers, which was the one she wore every day. With money so tight, she hadn't been able to buy herself a new winter coat for some time, and she was conscious that the cuffs were more than a little threadbare. Still, occasions when she needed smart clothes were few and far between…thankfully!

'Here, I'll lock the door.' Mark took the keys from her and quickly locked the front door. He bent to pick up Robbie, carrying him in one arm as he helped Laura to the car. Once they were safely strapped into their seats he set off.

'I need to stop for a moment on the way,' he told her. 'A bit of business that needs sorting out.'

He didn't explain what it was and she didn't ask him, although she was surprised when he pulled up in front of the offices of a local building firm. He went inside, reappeared a short time later and got back in the car.

'Is everything all right?' Laura asked, wondering if he had some sort of problem at his flat.

'Fine.' He didn't say anything more, asking her instead how

Katie had got on that afternoon. They chatted about work until they drew up in the car park of a local pub, which was renowned throughout the area for its bar meals.

Mark turned to her as he switched off the engine. 'Will here be OK?'

'Fine. I've been here a few times, although not since…' She stopped, wondering if she should mention her previous visits. However, Mark merely shrugged.

'Not since your husband died? Well, let's see how it stands up to past experiences, shall we?'

Opening the car door, he got out and undid Robbie's seat belt. Lifting the little boy out of the car, he took firm hold of his hand as another car pulled up alongside them.

Laura automatically glanced at the vehicle, smiling pleasantly as a couple with two small children got out. The other woman returned her smile and turned to include Mark in it. However, Laura saw her face change as soon as she saw Robbie.

The woman turned away at once, urging her children ahead of her as she whispered something to her husband and hurried him towards the pub. He glanced back, his gaze alighting on Robbie for a moment before he turned away.

'Kids like that are better off in a home….' His voice faded as the family entered the pub, but the damage had been done because it was obvious that he'd been referring to Robbie.

Laura took a deep breath, wishing she was immune to the pain it always caused when strangers reacted like that to the sight of her son. Had they any idea how hurtful it was and how unjustified their prejudices were? Robbie was a loving little boy but they never tried to look past his disabilities and discover that for themselves.

'Are you OK?' Mark's tone was gentle and she forced herself to smile as she saw the concern on his face.

'Of course.' She glanced down as Robbie came and slipped his hand into hers, feeling a wave of tenderness and fear overwhelm her. How could she protect *him* from the hurt people inflicted with their attitudes? It was hard enough to deal with it herself and Robbie was just a child.

'Why don't we go inside and have something to drink while we make up our minds what we want to eat?' Mark slipped his hand under her elbow, determinedly steering her towards the brightly lit building.

Laura hung back, no longer sure that it was a good idea. Although it hurt to see people's reactions to Robbie, she'd learned to deal with them on a practical level but Mark hadn't. Was it really fair to expose him to such unpleasantness and possible embarrassment?

'I'm not sure that it's a good idea...' she began.

'Why? Surely you aren't going to let other people's ignorance affect you, Laura? Because that's all it is—ignorance and fear of something they don't understand.' His voice grated with anger. However, the hand he laid on Robbie's head was so gentle and protective that Laura felt a lump come to her throat. How could she have imagined even for a second that Mark would feel ashamed to be seen with them?

'Thank you,' she whispered. 'I thought you might feel...well, uncomfortable.'

He bent and looked deep into her eyes so that there was no doubting that he was telling the truth. 'The only thing I feel at this moment, Laura, is pride that you and Robbie have agreed to spend some time with me.'

He suddenly grinned as he bent and swept the child into his arms. 'Now, let's get in there. I, for one, am starving!'

Laura laughed, feeling a new lightness in her heart. She didn't stop to examine it as she followed Mark into the pub, didn't need to. Mark was the cause of it, Mark and his attitude, his understanding, his compassion. What a truly wonderful man he was!

It was a lovely evening. The food was as good as she remembered it—the steak they both ordered cooked to perfection, the chips and salad which accompanied it both delicious. Good traditional British food was the order of the day there and the landlord and his wife had built up an appreciative clientele.

Robbie ate every morsel of his chicken nuggets and chips then polished off a dish of home-made ice cream while she and Mark had coffee. The family they had seen in the car park was seated at a table nearby and it was obvious that Robbie was dying to go over to play with the other children. However, bearing in mind what had happened earlier, Laura knew that it wouldn't be wise so she kept him occupied with a colouring book and crayons she'd brought with her.

'See, Mummy.' He held up the picture he'd coloured in to show her, smiling proudly as she admired his handiwork. Robbie was oblivious to the fact that he was supposed to keep within the black lines and had no inhibitions about the colours he used either.

Mark grinned as he saw the crimson grass and bright green sky. 'Very surreal. You have a real eye for colour, young man!'

Robbie grinned happily, not comprehending the words but understanding the warm tone in which they were said. He got up from his chair and went round the table to scramble onto Mark's knee. Wrapping his arms tightly around the man's neck, he kissed him on the cheek.

'Robbie love Mark,' he declared.

'And I love you, too, sunshine.' There was no hesitation as Mark returned the child's embrace. Laura felt tears prick her eyes as she watched them. It wasn't just an act—Mark really did care for the little boy. It made her start to believe that things could work out….

She sighed as she realised that was wishful thinking. Mark's attitude towards Robbie was certainly more than she could have expected from any man, but it didn't mean they had a future together. There were still so many other things to take into consideration like Ian and the guilt she would feel at replacing him, and the fact that Mark wanted children of his own. Both of those were major stumbling blocks and couldn't be dismissed.

They left the pub a short time later and got back in the car. Robbie was worn out by all the excitement and soon fell asleep. Mark took his time as he drove because the roads were still treacherous. Although the centre of the town was clear, once they reached the outskirts there was still a lot of snow about.

Laura rested her head against the seat, content just to sit quietly. She felt so warm and secure being with Mark, trusting him completely to get them back safely, although her heart sank at the thought of spending the night in the cold, damp house. Still, she had the whole weekend to work on the place so she should be able to achieve *something*….

She must have fallen asleep on that thought because the next thing she knew something was tickling her cheek. She brushed it away then found her eyes flying open as she felt a warm hand grip hers.

'We're here.'

Mark's tone was so deep and resonant that she felt a ripple run down her spine. Laura took a quick breath, struggling to surface through the layers of sleep. 'Here?'

'Home.' He gave her a slow smile then sat back in his seat and looked around. And there was something about the expression on his face….

She sat up, blinking the sleep from her eyes as she stared around her in confusion. It took a second before her addled brain absorbed the fact that they were parked in front of the building where Mark lived. She turned to him, her greeny-blue eyes awash with bewilderment.

'But this isn't my house.'

'No.' He gave her a slow grin. 'But it's where you'll be living for the next week, Laura.'

'Where I'll be living…? I don't understand.' She stared at him in shock, watching how his smile faded to be replaced by a look of determination. This was a different Mark to the one she was used to, a Mark who intended to get his own way, and her heart began to thump as she realised it.

'It's quite simple really. I phoned the builders while you were getting changed tonight and arranged for a team of men to go to your house and sort everything out.' He shrugged as he checked his watch. 'They should be there by now. I told the foreman that I wanted the work doing as quickly as possible so he promised to get onto it right away.'

'There? In my house, you mean? But how did they…?' She stopped, thinking back to what had happened on the way to the pub. She'd worked out the answer to her question even before Mark confirmed it.

'How did they get in? Simple. I gave them your keys.' He held up his hand placatingly. 'Don't worry. They're completely trustworthy. I know that for a fact because I used them myself when I moved into this place.'

'That isn't the point!' Funny how quickly her head had cleared. She glared at him, her stomach lurching as she considered the implications of what he'd done. 'Who gave you the right to do such a thing, Mark Dawson? I don't recall asking for your help!'

'You didn't. But, then, you're too damned independent for your own good.' He leaned over and gripped her shoulders to give her

a little shake. 'Be sensible, Laura! You can't possibly get tha
place straight all by yourself.'

He was right, of course. It would be hard enough to cope with
what needed doing even if she'd been at home all day, but with
her job and everything else it was nigh on impossible. However
there was one major point he'd overlooked, one which made he
feel sick as she thought about it.

'I can't afford to have people in to clear up, Mark,' she admitted
flatly, embarrassed at having to explain her straitened circum
stances.

'The insurance will cover it,' he began, then stopped. He uttered
what might have been a curse as his hands gripped her harder
'You aren't insured, are you? That's why you've been trying to
get everything done yourself.'

Laura shrugged, trying to make light of it. 'I let the insurance
lapse last year. The premiums were just too expensive for me to
keep paying them. My bad luck, I guess.'

'I should have guessed. I had a feeling that you were being
evasive the first time I mentioned it.' He sounded genuinely upset
that he hadn't worked it out before. However, his face was stil
set when she looked at him. 'Still, it makes no difference. The
work has to be done. And while your house is uninhabitable you
can stay here.'

'Oh, but I can't!' Laura forgot about her monetary problems a
she was faced with a far more pressing one. 'Look, Mark, it'
very kind of you but—'

'But nothing.' He opened the car door and got out, bending to
look back at her. 'You need a place to stay and I'm offering you
one. Simple, isn't it?'

'But…but what are people going to say? What am I going to
tell them when they find out I'm staying with you?' she asked
struggling to convince him that it wasn't a good idea, even though
she couldn't think of an alternative.

'Oh, that's easy.' Mark leaned back inside the car to lift the
sleeping child from the rear seat. He smiled at Laura and his gre
eyes were very soft in the glow from the interior light. 'Tell them
I kidnaped you!'

CHAPTER NINE

'HE COULD sleep for England! He hasn't stirred the whole time you were undressing him.'

Mark's tone was warm with amusement and Laura sighed. She couldn't decide if he was being deliberately obtuse or if he really *didn't* believe there was a problem about her staying in his flat! So far he hadn't given her a chance to voice her objections as he'd helped her put Robbie to bed, but somehow she had to make him see sense.

Leaving the bedroom door open just a crack so that the light wouldn't disturb the sleeping child, she followed Mark into the sitting-room, determined to get her point across. 'Look, Mark—'

'Fancy a glass of wine? I've a couple of decent bottles in the kitchen which my father gave me at Christmas.' He smiled as he waved her towards the sofa. 'He's a bit of a wine buff so I don't think you'll be disappointed. Sit yourself down and I'll fetch one.'

'Mark, I...'

She had no chance to finish yet again as he left the room. Laura raised her eyes to the heavens and sighed. Was he hoping to override her objections by ignoring them?

She sank onto the sofa and resolutely marshalled her thoughts for when he returned. She had to make him understand that it was out of the question for her and Robbie to stay here...although where they would go instead was another question. She couldn't impose on Claire for a whole week, neither could she invite herself round to any of her other friends' houses, willing though they might be to offer her a bed.

'Right, I decided on a *rosé*. I know a lot of people curl their lips at the thought of *pink* wine but I have to say that I find it more refreshing than red to drink on its own.'

Mark put two glasses on the coffee-table and filled them with wine. He offered her one, his brows drawing together as he saw her expression.

'What's wrong, Laura? Come on, out with it.'

'What's wrong is that you seem determined to bury your head in the sand about this, Mark!' She took a gulp of the rosy pink wine and paused. 'Mmm, that really is lovely.'

'Dad will be glad to know that you approve.' He sank onto the sofa, studying her with innocently clear eyes. 'Anyway, you were saying, sweetheart?'

Sweetheart? Laura gulped in a little air, feeling a sudden constriction in her lungs. The endearment had slid off his tongue as though it were the most natural thing in the world that he should call her that. Did Mark think of her as his *sweetheart*? she found herself wondering before she promptly ditched that idea.

Her mouth pursed as she looked at him, seeing past the guileless smile to the determination beneath. Pretty words were just a tool in his fight to get his own way! But if Mark thought that she was too naïve not to see through him then he was in for a surprise!

'I was saying that you're trying to ignore the facts, Mark, but they won't go away just because you don't want to face them.' She took another fortifying swallow of wine, feeling her arms and legs tingle as the alcohol started to find its way into her bloodstream. It gave her the rush of courage she sorely needed to carry on.

'People are going to start talking as soon as they hear that Robbie and I are staying here with you.' She held up her hand when he went to interrupt. 'No, I won't let you sidetrack me. Please, hear me out.'

'Of course.' He settled back against the cushions, propping his feet on the coffee-table and making himself comfortable as though prepared to sit there and listen for the whole night if need be.

Laura felt a little knot form in the region of her vocal cords, compounded of nervousness and a large dollop of suspicion. She hadn't expected him to be quite so…so *acquiescent*. Was it all an act and was he merely paying lip-service to the idea of listening to her objections?

She cleared her throat, determined to get her point across. However, it was funny how difficult it was to get the words to come out exactly as she wanted them to. 'Do you want people gossiping about us, Mark? Do you really think that it's wise in your position?'

She bit her lip as she finished, wishing her voice had sounded a little less quavery and a lot more forceful. She'd been trying to present the sensible voice of reason, but had it worked?

Mark didn't say anything for a moment, seemingly content to study the way the firelight shone through the rose pink wine in his glass. The silence dragged on for so long that Laura actually jumped when he suddenly sighed.

'I can't imagine that anyone is going to pass comment in this day and age about two people living together, Laura. But if it's a problem then we won't tell anyone.'

'That isn't the point!' she declared, jumping to her feet. Obtuse wasn't the word for the way he was acting, and she was more convinced than ever that it *was* deliberate! 'Although, frankly, whether or not we tell people about our arrangement is immaterial. You know as well as I do how fast gossip gets round a hospital!'

'And it bothers you what people are going to think?' he asked evenly.

'Yes, of course it does!' She strode to the window then turned and marched all the way back, too on edge to sit down and discuss the situation calmly any longer.

'Why?' He shrugged when she stared at him. 'It's a simple enough question, Laura. Why should it bother you what anyone thinks if we're happy with the arrangement?'

Put like that, her concerns seemed ridiculous, but it really wasn't as simple as he was trying to make it out to be.

'Because…well, because people will get the wrong idea.'

'You mean they'll start to wonder why I offered you a place to stay? They'll assume that it can't possibly be because I couldn't bear the thought of you and Robbie living in that house without any electricity? That it had nothing to do with the fact that I wouldn't have had a minute's peace, worrying about you both? Or that I wouldn't have offered *anyone* who found herself in a similar plight a bed for a few nights?'

He tilted his head and looked her squarely in the eyes. 'Do you really believe that the people we work with would think it wrong to offer shelter to a mother and child who desperately need help, because I don't.'

It sounded crazy to have doubts when he explained it like that, but was it really so straightforward? Laura swung round and went back to the window, trying to sort through the jumble inside her head. One part of her believed what Mark had told her—that he would have offered help to anyone in her situation—but she knew instinctively there was more to it than that.

'Laura, I just want to help you. That's all.'

She glanced around, seeming to feel her heart curl up inside her as she saw the bleakness on his face. She could tell that he was hurt by her seeming rejection of his help and that had been the last thing she'd wanted to do, to hurt him.

Her hands clenched into fists as she struggled to keep all emotion from her voice. 'Is it, Mark? Honestly?'

'Yes.' He stood and came over to her and she could see the sincerity in his eyes. 'I'm not trying to put you under any kind of obligation to me. This isn't an attempt to get you here so that I can seduce you.'

He must have heard her shocked gasp because he grinned wickedly. 'Although the idea is tempting, I must admit. However, you have my word that this won't change a thing, Laura. This is just a breathing space. You'll be free to leave as soon as your house is ready, and I won't expect anything from you.'

But would she be able to walk away so easily? Already she felt things for him that she wouldn't have believed possible a week ago. How much more difficult was it going to be when she'd grown used to having him around? Her life had been so empty since Ian had died and she knew deep down that Mark's warmth and compassion, his tenderness—just Mark as the man he was—could so easily fill the void. Would it be wise to risk that happening—to risk hurting them both—when there could be no future for them?

Her mind whirled, questions tossing around like a ship on a stormy sea, and she felt tears fill her eyes. Mark gave a gentle murmur as he drew her to him, holding her tightly against the warm strength of his body.

'Don't torture yourself this way, Laura! There's no need, I

promise you.' He lifted her chin and his eyes were both tender and sad. 'I'll be your friend if that's all you want me to be.'

Did she? Or did she want more than that? Could she have more? Was she entitled to take from this man when she had so little to give?

Her head hurt with the dilemma but somehow Mark seemed to sense her confusion because he didn't press her for an answer. He let her go and went to top up their glasses with more wine. And when he spoke, his tone was deliberately light.

'Come along, drink up. You don't want to run the risk of me having a hangover in the morning because you're not drinking your fair share, do you?'

Laura managed to laugh, relieved to take her lead from him. 'Well, don't expect any sympathy if you do have one. You should know your limitations at your age, Dr Dawson!'

'Oh, you cruel woman! That was below the belt. My age, indeed! I'm a mere thirty-two years old, I'll have you know.' He grinned as she went to join him. 'You make it sound as though I'm in my dotage!'

'Well, you said it!' She laughed as she saw his indignant expression. She sank onto the sofa and picked up her glass, sighing with pleasure as the fruity flavour of the wine burst on her tongue. 'This really *is* delicious.'

'Wine has become rather a hobby with Dad since he retired. He and Mum go off on regular jaunts to France, sampling the offerings of different vineyards. When they find a wine they particularly like they buy a couple of cases and bring it back home.' Mark laughed softly as he settled back on the sofa. 'Emma and I are only too happy to sample the fruits of their travels, too.'

'Emma?' she asked before she could stop herself. She felt a little colour touch her cheeks as it hit her that Emma might be the name of his girlfriend. That thought led her on to another, equally unpalatable one—had Mark found her concerns about staying in his flat odd in view of the fact that he had a girlfriend? Maybe he believed that she knew all about this Emma. After all, gossip was rife in any hospital and it was rare that anyone could keep their private life private. The thought that she might have misread the situation—and that he might have realised it—filled her with mortification so that she missed what he said.

'Sorry. What was that?' she asked miserably when she became aware of the silence.

'I was just saying that Em tends to wheedle more booze out of Dad than I do. She plays shamelessly on the fact that not only is she an impoverished medical student but the apple of his eye.' Mark grinned. 'Mind you, she knew how to twist the poor man round her little finger from the time she was in nappies. Mum always says that Dad took one look at Em when she was born and that was it—love at first sight!'

'Emma's your sister?' She couldn't keep the surprise from her voice and she saw him go quite still before he slowly put his glass on the table.

'Yes. She's twenty-two, ten years younger than me. Mum calls Emma her happy little accident as they weren't planning on having another child when she came along.' He took a deep breath but his voice seemed to grate. 'Who did you think she was?'

'Your...your girlfriend,' she admitted in a tone which was barely above a whisper. She took a deep breath but it was impossible to control the feeling of relief that flooded through her.

'I see.' He shrugged but there was the oddest light in his eyes as he studied her flushed face. 'I don't have a girlfriend, Laura. I would have told you if I had.'

It was said so calmly but she understood what he was telling her. He wanted her to know that he wasn't emotionally tied to anyone. She should have realised that. Mark wasn't the sort of man who would cause a woman unhappiness by stringing her along.

It was difficult to hide the sudden elation she felt. Maybe it was wrong to feel this way but she couldn't help it. Mark wasn't involved with anyone and it felt so good to know that. Maybe it was the sense of euphoria which gave her an unaccustomed courage to find out more.

'Is that out of choice or circumstance?' she asked quietly.

'A bit of both, I suppose.' He smiled when he saw her frown. 'Sorry, that was rather an ambiguous answer, although it wasn't really meant to be.' He lifted his glass to his mouth and took a sip of wine before continuing. 'I've had girlfriends in the past, naturally. And one long-term relationship that ended not long before I moved to this part of the world.'

'Oh?' She didn't realise that it had sounded like a question until he began to answer. Her cheeks warmed as she realised how rude it was to cross-question him. However, Mark didn't seem at all perturbed as he continued in the same easy manner.

'Mmm. Ruth and I met when we were overseas. We kept in touch when we came back to England and, as luck would have it, both found jobs in Colchester.' He shrugged lightly. 'We lived together for a couple of years and might even have got married if we hadn't both realised that we were doing it for all the wrong reasons.'

'The wrong reasons...?' She trailed off uncertainly, her brow puckering as Mark gave a rueful smile.

'Uh-huh. We felt so *comfortable* with one another, you see. I think that was the main attraction that held us together. We'd seen so many awful things through our work that it was a sort of bond. However, I think we both gradually realised that, although we were fond of one another, it wasn't enough. For a marriage to work it has to be based on love, nothing less.'

Laura couldn't think of anything to say. Mark didn't sound at all distressed about the ending of his relationship, and she was afraid that her relief would show. The thought of him pining for this other woman would have been almost too much to bear, although she shied away from wondering why.

'So now that I've told you a bit about myself, how about you? Do you have any family, for instance—brothers, sisters, aunts, even cousins twenty times removed?' He turned the question into a joke and she laughed, grateful not to have to dig too deeply into her own muddled feelings.

'Nobody, I'm afraid. I'm the only child of only children and my parents died when I was in my teens. I believe there *are* a few distant cousins somewhere about but as I've never met them they don't really count.'

'I see. How about your husband's family, then?' Mark continued curiously.

'Exactly the same situation as mine.' She laughed softly. 'Ian used to say that we were two orphans together.'

'It must have brought you even closer and made it very hard when he died,' he observed quietly.

'I suppose it did. I was eighteen when I met Ian. I had just started training and was working in A and E at the Royal when he was brought in with a badly sprained ankle from playing football.' She smiled reminiscently. 'He never stopped chattering the whole time I was trying to strap his ankle up. He confessed later that he was terrified of hospitals and that he'd had to keep on talking to take his mind off being there!'

Mark laughed at that. 'Well, that answers what would have been my next question, i.e., what did he do? Obviously nothing medical?'

'No way! He was in electronics, an engineer. Very good at his job, too. He'd just been promoted when…when he was killed.'

Her voice broke and she looked away in embarrassment. It wasn't as though it had happened all that recently. Ian had been dead almost two years, yet telling Mark about it seemed to have brought all the pain back. She didn't know whether or not to answer when he probed a bit more.

'Was it an accident? He couldn't have been very old.'

'Twen-twenty-nine. It was a car crash. Ian was…he was…killed when a lorry ran out of control on a motorway slip road. It crashed into his car as he was driving past the junction. He…he didn't stand a chance…'

She couldn't continue as a sob welled from her lips. She pressed a hand to her mouth but more kept coming. It was as though a dam had burst and all the grief she'd stored up suddenly spilled over.

Mark was on his feet in a trice, drawing her up so that he could wrap her in his arms. He rocked her gently from side to side, his hand soothing as he smoothed her ruffled curls. 'Let it all out, sweetheart. It will do you good to cry. Ian was too young to die and you have a right to feel bitter and hurt at the waste of his life.'

Laura never knew afterwards how long they stood there, Mark rocking her to and fro, holding her while she sobbed out all the bottled up grief. When it was over she felt completely spent. Her mind and body were numb yet somehow freed from the weight of misery which had burdened her for so long.

'Here you go.'

Mark put her away from him as he handed her a clean white handkerchief. Laura blew her nose then summoned a wobbly smile.

'Sorry about that. I didn't mean to go to pieces on you.'

'It's way past time you let it all out. I'd guess that you've been trying to put on a brave face for Robbie's sake, but everyone needs time to grieve, Laura.' His eyes were like smoke, soft grey and shimmering, as they studied her tear-drenched face. 'You need time to heal before you can move on.'

She knew what he meant, of course. That she had to work through her pain over Ian's death before she could look to the future. Did Mark hope that future would include him?

Laura sensed it was so but there were too many other things to take into consideration, like his longing for a family, and Robbie....

She took a deep breath, unable to cope with any more soul-searching.

'I think I'll go to bed now if you don't mind,' she told him quietly, avoiding his eyes. She was simply too vulnerable right then to run the risk of making a mistake they could both come to regret.

'Of course not. You must make yourself at home while you're here, Laura. I'm on duty this weekend so I don't expect I'll see you until tomorrow night. Have a good day, both of you.'

Mark bent and kissed her cheek. Maybe it was meant to be just a token but Laura felt her heart race like crazy as she felt the warm touch of his lips on her skin.

She hurried from the room and undressed then crept into bed beside Robbie, praying for the oblivion of sleep. Everything would look different in the morning, she assured herself as she rolled onto her stomach. She would have had time to work through what had happened and find a balance.

Laura closed her eyes, deliberately conjuring up a picture of Ian, as she so often did when times became particularly hard. However, it was impossible to picture him that night. His face seemed to float just out of sight, beyond her reach....

She bit her lip as another face imprinted itself on her mind, a strong face with its angular lines and clear-cut features. It was so easy to conjure up the image of Mark Dawson, easier still to dream about him...

'I'll feel better being back at work. I won't have as much time to brood.'

It was Monday morning and Laura had arrived on the ward to find that Rachel had come back to work. It had been a funny kind of weekend and not at all how she'd imagined it would be.

For a start she hadn't seen Mark at all. He'd telephoned late on Saturday evening to let her know that he was stuck at work because there had been an emergency admission sent up from Casualty. After that, he'd informed her, he was driving straight to his parents' house as he'd forgotten that it was his mother's birthday the following day and he would be in the dog-house if he didn't turn up!

Laura had laughed dutifully, but as she'd hung up she'd found herself wondering if it had been an excuse to avoid returning to the flat. Had Mark felt it better that he absent himself while she was there to avoid any awkward moments? Maybe he thought that she would prefer it if he weren't around? However, the thought that she might be responsible for chasing him from his own home made her feel guiltier than ever. She had made up her mind that she would move back home just as soon as it was feasible.

'So, how have things been? You've settled in OK, I hope.'

Laura returned her thoughts to where they should have been in the first place—on her work. She smiled as she answered Rachel's question. 'I have. I know it's a bit early to say, but I think I'm going to enjoy Children's Med as much as Maternity.'

'Great! It must have been a bit of a wrench, deciding not to go back there, but this is another string to your bow.' Rachel shrugged. 'I'm only sorry that the post isn't graded at a staff nurse's level. I know it's been a bit of a step down for you, Laura, but the board wouldn't agree to it.'

'That doesn't matter so much as the fact that I can work set hours. Shift work would be impossible in my case, with Robbie to take care of.'

She sighed. 'Not many childminders will accept responsibility for children with handicaps, which is why I'm so grateful that Claire offered to help. She's been marvellous, looking after Robbie while I did that refresher course and collecting him from school each day. I couldn't have got this far without her. Anyway, you don't need a staff nurse. You have one already.'

'Hmm. Enough said on that subject, I think.' Rachel pursed her lips as she looked down the ward. Cathy was supervising the morning drugs round and was standing beside Bethany's bed. Her impatience with the teenager was obvious even from where they stood, and Laura held back a sigh. Couldn't Cathy tell that she was simply getting the girl's back up by behaving in such an authoritarian manner?

Rachel was evidently of the same opinion because she excused herself and went to her niece's bed. There was a brief exchange of words before Cathy came storming back to the office. She glowered as she saw Laura there.

'Nothing to do? Or are you telling tales to try and get Rachel on your side?' She gave an ugly laugh. 'It will take more than a bit of boot-licking to convince me that you're fit to do this job! And if Fiona Watts asks for my opinion, I shall give it to her.'

The malice in the younger woman's voice shocked Laura. 'What have you got against me, Cathy?'

'Nothing, apart from the fact that I know what your game is, making sheep's eyes at Mark the way you've been doing.' Cathy smiled thinly. 'It can't be easy being a widow, especially not with a Down's syndrome kid in tow. Most men would run a mile to avoid getting involved. But Mark isn't like that, as you discovered pretty quickly. He's too nice for his own good, quite frankly. But if you imagine I'm going to let you take advantage of his kindness to get yourself a free meal ticket then—'

'Morning, folks. How are we today?'

Laura swung round at the sound of the friendly greeting. Had Mark overheard what Cathy had said? she wondered sickly. There was no sign of anything on his face but maybe he'd decided to play the innocent on purpose to spare her any embarrassment. Or maybe he was glad that Cathy had said what he hadn't liked to say?

It was that last thought that leached all the colour from her face, and she saw Mark frown. However, before he could say anything she quickly excused herself and hurried into the ward. Katie was sitting on the edge of her bed, carefully combing the tangles out of her doll's hair, and she smiled in delight when she saw Laura.

'Laura, I missed you!' Discarding the doll, Katie jumped up and hugged her, her thin little arms twining tightly around Laura's waist. 'I asked one of the other nurses but she said that you didn't work on Saturdays and Sundays,' she added accusingly.

'I'm afraid not. I have a little boy, you see, Katie, and I have to look after him then.'

Laura sat on the edge of the bed and popped the child on her knee, feeling her heart aching as Katie snuggled closer. It was obvious that the little girl was starved of affection, and it broke her heart to think about the life Katie led with her mother.

Deliberately blocking out all thought of what had happened a few minutes earlier, she concentrated on cheering up the little girl. 'So tell me what you did this weekend while I wasn't here. Did you eat all your dinners up?'

'Uh-huh…apart from the sprouts,' Katie mumbled. 'I hate them!'

Laura laughed. Out of the corner of her eye she spotted Mark making his way down the ward, and deliberately turned so that he was no longer in her line of sight. 'Most children do! Anyway, what else did you do? Play some games? Watch television? Colouring?'

Katie nodded to each question, although she didn't elaborate. Laura sighed, knowing how hard it must have been for the child to spend the whole weekend without any visitors coming to see her. Weekends were hectic on any ward as people had time off from work then to visit their friends and relatives, and children's wards were no exception. She was just wondering how much progress the police had made with their enquiries as to the whereabouts of Katie's parents when Mark interrupted.

'Good morning, Katie. How are you feeling today?' He sat on the edge of the bed and Laura flinched as the mattress dipped, bringing his hard thigh into contact with hers.

A wave of heat flowed through her from the point of contact and she surreptitiously edged away, somewhat hampered by the fact that the little girl was still cuddled up on her knee.

'All right.' Katie gave him a shy smile before she buried her face against Laura's bosom once more. Mark's brows rose questioningly and Laura summoned a smile even though her heart felt like a leaden weight.

Even if it hadn't crossed Mark's mind before that she might be abusing his kindness, there was a good chance that he might start thinking that way now if he'd overheard Cathy's comments.

The thought that he might imagine she was using him was more than she could bear, but she couldn't discuss it with him at that moment.

'Katie needed a cuddle,' she explained. 'It's been a long weekend.'

He nodded, instantly understanding. 'I imagine it has.' He took a deep breath and his eyes were very dark when he looked at her. 'It's been a long one for me as well, Laura. Katie isn't the only one who missed you.'

He stood up, smiling at the little girl as though he hadn't heard Laura's shocked gasp. 'There's a treat in store for everyone this afternoon, poppet. I won't tell you what it is because it's a surprise. But I know for a fact that you will enjoy it.'

'A surprise?' Katie stared at him with huge, excited, blue eyes, her melancholy forgotten. 'What kind of surprise, Dr Mark?'

Mark laughed as he ran a gentle hand over her hair. Laura's breath caught as she felt his knuckles skim the tip of her left breast. It was yet another assault on her senses, which were already raw from that confession. When she heard his sharp intake of breath she knew that he'd suddenly realised what he'd done.

His hand lingered for what could have been no more than a single heartbeat, although it felt much longer than that, before it fell to his side. Laura felt her pulse race as she heard the grating note in his deep voice. 'If I told you, it wouldn't be a surprise, would it? You'll have to wait and see, young lady!'

He moved away without looking at Laura again. She understood why. Both of them were simply too aware of one another to risk even eye contact at that moment!

Her head whirled as she replied to Katie's excited questions as best she could, but it was hard to ignore what had happened or to put it into perspective. Where Mark was concerned 'perspective' was a word she might be able to spell, but that was all!

CHAPTER TEN

'OH, HE'S gorgeous! Just like Sandy.'

Katie's delighted laughter rang around the ward and everyone smiled. Mark's 'surprise' certainly had been a huge hit with Katie, Laura thought. But, then, it had lifted all the children's spirits when Barney, a beautiful golden retriever, had been brought into the ward by his owner, Peggy Mountfield.

Peggy, a kindly woman in her sixties, smiled as Barney was hugged and patted by the delighted child. 'There's nothing like a pet to cheer up a sick child, is there?'

'There certainly isn't,' Laura agreed as Barney trotted to the next bed, which happened to be Daniel's. She'd been surprised to discover that the boy was still in the ward, but Rachel had explained that as he was still complaining of pain in his ears it had been deemed wiser to keep him in. However, there was little sign that Daniel was in any kind of discomfort as he offered Barney one of his slippers and began a tug of war with the big dog.

Laura squashed a few qualms about what Mrs Glover would say when she saw the state of her son's slippers and turned curiously to Peggy. 'Do you do this kind of thing very often, then?'

'Bring Barney round the wards, you mean? Oh, yes. Several times a month, more if need be. Barney and I are members of PAT.'

'PAT?' Laura frowned. 'What does that stand for?'

'Pets As Therapy.' Mark had come up behind them and she jumped as he added his voice to the conversation. Rachel moved aside to let him join them, smiling as she watched the excited children cluster around the dog.

'A good name for it. Pets are wonderful therapy for a sick child,' she observed.

'It isn't just children who benefit from the contact, though,'

Mark explained, turning to Peggy for confirmation. 'You go into the adult wards as well, I believe.'

'We certainly do. The animals have just as much impact on the adults as they have on the children. They're a particular favourite with geriatric patients, so we also take them to some nursing homes in the area,' Peggy added.

'Animals? It isn't just dogs, then?' Laura queried.

Mark shook his head. 'Oh, no. Hamsters, rabbits, guinea pigs…if you can pet it then PAT visitors will bring it along! It's a great scheme, I think.'

'Well, I don't think it's right. Heaven knows what patients could catch off those animals.' Cathy and Jane had come to join them, and it was Cathy who had spoken. Laura saw Jane raise her eyebrows, and smiled in sympathy. It was unfortunate that Cathy happened to glance her way at that moment.

The staff nurse's mouth thinned and Laura felt a shudder run down her spine. It wasn't pleasant to know that the other woman disliked her to such an extent.

Whether or not Mark had felt her reaction, he gave her a frowning look before turning his attention to the other woman. His tone was pleasant enough but there was no mistaking the authority it held.

'I don't think there's any danger of that, Staff. Obviously, we wouldn't allow any patient who might be susceptible to infection to come into contact with the animals, but there have been no recorded cases of anyone catching anything from them.' He smiled at Peggy. 'And from the look of Barney, he's in perfect health. He really is a beautiful dog.'

'Thank you, Doctor. I do my best to make sure that he's clean and well groomed before bringing him on a visit.' She gave Cathy a speaking look then went to retrieve the slipper from Barney's mouth, as he'd won the game of tug of war.

The group disbanded after that and everyone went about their business. Mark was waylaid by Mrs Collins with some query about Jessica's diet, and he took her to the office to speak to her in private. It was almost time for the afternoon drinks to be given out so Laura headed for the kitchen, pausing *en route* as she spotted Bethany's sad face. She made a detour to the girl's bed and smiled at her.

'Are you feeling all right, love? You look a bit down.'

Bethany stared at the magazine she'd been pretending to read. She had kept herself aloof from all the excitement, ignoring Barney when the dog had stopped beside her bed. Laura knew that, apart from that brief episode the previous week, no one had had any success in getting through to the teenager. However, she refused to be deterred.

'Bethany?' she prompted, when the girl didn't reply.

'Mum said that we might be able to get a dog.' The words were so low that Laura had to strain to hear them, but at least it was a start. She sat on the chair beside the bed, keeping her tone carefully neutral.

'Did she? I expect you can still have one when you leave here.'

'How? I can't imagine them letting you have a dog in a children's home!' Bethany's voice suddenly broke on a sob. 'Nothing is ever going to be right now, is it? And it's all my fault!'

'Your fault? What do you mean?' Laura leant forward and clasped the girl's cold hand in both of hers. She wouldn't let go when Bethany tried to pull it away. 'Come on, Bethany, you can't leave it at that. You have to explain what you meant.'

'Th-that it's my fault Mum died, my fault that everyone was hurt in that crash, my fault that I...I'm crippled. It's a punishment, you see, for what I did!'

Bethany was sobbing in earnest now and Laura saw the concern on Rachel's face as she glanced their way. However, when Rachel made as though she was going to join them, Laura shook her head. She simply couldn't risk Bethany clamming up, as she might do if Rachel was there.

Letting go of the girl's hand, she got up and drew the curtains around the bed then sat down again. 'Why don't you tell me everything, right from the beginning?' she urged gently.

There was a long pause, during which she held her breath. Would Bethany tell her what was wrong at last? She could have cheered when the girl suddenly began speaking and the words came rushing out as though a dam had burst.

'It was my fault that Mum crashed the bus that night. If she hadn't been so angry with me, she might not have been driving so fast.'

Laura didn't bother to explain that, according to the police reports, the minibus had been doing no more than twenty miles an hour at the time of the accident. She would make sure that Bethany understood that later, but it was more important right now to hear the full story.

'Why was she angry with you, love? Had you had an argument about something?'

'Yes.' Bethany could hardly speak through her tears. Laura frowned as the girl suddenly tossed back the sheet that was covering her and drew up the hem of her nightshirt. 'We argued about this. That's why it's all my fault....'

She couldn't continue as tears got the better of her. Laura took one look at what she had been shown and sighed. It wasn't a pretty sight, and it had doubtless been causing Bethany a great deal of discomfort as well, but she was sure that Bethany's mother would have got over her annoyance in time. After all, a lot of teenage girls believed that a pierced belly button was the ultimate fashion statement!

'I take it that your mum didn't know what you were planning on doing?' she said softly, passing the girl a tissue from the box on the bedside cabinet.

'No.' Bethany sniffed and wiped her eyes. 'She was furious when she found out. I'd only had it done the day before the accident when I went into town with my friend, Kelly. I didn't tell Mum because I knew she would be annoyed, but as I was getting changed to go out for the theatre trip she came into my room and saw it.'

The girl took a gulping breath. 'Th-that's why she wasn't concentrating properly and driving too fast, because she was still angry with me. So it's all my fault, you see...everything!'

'Oh, love, that just isn't true!' Laura hugged the unhappy girl to her. 'Yes, I imagine your mum was annoyed that you hadn't told her, but it certainly wasn't your fault the accident happened.'

She held Bethany away from her and looked her straight in the eye. 'If you want to blame anything then blame the weather. The police told us that the bus skidded on the snow and not because your mum was driving too fast. She was only doing twenty miles an hour but she hit a particularly bad patch of ice and the bus went out of control. There wasn't anything she could have done about it because it probably happened too fast.'

'Are you sure? I keep thinking that if I hadn't done this...' She pointed to the inflamed area around her navel and grimaced.

'You might not have been in so much discomfort, because I'm sure that must be sore. However, you couldn't have altered what happened. It was an accident, Bethany, and no one was to blame.'

Laura stood, deeming it wise to give the teenager time to mull over what she'd said. 'Anyway, how about if I clean that up and make you a bit more comfortable? I expect it's rather painful, isn't it?'

Bethany nodded, obviously too spent by her outpouring of guilt to say anything else. Laura gave her an encouraging smile then hurried off to find some surgical spirit. Rachel followed her from the ward, looking worried.

'Is everything all right? Bethany looked really upset....'

Laura patted her arm. 'Everything is fine, or it will be with a bit of luck.' She quickly explained what the girl had told her, sighing as she heard Rachel's shocked gasp.

'Oh, the poor thing! Fancy thinking that she was responsible? No wonder she hasn't wanted to talk about what happened.'

'It must have been awful for her.' Laura paused but there was no easy way to put it. 'She's also worried that she might have to go into a children's home. I suppose, knowing that her mother's dead and that her father has never bothered to keep in touch with her....'

'She can't believe that I would *ever* let that happen!' Rachel was aghast. 'Bethany will come to live with me and there's no question about it. I must go and tell her that straight away.' She turned to leave then stopped and hugged Laura. 'Thanks, Laura. I owe you one for this!'

'Don't mention it!' Laura laughed, only too pleased that there seemed to be a solution in sight.

'So what was that all about? Have you been working your magic once again, Nurse Grady?'

She felt her blood race as Mark appeared beside her. It was hard to behave calmly when he said things like that *and* in that tone of voice! She tried her best, willing her foolish heart to behave sensibly—something it had no intention of doing!

'I don't know about magic but there seems to have been a bit of a breakthrough with Bethany Jones.' She quickly explained once more and heard Mark sigh.

'No wonder the poor kid has been so withdrawn. She must

have been going through agonies, blaming herself for her mother's death,' he observed quietly.

'I know. Thank heavens we got to the bottom of it at last. Maybe now we can start to make some progress with her.'

'Thank heavens *you* got to the bottom of it, you mean.' Mark's smile was warm. 'You're a very special woman, Laura Grady. You have the rare gift of making people respond to you.'

'Oh…Thank you.' She blushed with pleasure, unable to hide her delight at the compliment. Mark had said that she was very special and that was how she felt when he was around…

'Barbara just told me what you said, Dr Dawson. I still don't think it's right. Are you *sure* that Jessica will need to be on this diet for the rest of her life?'

Les Collins's belligerent tones were a rude intrusion. Laura saw Mark take a deep breath before he turned and clapped the other man on the shoulder. She knew he felt the same way she did about the interruption, but, he was patience itself as he led the man towards the office.

'I think I'd better go through it all again with you, Mr Collins….'

His voice faded as the door closed and Laura smiled mistily. Not for the world would Mark let Les Collins know how he felt, but wasn't that typical of him? If he thought that *she* was special, she felt exactly the same about him!

'Are you going to stand there all day? If you need something to do, I can always find you a job.'

She sighed as Cathy's voice carried to where she stood. She didn't need to look round to know that the other woman was addressing her! Better to shelve any more thoughts of Mark until later, otherwise the staff nurse would be down on her like a ton of bricks!

She quickly explained what she was doing then went to collect the surgical spirit from the drugs cupboard. Rachel was just leaving Bethany's bedside and her eyes were damp with tears.

'OK?' Laura whispered, relieved when Rachel nodded. She set to work as Rachel hurried away to speak to Peggy Mountfield and thank her for coming. The children were loathe to let Barney leave, and those who were able to do so accompanied him and his owner to the door and waved them off.

Laura concentrated on what she was doing, carefully easing

the metal stud out of the inflamed flesh surrounding Bethany's navel and murmuring commiseratingly as the girl winced.

'I know it hurts, love, but it needs to come out so that it can heal. I think it must have become infected.'

Bethany gritted her teeth. 'I wish I'd never had it done in the first place! It's just that everyone has their belly buttons pierced.'

'And you didn't want to be the odd one out?' Laura teased, earning herself a shy smile. 'Understandable. And there wouldn't have been a problem if you'd told us because then we could have kept a check on it.'

She dropped the stud into a dish then quickly cleaned up the wound. 'Still, it will soon heal. And you can always have it done again when you leave here. Just be careful next time, though.'

'I can't see me going back there again.' Bethany's voice was flat. 'The place where I had it done is up a steep flight of stairs.' She poked disconsolately at her leg. 'I won't be able to go up stairs with this.'

'You'll be surprised. Once you get the hang of the artificial limb you'll be able to get around almost as well as before. No, *really*,' she added as she saw Bethany's scepticism.

'Sure. I can just see me hopping all the way up those stairs, I don't think. I hate that doctor who cut my leg off. Doctors are supposed to make you better, not worse!'

The girl's voice had risen and Laura smiled sympathetically, although she made sure that Bethany understood the true facts. 'That doctor saved your life, love. You would have bled to death if they hadn't got you out of the wreckage. Your leg was too badly injured to save it and that's why he amputated it.

'Anyway, that should do the trick for now. I'll make a note on your chart for the night staff to check how that wound is healing, but it should be better in a day or so.'

She quickly amended Bethany's notes to include the new treatment then took the surgical spirit back to the drugs cupboard and went to find Rachel. It was almost time for her break but she wanted to check that there were no more jobs which needed doing before she went to the canteen. Jane joined her by the lift, having been sent for her break as well.

'Of all the times for Tom to come into the ward! Did you see his face? I felt so sorry for him!'

Laura shook her head, not sure what the other nurse was talking about. 'Sorry, but what do you mean?'

'When you were talking to Bethany just now?' Jane sighed as she realised Laura had no idea what she was talking about. 'Tom Hartley came to see how Bethany was doing. He'd just set foot in the ward when all of sudden she shouted out how much she hated the doctor who'd amputated her leg. Tom obviously heard, although he didn't say anything, just turned right around again and left. You feel so sorry for him, don't you? Especially as he and Rachel have been going out for the past few months. It can't be easy for him.'

'It can't,' Laura agreed sadly, trying to imagine how the poor man must feel. Although Tom knew he couldn't have done anything else in the circumstances, it couldn't be easy for him. It must have put a great strain on his relationship with Rachel as well.

She sighed as the lift arrived to whisk them up to the canteen and a few minutes of peace and quiet. Relationships were difficult at the best of time without any outside influences. Look how hard it was for her and Mark....

She blushed furiously. There was no her and Mark! She would be wise to get that into her head straight away!

The rest of the day flew past so that it seemed to take no time at all before it was time to leave. Laura collected her coat and travelled down in the lift with Jane, wondering if Mark would be waiting for her.

Her heart lifted at the thought of seeing him, but when they arrived in the foyer there was no sign of him. She bit back a sigh, telling herself that it was presumptuous to expect him to be waiting for her.

She said goodbye to Jane then made her way to the bus stop. Luckily enough, a bus came along almost immediately. She paid her fare and took a seat by the window, shifting over as far as she could as a stout lady, carrying several large shopping bags, sat next to her. It was uncomfortable, sitting there with cans of beans digging into her ribs, and she thought longingly of the comfort of Mark's car.

Funny how quickly one got used to the little luxuries, she

thought wryly. But it would be dangerous to get too used to them. Once her house was ready there would be no reason for Mark to drive her home each night. The thought was oddly depressing.

The sound of a car horn suddenly woke her from her reverie. She glanced out of the window and gasped as she recognised Mark's car drawing alongside the bus. He waved and mouthed something but, for a second her addled brain couldn't work out what he wanted her to do.

'Wants you to get off at the next stop, love.' The elderly woman had been watching what was happening with interest. She elbowed Laura in the ribs as the bus slowed. 'Well, get along with you, then. Don't keep 'im waiting. If I 'ad an 'andsome young man like that offering to run me 'ome…or anything else…I'd be off 'ere like a shot!'

Laura blushed as the woman gave a cackling laugh which instantly gained the rest of the passengers' attention. She struggled out of the seat as her companion regaled everyone with what was happening. There was a good deal of head-turning while people peered out of the window as Mark drew up behind the bus.

Laura's cheeks were burning as she hurried down the aisle and alighted when the bus stopped. She knew that everyone was watching as she ran over to the car and got in.

Mark looked at her and raised his brows. 'You look all hot and bothered. Is something wrong?'

'No…' She sighed. 'Just something the lady sitting next to me said.' She managed to smile. 'She obviously took a fancy to you and told me that she'd have been off the bus like a shot if you'd been offering her a lift!'

'Did she, indeed? Shame I'm spoken for, then, isn't it?' He gave her a teasing grin and Laura swallowed.

'Spoken for,' she repeated numbly, staring at him with luminous green eyes.

'Uh-huh. Ever since we met I've had eyes for no one but you, my lovely Laura.' He bent and kissed her quickly on the mouth then grinned as the bus driver honked and gave him a thumbs-up sign as he pulled away from the bus stop.

'Hmm, I think we'd better move along before we attract any

more attention, don't you?' Chuckling, Mark started the engine and pulled out into the flow of traffic.

Laura quelled the urge to put her hand to her lips to see if they felt as hot on the outside as they did on the inside. It was an effort to act naturally when she felt so churned up that she could barely think straight.

'I wondered where you were when I didn't see you in the foyer,' she began, then realised how that must sound and blushed furiously again.

'I didn't mean that I *expect* you to drive me home. I don't want you to think that. And, of course, it isn't any of my business where you were or what you were doing....'

She broke off, realising that she was digging herself an even deeper hole. She shot an uncomfortable look at Mark and wasn't soothed when she saw the smile that played around his mobile mouth. However, he didn't labour the point, mercifully sparing her any further embarrassment.

'I got held up at a meeting with Roger Hopkins,' he explained, referring to the hospital's manager. 'With Simon away I tend to get roped into meetings which I normally wouldn't attend.'

'Oh, I see. Was it about something important? Oh, I shouldn't have asked that, should I? I'm sorry. I—'

'Laura, relax!' He covered her hands with his and smiled at her. 'Take a deep breath and count to ten then just let it all hang loose.'

'I'm not sure I know how to do that!' She couldn't help laughing, struck by the sheer ridiculousness of the phrase. 'Let *what* hang loose?'

'I've no idea, but it sounds great, doesn't it?' He grinned back at her, his eyes warm and teasing. 'Blame it on too many nights spent in front of the TV. I have a stock of wonderfully obtuse sayings like that, gleaned from all those dreadful sixties films they show late at night. Maybe I should get out more, get myself a social life. What do you think?'

'Might be a good idea. Still, you haven't been stuck in front of the TV this weekend. Did you have a good time at your parents'?' she asked, feeling easier all of a sudden. Mark had this wonderful knack of taking the sting out of embarrassing situations. She wondered how he did it before it hit her that it was simply that he cared too much about other people to want them to feel uncomfortable.

'Great. Em managed to take some time out from her studies and it's always fun when we get together. In fact, she promised that she'll come and spend a week with me as soon as she gets a chance.'

Had that been a gentle hint, a way of telling her that he wanted her to move back home as soon as she could? Maybe it was his way of making sure that she knew there was a time limit on her stay. She couldn't help thinking back to what Cathy had said that morning, about her taking advantage of Mark's generosity, as all her doubts came rushing back.

'I'll be leaving as soon as I can,' she said quickly. 'In fact, maybe it would be an idea if I found bed and breakfast accommodation—'

'No way!' Mark's tone was firm. His mouth compressed as he shot her a stern look. 'I know you're looking for an excuse to leave the flat, Laura, but I simply won't allow you to go to some seedy B&B.'

At any other time she might well have picked him up on that. After all, what right did he have to assume that she needed to ask his permission? However, she was more concerned with the rest of what he'd said.

'What do you mean, I'm looking for an excuse?' she demanded.

He shrugged, his attention focused on the road as they came to a junction. Maybe it was the fact that he needed to concentrate on what he was doing which made his voice sound so flat.

'You made it plain that you didn't like the idea of accepting my hospitality, so it's a simple matter of adding two and two.'

He was right, but *wrong*! She hadn't liked the thought of staying in his flat but she certainly hadn't been trying to use his sister's visit as an excuse to leave! Without stopping to think, she set him straight.

'It wasn't an excuse, Mark. I just don't want to abuse your kindness. There isn't enough room in the flat for your sister to stay, with Robbie and me being there.'

'Em won't be coming for weeks yet. And even if she turned up on the doorstep this very night, it wouldn't make a scrap of difference. I want you and Robbie there, Laura. I wouldn't have asked you if I hadn't,' he stated firmly.

'Are you sure? I did wonder if maybe you regretted it.' She shrugged when she saw his surprise. 'You stayed away all weekend and maybe that was because you found it...well, awkward having us around.'

'No way! Did you really think that? Oh, sweetheart, no!'

He stopped the car and turned to her. His eyes were very dark as they held hers and she felt her breath catch. When had anyone looked at her with such tenderness? she found herself wondering.

'I couldn't get back to the flat because I had to stay at work on Saturday evening.' He shrugged but she could see the regret in his eyes. A boy was brought in, only fourteen years old—he'd taken a drug overdose and didn't make it.'

'Oh, how dreadful!' Without stopping to think, she covered his hand with hers. 'It must have been awful for everyone involved, Mark.'

'It was. The family was distraught. They'd no idea he'd been using drugs, you see. I spent over an hour just talking to them and then, as I was about to leave, I suddenly noticed the date on the calendar and realised it was Mum's birthday the next day.'

He turned his hand over and captured hers, his thumb painting gentle patterns on the soft flesh of her palm. 'It's sort of an unspoken rule that Em and I try to get home for her birthday, so I headed straight off after I phoned you. My parents live in the north-east, just on the Scottish Border, so it's a bit of a drive.'

He took a deep breath. 'I did think about inviting you and Robbie to go with me, but I decided it was too soon.' He smiled at her, a world of tender understanding in his eyes. 'You aren't ready for that yet, Laura, are you?'

She didn't know what to say. How could she answer the question when the answer itself was fraught with danger? One part of her would love to meet his family while the other part knew that it would be giving out the wrong kind of signals. Even though she was over her guilt about Ian there were other obstacles in the way of their relationship...

She paused as the thought sank in. She *was* over Ian's death and no longer felt guilty at the thought of loving someone else. How had it happened so quickly when just a week ago the idea had been unthinkable?

She searched her mind and realised that the healing process had begun the night she'd told Mark about Ian's death. Until that point she'd kept all the pain and anger bottled up inside her so that she hadn't given herself the chance to heal. But telling Mark about it had been the catalyst which had set her free. Now she knew that she had a future to look forward to, not just a past to mourn. The realisation both scared and excited her because it made it that more difficult to act sensibly.

'Laura?'

Mark prompted her, making her aware that she hadn't answered his question. She withdrew her hand, knowing that she needed all her strength at that moment. She had to think about Robbie, about the fact that she had a handicapped child who would need lifelong care and that there was always the chance—slim though it might be—that she could have another child who wasn't perfect. She simply wasn't the woman Mark needed in his life!

'I…I'm sure your mother would have had a fit if I'd turned up unannounced,' she said softly, deliberately fudging the issue.

Mark's eyes blazed, making her see that he knew what she was doing. However, his tone was even enough. 'Mum loves company so that wouldn't have been a problem. Still, maybe next time, eh?'

He started the car while Laura turned to stare sightlessly out of the window. There wouldn't be a next time because she wouldn't let things progress that far! It wasn't fair to Mark to raise his hopes, neither would it be fair to take advantage of his feelings for her. Oh, she didn't doubt that he *felt* something, which was what made it all the more difficult to do what was right. But she wouldn't ruin Mark's life by grasping this chance of happiness. She cared too much about him to do that.

'Mark do, Mark do!'

Robbie jumped up and down, becoming more and more agitated in his determination to get his own way. Laura fixed a firm smile to her mouth as she took hold of his hand.

'Mark is busy, as I told you, darling. Now, come along.'

She attempted to lead him to the bathroom but the child struggled free and threw himself on the floor. Drumming his heels on the carpet, he screamed out his frustration.

'Want Mark! Want Mark…!'

'Hey, what's this all about? That's a dreadful noise. You'll frighten Lucy.'

Mark came out of the sitting-room and stared at the child lying on the floor. Laura was so mortified that she could have died as she wondered what he thought.

It wasn't like Robbie to behave this way. Normally, he was very even-tempered and there had been no sign of an impending tantrum when they'd collected him from Claire's house and brought him back to the flat. He'd seemed a bit tired over tea, had needed coaxing to eat up the spaghetti she'd made for them, but that was all. However, her refusal to ask Mark to bathe him had prompted this outburst.

She opened her mouth to apologise as Mark hunkered down beside the child, but he shook his head. 'Don't worry about it,' he said softly, then turned his attention to the little boy, who had calmed down a bit now. 'So, what's the matter, then? Tell me.'

Robbie stared up at him, his lower lip quivering ominously. 'Mark bath,' he said between hiccoughs. He looked round as the cat came into the hall and he held out his hand to her. However, she ignored him as, with a twitch of her tail, she stalked disdainfully towards the kitchen. His lower lip wobbled even harder as he repeated his demands in a shrill voice.

'Mark bath!'

Mark shook his head. His tone was kind but firm as he spoke to the little boy. 'No, Robbie. Your mummy has told you that I'm busy. Now, you must do what she says. Maybe I'll give you a bath tomorrow if you're a good boy tonight.'

Robbie stared at him, obviously weighing up whether or not Mark meant it. He smiled, his tantrum forgotten all of a sudden. 'Tomorrow?'

'That's right. Now, come, up you get. And no more of this naughtiness.' Mark grinned as Robbie scrambled to his feet. 'Lucy doesn't like people shouting. It scares her.'

Robbie nodded solemnly. He seemed his usual happy self once more as he ran to the bathroom. A few seconds later they could hear him brushing his teeth with great gusto.

'Thank you,' Laura said sincerely. 'I'm so glad that you didn't make the mistake of giving in just to stop him crying.'

'I guessed that would be the wrong thing to do,' Mark said wryly. 'Although I'm afraid I don't have a lot of experience in child-rearing!'

'Some people are just born with the right instincts and that's why they make wonderful parents,' she said without thinking.

'I can hardly wait.' His voice was very deep. When she looked at him there was an expression in his eyes that made her pulse race. 'I'm looking forward to having children of my own, Laura. But sharing Robbie with you is a bonus.'

'Mark, I...' she began, but he chuckled as he pressed a finger against her mouth.

'I know! I shouldn't say things like that. But can I help it if they just sort of slip out?' He grimaced, pulling such a comically contrite face that she couldn't help laughing.

'You're incorrigible, Mark Dawson. You have an answer for everything!'

'But you love me anyway.' It had been said lightly enough, the kind of off-the-cuff remark that people used all the time. But it hit Laura hard. Her heart seemed to skip several beats before it began racing like crazy.

'I...I'd better go and see what that little horror is up to,' she muttered, making a beeline for the bathroom. She closed the door and took a big breath but her heart was still having the time of its life, pumping away like mad. She pressed a hand to her chest and could feel it beating against her palm, tangible proof of how Mark affected her...

Laura let her hand fall to her side, not needing any further evidence. She could tell black from white—she wasn't stupid. She was on the brink of falling in love with Mark Dawson, maybe even halfway there already, but it had to stop!

End. Terminate. Cease. Finish. There must be dozens of different words to describe what had to happen. Not one of them sounded in the least bit appealing, funnily enough!

CHAPTER ELEVEN

MARK was sitting at his desk when Laura went into the sitting-room a short time later. He removed his spectacles and tossed them onto the pile of papers he'd been working on when he saw her.

'Everything all right now?'

'Fine. Robbie's fast asleep. He seems to have got over his tantrum, thank heavens.'

She looked around uncertainly. Getting Robbie bathed and ready for bed had helped calm her jittery nerves. However, it wasn't easy to ignore the volatility of the situation now that she and Mark were alone. Just being in the room with him made her feel all churned up again, and that was the last thing she could afford. She had to be sensible, if not for her own sake then for his.

'I can see you're busy so I won't interrupt,' she said, edging back out of the room.

'I'll be finished with this very shortly.' He glanced at the papers and sighed. 'I promised Simon weeks ago that I'd dig out some statistics for him, but I haven't had the chance until now to start on it. Still, it's not so bad when you set your mind to it…or that's what I'm telling myself!'

Laura laughed dutifully, although she wasn't convinced that it would be wise to hang around too long. 'It can't have been easy, covering for him. Children's Med is such a busy department.'

'Which is why Simon wants these figures.' Mark tapped his pen on the papers. 'This is a breakdown of the number and variety of cases we've dealt with in the last six months, compared with the same period for the past three years. From what I can tell, there has been around a twenty per cent increase in our case load.'

'Really? That's an awful lot. Is there a reason for it?' Laura asked, interested despite herself.

'Yes. The area health authority has been running down services at the Royal for the past few years, although they've taken care that the public doesn't know that. Simon suspects that they'll close the Royal eventually and transfer everything to us.'

He shrugged philosophically. 'Cuts to services are commonplace nowadays and it could work out for the best, concentrating resources in one hospital rather than trying to find sufficient funding for two. However, it means that in the interim Dalverston is being put under increasing pressure. Simon wants all the ammunition he can get to take to the hospital board and ask them for extra funding.'

'Is that what you had to see Roger Hopkins about?' Laura guessed.

'Yes. Roger's as worried as we are. We're already at our limit and if the situation continues there's a very real danger that we won't be able to cope. Roger has offered his support when Simon puts his case to the board. Once they see these figures we're hoping they'll put pressure on the health authority to come up with extra cash for more staff and to improve facilities.'

'It would be a help, wouldn't it? There are a lot of things which need replacing, for instance,' she agreed thoughtfully.

'Exactly. I'd like to see the whole ward closed and a new one built, but that's a little *too* ambitious perhaps.' He grinned as he picked up his spectacles and put them firmly back in place. 'In the meantime, I'd better get down to it!'

He turned his attention back to his task and was soon engrossed. Laura hesitated but there seemed no real reason to hurry away now that Mark was fully occupied with what he was doing. She went and sat on the sofa, taking a magazine from the shelf beneath the coffee-table. It was an old copy of *Lancashire Life* and she flicked through its pages, pausing when she came to an article about Dalverston.

She settled down to read it and was soon caught up in a story about a local highwayman who had roamed the area surrounding the town many years before. It was a story she'd heard before, but the writer had a particularly nice turn of phrase and had added several new twists to the tale so she was soon absorbed.

It was quiet in the room with just the crackling of the logs in the grate to provide a background. When Mark tossed down his pen she jumped. She glanced at the clock and was surprised to find that a good hour had passed. Funny, she wouldn't have imagined they could spend so much time together so comfortably, but wasn't that just another facet of Mark—the fact that he could be such an easygoing companion as well as an exciting one?

'I think I've just about cracked it!' He sounded relieved as he got up from the desk. He flexed his back and groaned. 'Oh, wow, I'd forgotten how tiring it can be, poring over a stack of papers.'

Laura put the magazine down and smiled sympathetically. 'Cramp? Nothing worse, is there?'

'There certainly isn't...' He gritted his teeth, rolling his shoulders back and forth in an effort to loosen the knotted muscles, but it didn't seem to have much effect.

Laura hesitated but concern for the discomfort he was in wouldn't let her rest. She patted the cushion next to her. 'Here, sit yourself down and I'll try to massage it away.'

'Would you?' He hesitated only a moment before he came over to the sofa and sank gratefully onto it.

Laura stood and went round the back of the sofa, running her hand experimentally over the corded muscles at the base of his neck. Her heart gave a small bump of awareness but she ruthlessly suppressed it. She'd offered the massage in a purely *professional* capacity, she told herself sternly. And that was the way she intended to conduct it!

'Can you undo your top buttons?' she requested in her calmest tone.

'Sure.' Mark flicked open the top three buttons of his pale blue shirt and settled back in his seat. Closing his eyes, he let his head loll forward as Laura put both hands on the nape of his neck and began to knead it gently. 'Oh, does that feel good!'

She smiled as she heard the genuine appreciation in his voice. 'It should do. I did a course on massage when I was a midwife. I used to teach the expectant fathers how to rub their wives' backs while they were in labour!'

'I hope you're adapting the technique. The circumstances aren't *quite* the same in this case, Laura.'

She chuckled at the wry note in his voice. 'No? I disagree.' She ran her hands experimentally across the width of his shoulders, feeling the knots in them. 'Tension is tension, no matter what causes it, so the remedy is much the same.'

'Is it?' There was a taut edge to the question which made her pause, but there was no sign of it as he added, 'Well, I'll have to take your word for that as you're the expert.'

He fell silent after that, seemingly content to let her get on with the job of working all the kinks out of his neck and shoulders. Laura worked methodically, finding a knot of muscle and working away until she felt it relax beneath her hands. She found that she was enjoying it as much as Mark was. There was something deeply *satisfying* about the feeling it gave her to know that she could ease his discomfort this way.

Her hands worked their way along his shoulders then worked their way all the way back to the nape of his neck once more. His shirt had fallen open and she felt the warmth of his skin as her fingers glided inside his collar. She pressed her fingertips into the column of his neck, hearing him groan as she delicately probed each separate vertebra.

Her hands stilled as a frown puckered her brow. 'Sorry. Does that hurt?'

'No.' His voice seemed to crack on the word and she heard him clear his throat before he suddenly leaned forward out of her reach. He stood up, keeping his back towards her as he buttoned the neck of his shirt. 'Thanks, Laura. That was great…really.'

She frowned again, wondering why a small voice was telling her that he was feeling far from 'great'. 'Sure? I could massage lower down your back if—'

'No!' He spun round so fast that she actually backed away because he'd startled her that much. He took a deep breath and she could see the effort it cost him to speak in what was meant to be a normal tone of voice. 'As I said, that's helped a lot.'

He was saying one thing but giving out entirely the opposite signals! Laura stared at him in confusion and heard him sigh.

'Sweetheart, do I really need to spell it out for you?' he asked with what sounded suspiciously like exasperation. 'You've managed to cure the ache in one part of me but I'm having the devil's own job with another!'

'Oh!' Her gasp echoed around the room as it hit her what he meant. Her eyes flew downwards then flew straight back up because she didn't need to check if he'd meant what he'd said. The very air seemed to pulsate with emotions all of a sudden, new, different ones to those that had been around just a few seconds before.

Laura felt her heart give a sharp lurch so that it felt as though it had plummeted down and bounced back off her diaphragm. She knew that she should say something—something light and witty—to ease the tension, but nothing came to mind. Her mind was a huge void, every rational thought sucked from it by the sheer force of feeling which hit her. She didn't want to find the exact *bon mot* to smooth over this moment! She didn't want to rationalise it with perfect grammar. She didn't want to have to think at all and thereby deny herself what she suddenly wanted to *feel* so much!

'Laura?' There was a thread of uncertainty in Mark's voice as he said her name, but none at all in the way he came round the sofa and took hold of her hands. If he was wondering if this was a wise thing to do then it certainly didn't show, she realised with a humour which should have shocked her, only she refused to be shocked.

When he pulled her into his arms and held her so that she could feel the urgency of his body pressing against hers, she sighed with pleasure and no trace of regret. Regret was something she would deal with later, but for now it wasn't on the agenda. There were too many positive emotions to enjoy, rather than worrying about negatives. For too many long and lonely months she'd denied her normal womanly instincts, told herself they were dead. Now, as Mark held her, she felt more alive than she had in ages. How could she possibly regret feeling like this?

His lips were hard and warm, demanding a response which she gave him eagerly. As his mouth took hers, Laura's took equal delight in drawing a response from his. They were both trembling when the kiss ended, both of them stunned by the force of their passion, and yet even then Mark took the time to make sure she knew what was happening.

'Laura, you know where this is leading, don't you?' He cupped her face between his hands, staring deep into her eyes and making her look into his so that he could tell she understood.

'Yes, I know.' She raised her head and faced him proudly. 'I want you to make love to me, Mark. I...' Her voice cracked, but she recovered immediately. 'I want to make love to you.'

He closed his eyes as though he was afraid of what she might see in them at that moment, but when he opened them again it was still there—all the joy, all the tenderness, all the love.

'Laura, I—'

'No.' She pressed her fingers against his lips, stopping the words before they could emerge. It didn't make them any less real, couldn't change things, but it was for the best. She didn't need to hear him say that he loved her to know that it was true, and she felt a momentary chill. When this was over, would *he* regret it? Was she wrong to run the risk of hurting him, even though it was the last thing she wanted to do?

Her mind veered towards common sense before it abruptly changed course once more. She would think about that later as well. She rose on tiptoe, twining her arms around his neck as she pressed her lips to his in an invitation neither of them could resist.

'Laura…Laura!'

There was joy in the murmured sound of her name and tenderness as well but, then, she'd expected nothing else. Mark would love her like the man he was, tenderly and with the utmost caring, and it would be all the more special because of that. How could she ask for anything more?

Firelight flickered over their bodies as they slowly undressed one another. They shared the pleasure, each taking a turn. Mark unbuttoned her blouse and slid it off her shoulders, pausing to kiss her throat and collarbone before letting it fall to the floor. Laura unfastened his shirt, letting her palms rest on the warm muscles of his chest for a few delicious seconds before she slid the soft cotton off his shoulders.

Mark smiled but his eyes were so dark and burning with heat that her breath caught. 'I get the best out of this deal.' He ran a teasing finger around the lace covering her breasts. 'I get to remove more than you do!'

Laura smiled then gasped as his head dipped while he pressed a kiss to her warm skin. She was shivering uncontrollably as his hands slid behind her back to undo the hooks on her bra. He fumbled with the tiny fastenings for a moment then gave a murmur of triumph as he managed to work them free at last.

White lace rustled as he drew the straps down her arms, slowly inch by delectable inch. There was just a tiny scrap of material covering her breasts now and she found that she couldn't drag her eyes away from the sight of what was happening. The blood was drumming in her ears, pounding at her temples, making her legs feel weak and her head dizzy.

Why didn't he take it off and stop this torment? she found herself thinking just a millisecond before he complied and the ability to think disappeared. There was just the warm, caressing touch of Mark's hands on her sensitive skin, the expression of reverence on his face as he bent towards her, then a feeling so intense, so powerful that she cried out as his mouth found her. It was just a foretaste of the long hours of pleasure to come....

Grey morning light crept through a gap in the velvet curtains, chasing away the last of the night. Laura closed her eyes, not wanting to let it slip away. Day was upon them and inside she was afraid of what would happen when they had to face what they had done. She wanted to cling to the memories as long as she could....

'Are you awake?'

Mark's voice was low enough not to wake her if she had been sleeping, but she still jumped. She opened her eyes, all her doubts clear to see in their shadowy depths.

'Don't!' He scooped her towards him, his big warm arms holding her close as he covered her face with kisses. They had made love on the sofa, staying there afterwards to sleep, so there was little room to move, yet somehow Laura managed to draw back.

'Should we have done what we did, Mark?' she asked in a small voice that betrayed her uncertainty.

'Yes! How can you doubt it?' He rolled her over, looming over her so that she was forced to look into his eyes. 'Wasn't it as wonderful for you as it was for me, Laura?'

'Yes, but—'

'But nothing!' He kissed her hard, hungrily, groaning deep in his throat as he felt her immediate response. She could feel the tremor which ran through him and knew what an effort it cost him when he pulled back.

'I could stay here all day, convincing you, but duty calls, my love. And if I'm not mistaken, it sounds as though your son is awake and raring to go!' He grinned as the unmistakable sound of bed springs being put through a severe testing issued from the bedroom. Planting a last kiss on Laura's parted lips, he rolled to his feet and groaned dramatically.

'Oh, my poor aching back! That sofa certainly wasn't made for someone my size. I'd ask for another one of your wonderful massages only, remembering what happened last night, I don't think we have time!'

Laura summoned a smile, trying her best to behave as positively as Mark was doing. 'Not if we aim to get to work this side of lunchtime! Anyway, I'd better go and stop Robbie using your bed as a trampoline. There won't be any springs left in it at this rate!'

She started to rise then stopped as she realised her state of undress. Mark had pulled the chenille throw over them for warmth before they'd fallen asleep, but now she was suddenly conscious of her nakedness.

'I'll get you my robe from the bathroom if you hold on.' He seemed to guess her predicament and once again made sure that she wouldn't feel embarrassed by it. Laura sank back into the warm cushions as he left the room, a smile playing around her lips. Was it her besotted imagination or was Mark *really* perfect? Kind, considerate, tender and gentle, not to mention the most exciting lover....

A flush heated her cheeks and she quickly buried her face in the cushions as her mind was flooded with images of the previous night. The velvet smelt of Mark's aftershave and she drew in a deep breath, letting the delicious aroma fill her. Maybe she should feel guilty about what had happened, but she refused to be a hypocrite. Neither would Ian have wanted her to be one. Her love for Ian hadn't been diminished in any way because of her love for Mark....

The thought slipped in and was suddenly there, slap bang in her head in all its glory. She loved Mark. So much for all her vows not to let it happen! Yet, oddly, she didn't feel shocked by the discovery or scared. It felt too good, too right, too...too wonderful!

'Here you are.' Mark came back with the robe and held it out for her. Laura stood up, forgetting her shyness as her mind rejoiced at its new revelation. She loved him. He loved her. They loved each other. Just conjugating the verb gave her so much pleasure!

'Mmm, I think I could take to this very easily.' Mark wrapped the robe around her as she slid her arms into the soft towelling. He turned her round and neatly tied the belt in a careful knot. His grey eyes gleamed with laughter and a host of other things as he looked up at her. 'I have a vacancy for a full time house-guest if you're interested. The terms are reasonable and you get all sorts of privileges.'

'Such as?' She hadn't felt this light-hearted in ages, she realised as she responded to his teasing banter. There had been too many other things to think about, to worry over. Now it was joy itself just to play the fool with Mark like this.

Her delicate brows pleated as she mockingly demanded an explanation. 'What privileges, pray, Dr Dawson?'

'Oh, things like being allowed the run of the place and unlimited use of the Jacuzzi.' He sighed when she sniffed her disdain. 'Hmm, I can see you aren't impressed. How about the chance to share my bed…or, in this case, my sofa…each night? How does that sound to you?'

'You really think that's a privilege—' she began, then gasped as he swung her up in his arms. 'Mark! Put me down before you drop me!'

'Unlikely.' He grinned at her. 'You weigh next to nothing so I don't think you're in any danger of being dropped, my love.'

He dropped a smug kiss on her nose, obviously enjoying the chance to show off his superior strength. However, there was a light in his eyes that told her he meant what he'd said as he continued quietly, 'And, yes, I really do believe that sleeping in my bed is a privilege because it isn't an offer I've made to all that many women, Laura.'

He took a deep breath and she felt his chest rise and fall. 'In fact, I don't expect to make it to anyone else after this.'

She knew what he was saying and her heart tumbled around inside her as she realised its implications. 'Mark, I—' she began, but he wouldn't let her finish.

Setting her carefully on her feet, he kissed her hard, his grey eyes full of determination. 'No. I don't want you to make up your mind now because it's too soon.'

He let her go, walking quickly to the door before he glanced back, and it was obvious that he had no intention of listening even if she had tried to make him understand that she wasn't ready for any kind of commitment just yet. 'I'll put on a pot of coffee and rustle up some toast while you sort Robbie out. OK?'

'OK,' Laura replied softly. She bit her lip as he disappeared from the room. Suddenly her mind was awash once again with all the old doubts. Mark seemed to believe that they had a future together but she wasn't convinced. She never had been, even though one of her main objections had been ruled out.

She no longer felt guilty at the thought of forming a relationship with another man. Ian wouldn't have expected her to spend the rest of her days mourning him and would have been pleased that she'd found happiness again. However, that had never been the only reason against her allowing Mark into her life....

'Mummy, me hungry.'

She turned at the sound of the child's voice and her heart began to ache as she saw Robbie standing in the doorway. There was another reason why there couldn't be a happy-ever-after for her and Mark, one that couldn't be changed. She couldn't put upon him the burden of looking after her son, especially not when she could never risk giving him a child of his own. It wouldn't be fair. She couldn't take everything from Mark and give him nothing in return!

'I don't think there is anything to worry about, Mrs Glover. Daniel seems happy enough now, doesn't he?'

Laura summoned a smile but it was an effort. Her mind was still awash with what had happened the night before, despite the fact that it was now mid-morning. She hadn't seen Mark since he'd driven her to work that morning because he'd been caught up in yet another meeting, but in one way she was glad.

It wasn't going to be easy to make him understand how she felt yet she shied away from telling him the truth. Mark would overrule her objections and that was the last thing she must let him do. She wouldn't *hurt* Mark by grasping her own chance of happiness when it would mean him losing out on so much....

'He should be better by now. I just can't understand what's gone wrong.'

Laura took a deep breath and determinedly focused on the problem of Daniel. 'We don't think anything *has* gone wrong, Mrs Glover. Dr Dawson is confident that Daniel's operation went completely to plan.'

'But he keeps on saying that his ears hurt!' Josephine Glover sighed as she looked over to where her son was laughing with Tim Matthews. 'Not that there looks much wrong with him, as you say, nurse. If I didn't know better, I'd say he was having us all on. He wasn't too keen on the idea of going to stay with his gran when he came out of here, but there wasn't anything else I could think of. His dad and I can't afford to take any more time off work to look after him, you see.'

'I do,' Laura agreed, wondering if Mrs Glover might have shed some light on the problem. Everyone had been perplexed by Daniel's repeated claims that his ears were hurting, because there was no reason why they should be. Could it be that Daniel was having more fun in hospital than he would have had at his grandmother's house?

Laura sighed as she looked at the two boys. They had their heads together and were obviously plotting some new bit of mischief. So far Daniel had notched up quite a list of incidents ranging from the Rice Crispie experiment to another involving how fast a bath could fill with water.

They had been spared a flood only because Rachel had happened to hear the water running and had gone to investigate. She had found Daniel—complete with stop-watch—timing the proceedings and oblivious to the fact that water was ready to pour over the side of the bath at any moment!

Rachel had given him a good telling-off but none of them believed it would have much effect. Daniel had the sort of enquiring mind which meant that trouble followed him around!

Laura made a mental note to mention what she'd learned. However, there was no opportunity for the rest of the morning because it was so busy. Two of the children from the minibus crash were discharged, but they had three new admissions, which stretched them to the limit. And, to cap it all, Bethany was in a great deal of pain.

Laura spent some time with the teenager but it was hard to watch her suffer. Phantom pain from an amputated limb was a well-documented problem. However, Laura suspected there was more to it than that. Bethany's usual pain relief didn't seem to be having any effect and she found herself wondering if perhaps a neuroma had formed. That kind of benign tumour, made up of nerve tissue, could develop on occasion, despite every precaution being taken.

She decided that it should be investigated and went to find Rachel, only to discover that she had taken an early lunch-break.

Cathy was covering for her and she made no attempt to disguise her hostility when Laura went to the office.

'Yes? What is it now? Maybe you don't have anything to do but I have so get on with it.'

Laura took a calming breath, refusing to sink to the other woman's level despite such provocation. 'Bethany Jones is in a lot of pain and I think she needs someone to look at her leg. I know Mark is in a meeting so perhaps we should get Tom Hartley down here. It could be a neuroma.'

'Could it indeed? And since when have you been qualified to make such a diagnosis?' Cathy laughed scathingly. 'Just because you're sleeping with Mark Dawson, it doesn't make you an expert!'

Laura's stomach turned over. How did Cathy know what had happened? Unless…unless Mark had told her? Her mind grappled with that thought, but before she could convince herself how unlikely it was Cathy continued.

'I thought so. I could tell what your game was from the moment I met you. Nice move, Laura. I bet Mark didn't know what had hit him, did he?'

'I…I don't know what you mean…' she began, but once again Cathy didn't let her finish. There was the gleam of malice in her eyes as she treated Laura to a scornful stare.

'You look as though butter wouldn't melt in your mouth, but we both know the score. You must have thought all your Christmases had come together when Mark dropped into your greedy little hands. The trouble is, as I've said before, that he's just too nice for his own good. He can't see what you're up to.'

'How dare you?' Suddenly Laura had had enough. She might have been willing to ignore Cathy's spiteful comments about her work, but there was no way she was prepared to let her make any more such remarks about her private life!

'So I slept with Mark as a means to an end? Is that what you're saying?' She gave a scornful laugh, watching the ugly colour bloom in the other woman's face. 'After all, it's what you'd do given the chance, isn't it, Cathy? And I have a much greater incentive to try and land myself someone like Mark. I mean, how many men would be willing to take on a handicapped child? But Mark is different, isn't he? He's kind and caring and it didn't take much to convince him what a wonderful human being I am

Sleeping with him was little enough repayment for the chance of a free meal ticket!'

She paused to draw breath, barely aware that she was trembling all over. How could anyone accuse her of such dreadful deeds? She was just opening her mouth to tell Cathy in no uncertain terms how wrong she was when she caught a movement out of the corner of her eye.

She glanced round and her heart seemed to grind to a halt as she saw Mark standing by the lifts. It was obvious from his face that he'd heard every word she'd said and how he'd interpreted them.

There was a moment when his eyes held hers before he abruptly turned and strode towards the stairs. The door slammed shut behind him and the noise it made seemed to release her from the spell.

Ignoring Cathy's mocking, triumphant laughter, Laura raced after him. He had a head start on her and had reached the ground floor before she managed to catch him up.

'Mark, wait! Please!'

He stopped, his hand resting on the doorhandle as she arrived, panting, at his side. 'I'm on my way to A and E,' he said flatly and the tone of his voice made her feel chilled to her soul. Surely he didn't believe that she'd *meant* any of those things she'd said? He couldn't! And yet there was something about the way he stood there, looking so distant and aloof, which made her fear the worst.

Reaching out, she laid her hand on his, beseeching him to listen to what she was saying. 'It won't take long but I have to explain what you heard—'

He shook his head. 'There's no need. Anyway, this is neither the time nor the place to discuss this.'

'Then when can we talk about it?' Her fingers gripped his harder when he tried to withdraw his hand because she was suddenly afraid. Mark couldn't possibly believe she would do that to him—make use of him—surely?

Her voice took on a new urgency as she struggled to make him understand what had been going on. 'What I said just now wasn't true! It was Cathy, you see. She'd said some horrible things about you and me, and I—'

'And you were what?' His tone was glacial all of a sudden. 'Trying to set her straight so that she understood the situation?'

He shrugged but she could see the pain in his eyes and her heart ached at what he must be going through. 'Fine. It's always better to get things out into the open, I find. It saves a lot of problems in the long run.'

'No! You've got it all wrong!'

Why wouldn't he listen to her? Why wouldn't he believe what she was telling him? Even as her mind screamed out the questions she knew the answers. Mark was deeply hurt by what he'd seemingly overheard and he was reacting to it as anyone would.

She took a deep breath, struggling for control as she tried to convince him that he'd put the entirely wrong interpretation on the conversation. 'I was furious that Cathy should imply that I was trying to…to trick you. It wasn't the first time that she's passed such comments but I was determined that it would be the last. I was trying to make her see just how ridiculous she was being.'

'Really? And in the course of doing so you thought it necessary to tell her that we had slept together?' His brows rose steeply, and the look he gave her was so cold and clinical that she shuddered. 'That isn't the sort of confidence people normally share with someone they don't like. But perhaps you used it more as proof of just how deeply involved we are? A sort of warning that it was a waste of time her making waves because I wouldn't believe her?'

'No! I didn't confide anything in her. She just…well, she just guessed!'

Laura could hear the panic in her voice and fought to control it. However, it wasn't easy when Mark was acting like this. 'I never said anything about last night to Cathy, or anyone else,' she said flatly, desperate to convince him.

'No?' He shrugged, his shoulders rising and falling dismissively. 'Maybe you didn't and it was just a lucky guess on her behalf. After all, my interest in you must have been apparent to everyone, I imagine?'

He must have seen the blush that swept up her face because his laughter was sardonic. 'I can see that I'm right. I was never very good at hiding my feelings, Laura, so it didn't take an expert to see that I was falling for you. You soon realised what was happening, although in all fairness you did try to warn me that you weren't interested. I suppose I can't blame you for taking advantage of the opportunity when I refused to be convinced.'

'What opportunity? What are you saying, Mark?' Her tone sounded almost as cold as his had done, but she couldn't seem to add any emotion to it when her very bones felt as though they had turned to ice all of a sudden.

Mark smiled thinly and the expression in his eyes made her want to weep. It was as though all the warmth had seeped away, leaving them cold and empty, like the eyes of a stranger. 'That maybe you eventually saw me as the answer to your problems if not your prayers. It can't have been easy, managing on your own. In fact, I know how hard it has been because you told me so yourself. So why not take advantage of my interest in you?

'I'm not rich but I have a steady job. And I'm kind to old ladies and children. I'm not *too* bad a catch at the end of the day, even if I could never match up to your husband. Once you'd subdued your guilty conscience then it wasn't too hard to play along, was it, even though you had a few qualms this morning? Still, maybe sleeping with me so soon hadn't been part of the plan, but these things happen. I only hope that you didn't find it too distasteful.'

There wasn't anything she could say. Words weren't enough to describe how it made her feel to have him accuse her like that. Laura was too numb to cry, too numb to feel anything much. It was as though the world had caved in around her and she'd been left staring into a great dark pit from where there was no escape.

Without a word she turned and made her way back up the stairs, and the sound of her footsteps mocked her. Every step was a step away from Mark but, then, the distance between them couldn't be measured in feet or even miles. How could he believe her capable of such *deceit*? She had no idea but, then, she really didn't know him all that well, just as he obviously didn't know her.

CHAPTER TWELVE

'I'M PLEASED to say that there's no sign of renal scarring. Katie has been extremely lucky and our main concern now has to be to ensure that she's not placed at risk again in the future.'

Mark tossed his spectacles onto the blotter and looked round. There was a small crowd gathered in the office that afternoon for the team meeting. Laura was there to add her comments about the children under her care, and she was trying to keep her mind on what was happening rather than on what had gone on that morning. This was the first time she had seen Mark since their conversation, and it wasn't easy to blot it out of her mind. Recalling what he'd accused her of doing was just so painful.

Tears stung her eyes and she quickly looked down at the notes she'd been making. Thankfully, everyone seemed too concerned about Katie to notice her distress.

'The police have tracked down her mother at last.' Gill Marsh, the hospital's social worker, sighed as everyone looked at her. 'Yes, she's on holiday. She's in Gran Canaria with her boyfriend. According to my contact at the police station she'll be flying home later today, although it took a bit of *persuasion* to get her to cut short her stay.'

'Incredible, isn't it?' Rachel voiced all their thoughts. She sighed as she looked at Gill. 'How about Katie's father? I shudder to think what will happen to the poor kid if the mother is left to look after her on her own again.'

'The police have a lead which they're following up. Evidently, they think that Gary Watson is in Ireland. And as for Lisa Watson getting Katie back, well, that's something the courts will decide. The police have said that they'll be prosecuting Lisa for child abandonment, so Katie will probably be placed under an interim supervision order until a decision is made about her future.'

'Poor little thing! As if she hasn't enough to cope with,' Laura murmured, her heart going out to the poor child.

'Not everyone shares your devotion to their children, Laura. Neither are they willing to make the kind of sacrifices you make.'

Mark's tone was level yet she knew that what might have sounded like a compliment to the others was a world away from being that. It was a reference to the previous night and, specifically, to the fact that he believed that she'd slept with him purely as a means to an end.

She felt sudden anger compounded of pain and a deep sense of injustice. 'Probably not. But my view is that you do whatever it takes even if you might find it personally abhorrent.'

His eyes flashed as the jibe hit home, although his tone didn't alter. 'Then all I can say is that I admire your dedication.' He took another set of notes off the pile but not before she'd seen the expression of pain that crossed his face.

Laura took a deep breath, feeling her heart aching. Suddenly the urge to retaliate had disappeared as fast as it had come. Knowing that she was hurting Mark was more than she could bear. She loved him and the last thing she wanted was to cause him any pain!

'So, on to Bethany. How has she been today?' Mark checked the girl's notes and nodded. 'Everything looks fine. She doesn't appear to be experiencing any problems so I think we're looking towards her being fitted with a temporary prosthesis in a week or—'

'Excuse me.' Laura spoke up, jolted out of her own unhappy thoughts by what he'd said. 'Bethany was in a great deal of pain this morning!'

'Then why didn't you see fit to tell anyone?' Mark's tone was glacial and Laura felt her heart start to pound. He was speaking to her in a purely professional capacity now and it was obvious that he was angry by what he saw as a lapse by her.

She hurried to set matters straight. 'I did! I told Cathy that I was concerned about her. You were in a meeting so I suggested that we should contact Tom Hartley and ask him to see Bethany. I wondered if perhaps a neuroma had formed.'

'There's nothing down here to suggest that Tom saw her or

that he was asked to.' Mark's face was set as he turned to Rachel. 'Did Cathy mention any of this to you?'

'No. Obviously, I would have done something about it if she had, although Cathy is perfectly capable of contacting Tom herself if she thought it urgent that Bethany be seen,' she replied, looking worried.

'We need to have a word with her so that we can get to the bottom of this. However, my main concern right now is Bethany.'

Mark got up and abruptly left the office. A small silence fell after his departure. Laura took a deep breath, wondering if it was her imagination or whether the others seemed to believe that she was at fault.

She glanced at Rachel but the other woman avoided her eyes as she excused herself and left. Gill Marsh had gathered up her papers and she, too, disappeared. Penny Carmichael, the physiotherapist, cleared her throat.

'Looks like a bit of a mix-up, doesn't it?'

Laura nodded miserably. 'Yes, it does. I can't understand why Cathy didn't contact Tom....'

She tailed off, remembering what had happened earlier when she'd spoken to the staff nurse. Had Cathy forgotten about contacting the surgical registrar in the heat of the moment? It was the only explanation she could think of, although she doubted whether Mark would consider it a valid excuse.

He came back just then. His face was set as he went to the phone and dialled. 'Tom Hartley, please.' He paused, a frown darkening his brow. 'Then ask him to call me as soon as he can. It's urgent.'

The phone went down with a thud which reverberated around the room. Laura realised that her palms were damp and ran them down her skirt. Mark's expression was thunderous as he turned to Penny and quietly informed her that the meeting was over. However, when Laura got up to leave he stopped her.

'I want a word with you, Nurse Grady.'

Penny shot her a sympathetic smile before she hurried out of the door. It was obvious she believed that Laura was in for a telling-off, although for the life of her Laura couldn't see how she was at fault. She had informed her superior, Cathy, about her concerns, so surely it had been up to Cathy to follow through on them?

'Mark, I—'

He held up his hand to stop her saying anything. 'I would prefer it if we waited until Staff Nurse Williams joined us. Please, take a seat.'

Laura sat down, suddenly glad to do so as her legs began to tremble. It was difficult to remain calm in view of the disapproving atmosphere in the room. However, there was no trace of nervousness on Cathy's face as she tapped on the door and came into the room.

'You wanted a word with me, Mark?' she asked brightly.

'Please.' He waited until Cathy had sat down before continuing, 'I'm extremely concerned that no action was taken when it was discovered that Bethany Jones was experiencing severe pain this morning. Nurse Grady informs me that she told you about the situation and suggested that you ask Tom Hartley to see Bethany as I was unavailable. Is that right?'

'I'm sorry, but I'm afraid I don't understand.' Cathy's voice had risen in surprise. However, it was nothing to what Laura felt as the other woman turned to her. 'Exactly when were you *supposed* to have told me about this?'

Laura felt sick as she heard the disbelief in the other woman's voice. Cathy sounded so convincing that she actually began to doubt herself. Had she *really* told her about Bethany?

It was obvious that Mark had sensed her uncertainty. 'You are sure that you discussed this problem with Staff Nurse Williams?'

Her mind cleared as she heard his sceptical tone. It was obvious that Mark didn't believe her, and it stung to realise it. 'Of course I'm sure!' She gave a discordant little laugh. 'I told her about my concerns this morning. In fact, you overheard what I said!'

'I didn't hear you making any reference to Bethany,' he stated flatly.

Cathy gave a tinkly laugh. 'That's because she never mentioned her!'

She turned to Laura with an expression of bewilderment on her face. 'I really can't believe that you're trying to blame me for your incompetence. I know we haven't exactly hit it off—

understandable really, because I'm a stickler when it comes to work. However, I think it's deplorable that you should try to lay the blame at my door, especially as the one who has suffered in all this is poor Bethany.'

Laura gasped. 'How can you say that? You know that I told you she was in pain.' She turned to Mark when Cathy shrugged. 'I did!'

'I'm afraid it's your word against Cathy's,' he said repressively, his face taut with disapproval and something which looked suspiciously like pain. It was obvious that he thought she was lying, Laura thought miserably. Didn't he know anything at all about her, know that she was incapable of doing that? Bearing in mind what he'd said to her earlier, it seemed unlikely, and her heart ached even more.

She got up, realising there was little she could do to convince him if he was set on thinking the worst. Whether or not this would have repercussions in the future, she had no idea. She was working a three-month trial period and the hospital board had the option to dismiss her at the end of it if they chose to. Would this count against her? she wondered miserably as she left the office. It might.

'Sorry you decided not to take my advice now, are you?'

Cathy had followed her from the room and Laura turned to face her. 'What advice? I don't know what you're talking about any more than I understand why you lied to Mark just now! You know as well as I do that I told you about Bethany.'

'But it's what Mark believes that counts, isn't it? And it's obvious that he doesn't believe you, Laura.' Cathy smiled mockingly. 'What a shame that all your plans have gone to waste. You should have done what I told you to and steered clear of him.'

She shrugged. 'There are other fish in the sea and you might have been able to snare some other poor unsuspecting soul, but not now. Your name is going to be mud once this story gets round. There's an awful lot of sympathy in this place for Rachel and her niece, and folk won't take kindly to the fact that you failed to do what you should have done.'

Cathy walked away, letting the doors to the ward snap shut behind her. Laura took a steadying breath but her heart was racing crazily. She didn't doubt that the story would be all round the hospital very shortly. Cathy would enjoy being the bearer of such bad tidings! What if people did turn against her? What if Fiona Watts heard the story and let it influence her? She could find herself out of a job before the three months were up! How was she going to manage to pay her bills, not to mention the repairs to her house?

Panic filled her and she had to bite her lip to hold back a sob. This, coming on top of what had happened between her and Mark earlier, was just too much!

'Are you all right?'

The concern in Mark's voice as he came out of the office and found her standing there almost tipped her over the edge. It was only pride that gave her the strength to hold onto the shreds of her composure—that, and an unwillingness to let him think that she was trying to play on his sympathy!

'Fine, thank you,' she said tautly, turning away.

'Laura, I...' He stopped, shaking his head when she glanced back, and she couldn't recall ever seeing such agony on anyone's face as she saw on his at that moment. 'Nothing. Forget it.'

He walked away, summoning the lift and disappearing into it as soon as it arrived. Laura took a deep breath but it couldn't fill the emptiness which seemed to run soul-deep. Without Mark in her life, her world seemed emptier than ever.

The next few days were a nightmare. Laura began to dread going into work each day. True to her threat, Cathy had started spreading rumours and Laura soon found that she had to steel herself to face the hostile stares when she went to the canteen for her breaks. In the end she started taking sandwiches for her lunch and eating them in the staffroom to spare herself the daily ordeal. Maybe it was the wrong thing to do because it probably made her appear even more guilty, but she simply couldn't face the hostility day after day.

What hurt most, however, was that Rachel was so cool with her. She wished she could make Rachel understand that she wasn't at fault but, with Cathy embroidering the story, it wasn't going to be easy. The fact that Tom Hartley had agreed with her diagnosis and had decided that Bethany did have a neuroma which would need to be removed surgically was no consolation.

It just made Laura wish that she'd made sure that the surgical registrar had been called in the first place.

As for Mark, he was so distant whenever he came into the ward that it was pure torture just having to speak to him. She found herself going to all sorts of lengths to avoid him. It was one of the blackest times in her life and she found herself wondering if she would ever come through it.

She moved out of Mark's flat because it would have been impossible to remain there in the circumstances. He wasn't home when she packed up her few belongings, and she was glad. Having to say goodbye to him would have been far too painful in the circumstances. In the end she wrote him a stilted little note, thanking him for his kindness, and left it in the kitchen where he would be bound to see it.

Although she hated having to do it, she had no choice but to ask Claire if she would put her and Robbie up until her house was ready. Claire agreed without hesitation and went out of her way to make them both feel welcome. Laura knew that her friend was curious about what had happened but she couldn't bring herself to talk about it. Just the thought that Mark believed her capable of being so deceitful was more than she could bear— she certainly didn't want to discuss it.

By the end of the week Laura was close to despair. It was hard to put on a brave face when she got back to Claire's that night. It had been a particularly bad day because she'd seen Mark several times and he'd been very distant. Added to that, Cathy had been particularly obnoxious, taking her to task at every opportunity she got. Laura had reached the point where she'd started to think it might be better if she handed in her notice because she couldn't take much more.

Claire took one look at her dejected face as she opened the front door and sighed heavily. 'Look, tell me to mind my own business if you want, but what's wrong, Laura? It's obvious that you're upset, and it doesn't take much to work out that it's got something to do with Mark. Can't you tell me what's happened? It might help.'

'I don't think anything can help. It's like some sort of horrible nightmare....' She broke off as tears began to stream down her face. She was barely aware of what was happening as Claire chivvied her into the sitting-room and made her sit down.

'Come on, tell me what's wrong, love. I don't want to pry but I can't bear to see you like this,' Claire said worriedly, patting Laura's hand.

Suddenly Laura knew that she had to get it all off her chest. She told Claire everything. When she'd finished, Claire shook her head.

'I can't understand how anyone could be so nasty! I've heard rumours about that Cathy Williams, but even so…' She sighed. 'But what is more important is Mark and what he believes—although I could shake him for being such an idiot! How on earth could he think that you were trying to take him for all you could get?'

'Because he doesn't know me all that well. Everything happened so fast…' Laura tailed off and gulped.

'Hit you both for six, didn't it?' Claire smiled as she saw Laura blush. 'I could tell from the word go that Mark was smitten with you, but I wasn't sure you were ready for another relationship, even though I tried to spur you on!'

'I didn't think I was,' she confessed quietly. 'I certainly wasn't looking for one. At first I felt so guilty and tried to deny my own feelings.'

'And now?'

Laura smiled, although her eyes were sad. 'Now I know that I'm in love with Mark, but that still doesn't change the fact that there isn't a future for us.'

'You mean because of what's happened? Look, Laura, I'm sure that Mark just needs time to think this all through. Falling in love with you has obviously hit him hard because it seems to me as though a few of his brain cells must have short-circuited!' Claire's tone was wry. 'But once he realises the mistake he's made, he'll come to his senses.'

Laura shook her head. 'There isn't going to be a happy-ever-after for Mark and me. There can't be.'

'But you said that you've got over your guilt about Ian and that you love him!' Claire exclaimed.

'I have and I do. But it still isn't going to happen.' Laura took a deep breath as she felt the pain hit her afresh. 'Mark loves children and he would make a wonderful father.'

'So? That seems like a plus factor from where I'm sitting. I mean, I've seen how marvellous he is with Robbie.…'

'Yes, he is. But don't you see that it's Robbie who's the stumbling block in all this? How can I expect Mark to take on the responsibility of caring for Robbie? It's difficult enough for anyone to take on somebody else's child, let alone when it's a child with handicaps!'

She shook her head. 'It wouldn't be fair. Not when we could never have children of our own. That's a risk I can't take. I would be denying Mark a normal family life and the children he longs for. I just can't do it.'

'But there's no proof that you would have a second Down's child! You know the odds better than I do, Laura. For someone of your age—'

'It shouldn't happen?' She laughed flatly. 'Maybe not, but it did. Don't get me wrong. I love Robbie and I wouldn't want to be without him. But would it be right to run the risk of having another child like him and spoiling all Mark's dreams? I don't think so.'

Claire shook her head. 'I still think you're wrong but it's a decision only you can make at the end of the day. I shall just keep my fingers crossed that you'll come to your senses…both of you…before it's too late!'

She got up and grimaced. 'Oh, that wretched twinge is back again. I've had it on and off all afternoon long.'

She rubbed the small of her back then sighed. 'Still, not long now and then Braxton-Hicks and his rotten contractions can go take a running jump! Right, Sean is on lates today and won't be back till eleven. Why don't we have something to eat then get ourselves a video to watch? Something nice and light, not one of those all-action movies the boys love!'

'Sounds good to me.' Laura managed to smile, knowing that Claire was doing her best to cheer her up. She got up and hugged her, laughing at the effort it took to get her arms around Claire. 'It's great to have friends like you, even though there does seem to be an awful lot of you at the moment!'

'Cheeky monkey!' Claire laughed as she led the way from the room more at a waddle than a walk. She seemed to be finding it a lot more difficult to get around than she had the previous week, Laura realised, thinking back to the snowball fight and the very active part Claire had taken in it. That had been the night Mark had kissed her and admitted how he felt….

She sighed, consigning the memory to her mental waste bin. It certainly wouldn't help to think back over all the happy times at this point!

It was a pleasant evening after all. Once the children were in bed, she and Claire settled down to enjoy their film, a romantic comedy which had been a big hit at the box office. It helped keep her mind off her problems, which was a relief.

Sean telephoned just before eleven to say that he would be late as one of the junior doctors had been sent home with flu and they were short-staffed. They went up to bed soon after that as they were both tired, and Laura fell fast asleep almost as soon as her head hit the pillow. She was dreaming some complicated dream where she was running down a long corridor when a thumping on her bedroom door woke her.

'What is it?' she asked, jumping up and rushing to the door as she recognised Claire's voice calling her name. She put a steadying arm around her friend and helped her over to the bed.

'I think I'm in labour,' Claire panted, her face contorting with pain. She breathed deeply, waiting until the spasm had passed. 'My waters have broken so I don't think it's a false alarm this time.'

'Right, let's get you to the hospital straight away.' Laura tried to hide her concern but she couldn't deny that she was worried. Claire still had a month to go before the baby was due.

She quickly debated whether she should call an ambulance then decided that immediate action was called for as Claire gasped. Her contractions were coming so close together that it was obvious the baby would be born very shortly, and Laura didn't want to take any chances. The child would be far safer coming into the world in a well-equipped maternity unit rather than the bedroom!

The children were very excited when she woke them and told them what was happening. They hurriedly got dressed while she pulled on a pair of jeans and a sweater. Claire was in no state to change out of her nightclothes so a coat thrown over her robe was the solution.

Ben helped her get his mother into the front seat of the car, his small face full of concern as he saw that she was in pain. 'Does it hurt a lot, Mum?' he asked anxiously.

'Quite a lot,' Claire answered truthfully. She managed to smile as the spasm passed. 'But it will be worth it!'

Ben seemed happier after that. He got into the back of the car and made sure that his and Robbie's seat belts were fastened securely. Laura set off, thanking her lucky stars that the snow had almost gone. It took them very little time to reach the hospital and she rang the bell on the maternity-unit door to summon assistance.

Claire was taken straight to a delivery suite. She looked pale and drawn and a little apprehensive. 'It's so early for the Blimp to be born, isn't it?'

Laura patted her hand. 'Only a few weeks. Everything is going to be fine, Claire. In a short time you'll have your new baby.'

'Yes... Oh, but Sean doesn't know that I'm here...!'

'I'll go and tell him. Don't worry. You just concentrate on what needs to be done.' Laura kissed her cheek then stepped aside as the trolley was wheeled into the delivery room. Mentally crossing her fingers that things would go smoothly, she glanced down at the two children.

'Right, gang. First things first. Shall we go and find your daddy, Ben, and tell him what's happened?'

'Please!' The boy looked happier once he knew he would see his father. They left Maternity and trailed round the building to the entrance to A and E. Sean was just crossing the waiting area and he stopped dead when he saw them.

'Laura, what's happened?'

She grinned at him. 'Guess!'

'The baby? Really?' He sounded momentarily stunned before he quickly collected himself. 'Right, I'll get straight over there.'

'Can I come, too, Dad?' Ben asked in an anxious little voice.

'Of course you can.' Sean put his hand on his son's shoulder and smiled at him in a way that brought a lump to Laura's throat. There was such pride in that look, such love. How would it feel to see Mark look at his son that way? she couldn't help thinking, then realised sadly that it was something she would never experience.

It took a few minutes before Sean was free to leave the department. He kissed Laura quickly on the cheek on his way to the door. 'Thanks, Laura. I'm so glad you were there!'

'My pleasure!'

She smiled as she watched the man and boy hurry away. That both of them were excited about the impending birth was in little doubt. She sighed, feeling rather deflated now that the excitement was over. It was gone two o'clock in the morning—definitely time to go home to bed!

She looked round for Robbie, wondering where he'd got to. He'd been playing with the toys in the corner but he was nowhere in sight now. She went into the treatment area and quietly called his name, but he didn't appear from any of the cubicles.

Laura's heart skipped a beat as she hurried back to the waiting room but there was still no sign of him. A and E was almost deserted at this hour of the morning and there were just two other people there, an elderly man and woman.

The old lady beckoned and Laura hurried over to her. 'If you're looking for the little lad, he went in there.'

She pointed to the lift and Laura frowned. 'Are you sure?'

'Aye. I may be getting on but there's nowt wrong with me eyes,' the old lady assured her tetchily. 'He got into the lift while you were talking to that nice young doctor who bandaged me leg.'

She lifted a gnarled leg, resplendent with its newly applied crêpe bandage, and sighed. 'Waiting for an ambulance now. Could be 'ere all night at this rate.'

Laura paused just long enough to thank her before she hurried to the lift. Her heart was hammering as she realised that Robbie could be anywhere in the building by now! She checked the display over the lift doors and saw that it had stopped at the third floor, which was where Children's Med was situated. Was Robbie there?

It took her only a few seconds to reach the floor and she felt her knees go weak with relief when she spotted a small familiar figure happily playing in the corridor outside the ward.

'Robbie! Why did you wander off like that?' she exclaimed, hurrying over to him. 'It was very naughty of you. I was worried.'

'Me play with the boy,' Robbie said, smiling guilelessly up at her.

'Which boy?' Laura asked, looking around.

'Daniel,' Robbie informed her importantly. He pointed to the kitchen. 'He in there.'

Laura shook her head in exasperation. It had to be Daniel Glover, of course. Who else could it be, although what the child was doing wandering around at this hour was anyone's guess!

'Right, I think I'd better make sure young Daniel gets himself back to bed.' Taking a firm hold of Robbie's hand, she hurried to the kitchen and opened the door then gasped as she was met by a cloud of thick black smoke. Flames were licking towards the ceiling, spurting out from something on one of the counters which was on fire.

Laura couldn't tell what was burning and didn't waste time trying. Her main concern was Daniel. She turned to Robbie, bending down so that he would understand how serious the situation was.

'Robbie, go into the ward and tell one of the nurses there's a fire in the kitchen.'

Robbie nodded. He seemed quite happy to be sent on the errand and was obviously unaware of the danger. Laura, however, wasn't. The fire was starting to spread as it gained hold, rivulets of flame running along the joints in the ceiling tiles. The whole room would be alight soon and her heart turned over at the thought of the child who was trapped in there.

'Daniel!' she shouted as she stepped inside the room. 'Where are you?'

There was no reply so she stumblingly made her way further into the room. The heat was growing more intense as the fire spread. Flames had danced down the curtains and were racing along the worktop like a red-hot river. Fumes and smoke stung her eyes, making it difficult to see, but she refused to give up until she was sure the child wasn't still in there.

'Daniel! Daniel!' she cried again, then coughed as she sucked in a lungful of smoke. The fire alarm was ringing in the background now, its shrill sound increasing her sense of urgency. When her foot caught on something lying on the floor she could have wept with relief as she realised it was the little boy.

She knelt beside him, her head swirling from lack of oxygen as she attempted to pick him up. He was sturdily built and quite big for his age, and she couldn't seem to lift him up from the floor. Summoning all her reserves, she tried again but she just didn't have the strength to pick him up. The acrid fumes were clogging her lungs now, making her head feel woozy, and she knew that she was going to pass out. Somehow she had to summon assistance before it was too late.

'Help! Someone, please, help me!'

The words were hardly out of her mouth when she felt herself being lifted into the air. In a daze she stared into a pair of familiar grey eyes, wondering if she were dreaming.

'Mark...?' She couldn't go on as a cough racked her.

'Don't try to talk, darling,' he ordered thickly, carrying her into the corridor. 'You're safe now. I've got you.'

'Daniel...' she began, struggling to make him understand, although it was an effort to speak. Her lungs seemed to be full of liquid fire, burning each time she tried to draw any air into them.

'Tom's got him. He'll be fine.' Mark's tone was so grim that her heart seemed to shrivel inside her. Would he ever forgive her for what he thought she'd done?

It seemed unlikely and she felt tears fill her eyes. Suddenly it was all too much to cope with, Mark's anger and the fire. She turned her face into his chest so that he couldn't see her tears. She was vaguely aware of other people milling about as he carried her along the corridor...firemen, staff, some of the children...

She gasped, struggling frantically to be put down. 'Robbie! Where is he? I have to find him....'

'He's fine, Laura. Madge Bickerstaffe has him. Everyone is safe.'

Mark didn't falter, looking neither to left nor right as he carried on walking, and the crowd parted as though by magic to let him through. Laura had no idea where he was taking her and didn't ask. It didn't seem to matter so long as Robbie and Daniel and the other children were safe.

Mark kicked open the door to the doctors' lounge with scant regard for the paintwork. Putting Laura down on one of the battered old couches, he went straight to the phone. His tone was terse to the point of rudeness as he spoke into the receiver.

'I want oxygen brought to the doctors' lounge immediately. And tell James Kershaw to get down here as fast as he can.'

He replaced the receiver then came back to the couch and

stared down at her with an expression on his face she found impossible to interpret. She closed her eyes in sudden agony, wondering why she was even bothering to work out what he was thinking. In the past few awful days, Mark had made it only too clear what he thought of her!

'If you ever do anything like that to me again, Laura, I promise you that I won't be held responsible for my actions! I thought I'd lost you.'

Her eyes flew open as she heard the anguish in his voice and she felt her heart lurch to a stop. She didn't want to believe what her eyes were telling her because if she was wrong then it was going to be too painful....

She wet her lips but her voice sounded so thin and cracked when it emerged that she barely recognised it. 'W-would it have mattered, Mark?'

'Of course it would!' He sank down onto the cushion beside her and dragged her into his arms, holding her so tightly that she could feel his heart pounding beneath her breasts. 'Don't you know how much I love you, Laura? Don't you realise that you're the most precious thing in the whole world to me?'

Her eyes misted as she heard what he said. It was more than she could have hoped for in view of what had happened. Had he realised at last that she'd never tried to deceive him?

Her body shook because the answer was so important to her that she hardly dared ask him. 'But what about the other day and what...what you said?' She couldn't bring herself to repeat the accusations he'd made, didn't need to as she heard him groan.

'I was hurt and confused and I should be shot for saying something like that to you, my love! But I've come to my senses now.'

He tipped her head up so that he could look into her eyes, and she felt her pulse leap as she saw the sincerity in his. There was no doubting that he meant every word he said. 'I know you didn't make love to me for any reason other than it was the right thing to do. I know that you weren't trying to find yourself a meal ticket because it would never enter your head to do such a thing.'

He took a deep breath and his voice seemed to grate with a new depth. 'I know that I love you, Laura. That I need you. That

I can't face the thought of a future without you in it. I know all that but I don't know how you feel.'

She bit her lip as the old fears resurfaced for a moment. Yet as she looked into Mark's eyes she knew that she was lost. Right or wrong, she couldn't lie to him about something so important!

'I love you, too, Mark,' she admitted softly. She smiled as she raised her hand and cupped his cheek. 'I love you so much that it hurts!'

'Oh, darling!'

His lips were hungry and full of passion yet the kiss was laced with that tenderness which was such an intrinsic part of him. Laura responded blindly, willingly, but it was over all too soon.

Mark determinedly set her away from him, although she could see lines of strain bracketing his mouth. 'No, I can't do this!'

'Do what? Kiss me?'

She couldn't hide her surprise and she heard him laugh. There was a wicked gleam in his eyes but it didn't disguise all the other things she could see there as well.

'Uh-huh. It would be totally unethical to take advantage of a sick woman!' He looked round as a knock came at the door, sparing her from having to think up a suitable retort. 'That will be the cavalry, I expect. We shall continue this later—when you're in a fit state.'

He treated her to a smile which almost made her melt, then turned to greet the dark-haired man who had put his head round the door. 'Glad you could make it, James. Laura has been playing the heroine and I want you to check her over. She must have inhaled a lot of smoke in that kitchen.'

'Mmm, I heard you'd had a bit of a fire.' James Kershaw, the senior registrar on the chest ward, grinned as he came over to the couch. 'Hi, Laura. From the look of you, you don't appear to be suffering too many ill effects from your escapades, although I'll need to keep you in for observation just to be on the safe side.'

He glanced at Mark and winked. 'A bit of my skill and a large dose of TLC and she should be right as rain tomorrow.'

'Well, I'm more than willing to provide the TLC, although maybe it would be better to wait until she's discharged from your ward, James. We might raise a few eyebrows if I got too carried away with my role!'

James laughed as Laura blushed furiously, although her heart was behaving shamelessly at the thought of the tender loving care Mark intended to dole out!

A nurse appeared just then with a wheelchair, and Mark helped her up from the couch. Within a very short time Laura found herself sitting in the chair, an oxygen mask over her nose and mouth assisting her breathing.

Mark dropped a kiss onto her forehead, totally unconcerned by the amused glances James and the nurse exchanged. 'Just take it easy and rest, darling. I'll be in to see you tomorrow morning. Now, I'd better collect Robbie and take him home.'

Laura's eyes said what she couldn't over the mask, and he squeezed her hand. They didn't need words, she realised, her heart overflowing as she saw the love in his eyes. They didn't need anything so mundane to say what needed to be said. Her lungs might be suffering but her heart felt better than it had felt for ages!

She turned to wave before she was wheeled into the lift and felt herself fill up with emotion when she saw him standing there, holding Robbie's hand. They looked so right somehow, as though they were meant to be together. Maybe they were. Love had a knack of overcoming all kinds of obstacles. Suddenly she knew that her fears were just that, fears, not realities. As long as she and Mark were together, they could work *anything* out!

EPILOGUE

TWO MONTHS LATER...

'So, what do you think? Is it or isn't it just perfect?'

Mark made no attempt to hide his delight, and Laura smiled. He'd been very secretive ever since they'd set off that morning, telling her that he had something he wanted to show her and that it was a surprise. She'd been on pins as they'd driven across town, wondering what it could be, but she'd never dreamed it would be anything as wonderful as this!

'It's beautiful…really lovely, but—'

'But me no buts, as the saying goes!' He kissed the tip of her nose then took hold of her hand. 'Just tell me that you would love to live here as much as I would.'

'Of course I would! Who wouldn't?' She took a deep breath as she stared at the exquisite little stone cottage in front of them. Sometimes she felt that she should pinch herself to make sure she wasn't dreaming because the past two months had been, quite simply, the best time of her life.

When she'd left hospital after being given the all-clear after the fire, she'd moved straight back into Mark's flat. He'd insisted and, frankly, Laura had seen no reason not to. She'd wanted to be with him as much as he'd wanted her there, so what would have been the point in waiting?

However, it had soon become apparent that living in the flat would have to be a temporary measure as it had simply been too crowded with the three of them there. It had been Mark who'd suggested that she should think about selling her house. He would sell his flat and they would buy another property together.

Laura had agreed without hesitation. It was time to move on and build a new life for herself. She would never forget Ian and would always cherish the time they'd had together, but she couldn't live in the past and waste the future, the future she and Mark were planning together.

With them both working, and looking after Robbie in their free time, it hadn't been easy to go house-hunting so she'd never suspected that *this* was the surprise Mark had had in store for her. Now she turned to him with a mock-ferocious scowl.

'How come you managed to find this place without saying anything to me?' she demanded.

'Oh, I have my ways!' He pulled her into his arms and kissed her, grinning as he felt her immediate response. He rubbed his lips up the side of her cheek, let them drift to the soft curls at her temples, let them linger…

Laura pulled back and glared at him, although her heart was beating so hard that he must have heard it. 'You are *not* going to sidetrack me this time, Mark Dawson!'

'I see. Well, if I can't have my wicked way with you, I suppose I'll have to tell you the whole story.' He smiled as he took hold of her hand again and led her up the path to the door of the cottage, where he produced a large iron key. 'Let's go inside and make ourselves comfortable first, though.'

'But won't the owners mind…?' she began, and heard him chuckle. She turned to face him, her hands on her hips. 'Come on, you wretched man, tell me what's going on!'

Mark led the way inside and walked right to the centre of the first room they came to. He took a long look around before he spoke. 'The owners won't mind because we're the new owners, Laura. Or we shall be if you decide you want the cottage. It belongs to Tom Hartley but he's decided to sell it and has given us first refusal.'

'Really?' Laura gulped. She looked round in a daze, taking stock of the oak beams and polished wooden floor, the diamond-paned window which gave a wonderful view of the river. 'I don't know how he can bear to sell it,' she exclaimed.

Mark shrugged, although his expression was momentarily sombre. 'With Tom going to Boston on the exchange pro-gramme, he won't have any need of the place. He was thinking about renting it out but suddenly decided that he would sell up as he isn't sure he wants to come back here.'

Laura sighed as she went to the window. 'Because of him and Rachel splitting up, you mean?'

'Probably. I wish things could have worked out for them but Rachel seems to think it would be impossible in view of Bethany's animosity towards Tom. Even though she's slowly getting used to the artificial limb, it can't be easy for the poor kid, I don't suppose,' he added.

'And, typically, Rachel has put Bethany's feelings first.' Laura sighed then shrugged philosophically. 'Well, only Rachel can decide what she must do, even though I wish things could have worked out for her and Tom. However, if Tom is set on selling the cottage then I can't think of anywhere I would like to live more. Robbie will just love it here!'

'Won't he just?' Mark smiled as he slid his arms around her waist. He nuzzled the nape of her neck with a loving kiss then let his chin rest on the top of her head. 'This is the perfect spot for children, Laura.'

She heard the question in his voice and took a deep breath. They had talked through her fears at length, and talking about the problem had clarified her feelings and helped her put them into perspective. 'It would. When we start a family of our own, there'll be plenty of space for them to play.' She turned into his arms and kissed him quickly. 'However, there's one very important thing we need to decide first.'

Mark's face darkened with momentary pain. 'Darling, you aren't still worried about having another handicapped child, are you? You know what Niall Gillespie said—that the chances of you having another Down's child are very remote and that you'll be offered all kinds of tests.'

He brushed a kiss over her mouth, although he was still frowning when he drew back. 'And you know how I feel, that I would love our child unconditionally, just as I love Robbie.'

'I know.' She slid her arms around his waist and hugged him, wondering how she'd been so lucky as to find such a wonderful man as him.

'So what is it, then? I love you, you love me, we love each other—what more do we need?'

Laura laughed softly as he calmly dismissed the idea of there being any problems in the way of their happiness. 'Nothing, except that I'm a bit old-fashioned in some respects. I want us to be married before we have this great big family you're planning, Mark Dawson. Is that a problem?'

'Not from where I'm standing. In fact, I'm way ahead of you.'

He suddenly dropped onto one knee, his expression both tender and comical as he looked up at her. 'Will you do me the honour of marrying me, Laura?' He fumbled in his pocket and withdrew a small velvet box, opening the lid with a flourish. 'As an added inducement, I bought you this.'

Laura gasped. 'This' turned out to be the most exquisite solitaire diamond ring she had ever seen! She couldn't think of a thing to say as Mark rose to his feet and took her hand. Easing the ring from its satin cushion, he slid it onto the third finger of her left hand and, of course, it was a perfect fit! Raising her hand to his lips, he kissed her knuckles and there was no hint of teasing in his voice now.

'I want this ring to be a symbol of how much I love you, Laura. I want you to know that finding you has made my life complete.'

'Oh, Mark!'

She kissed him, tears of joy and happiness streaming down her face. She laughed as he handed her his handkerchief.

'Thanks! Silly to cry when you're so happy, isn't it? The ring is just lovely and, yes, I'll marry you. I can't think of anything I want more. I feel the same about you, that finding you has made my world complete.'

She blew her nose then laughed again. 'Wait until Robbie finds out about this. He loves weddings!'

'Oh, he already knows,' Mark informed her airily. He grinned when she opened her mouth. 'I explained it to him this morning on the way to Claire's. I expect she and Sean know all about it by now, not to mention Ben and little Amy, although maybe the baby won't find the news all *that* exciting.'

'You did? And they all know? But…but you didn't know if I would say yes…' she began, but he just grinned.

'Didn't I?' He hugged her close, stopping her from saying anything else in the most satisfying way possible. His eyes were shimmering when they drew apart, full of love and a wealth of tenderness. 'I know how much you love me, Laura. That isn't bragging or being blasé, just a statement of fact.'

'Mmm, and to think that a couple of months ago you were worried that I was only after a free meal ticket,' she teased, loving the fact that they could now joke about it.

'I still can't believe that I was such an idiot! Although I had come to my senses—and *before* the fire, I might add.'

'Had you?' A frown puckered her brow.

He sighed as he led her to the sofa. 'Yes. I know we haven't really spoken about this since then. We didn't need to because you realised that I knew I'd been wrong.'

His face darkened. 'I should have guessed that Cathy had been causing trouble, but I was just so shocked when I overheard what you said that day that I couldn't seem to think straight. I suppose it had something to do with how fast it had all happened. I never expected to fall in love virtually at first sight, but that's what happened when I met you.'

'Was it?' Laura smiled smugly at him.

'You know it was!' he retorted with a rueful laugh. 'You dropped into my arms that first morning and from then on I was putty in your dainty little hands!' He kissed her quickly then drew back, a slight frown marring his brow.

'When we made love that first time it was so wonderful that it felt like a dream. And yet the following morning I sensed that you were troubled by what we'd done. I tried to dismiss your fears because I couldn't understand how you could have any reservations. Then I overheard what you said to Cathy and it made me wonder if I'd been deluding myself all along. It knocked me totally off balance for a few days so that I was no longer sure of anything any more.'

'Oh, Mark.' She heard the pain in his voice and her heart ached at what he must have gone through. 'The only reservations I had by that stage were about hurting you. I…I just thought that you deserved better than what I could give you. It worried me that I might end up ruining your life. Then Cathy began making all sorts of spiteful comments and I knew that I couldn't let her get away with them. I hurled all her horrible allegations back at her, only you overheard and misunderstood. I don't think I shall ever forgive myself for that!'

'You must!' His tone was urgent. 'It was just a silly mix-up and it's all over and done with now. I don't want you to think about it ever again. Promise?'

'Yes, if that's what you want.' Laura kissed him tenderly then drew back with a sigh. 'But I have to admit that I'm not sorry Cathy left.'

'I don't think any of us were. Once everyone realised that Cathy had been spreading a pack of lies about you being incompetent, nobody had any time for her.' Mark's tone was grim. 'She did the right thing by resigning. Deliberately withholding information about Bethany so that she could get you into trouble was way out of order. Fiona Watts told me that Cathy would have been dismissed if she hadn't chosen to go.'

'It's incredible to think that anyone could be so spiteful, isn't it? Thank heavens that Daniel Glover happened to be outside the office that day and overheard me telling Cathy that Bethany was in pain and that I was worried about it being a neuroma.'

'I know. He asked Madge what a neuroma was that night and told her what he'd heard when she queried why he wanted to know. It was just a pity that Madge was off duty the next few nights so that it didn't come to light sooner.' Mark laughed ruefully. 'That boy has some good points even if he did nearly manage to burn the place down!'

'He didn't mean to, though.' Laura found herself defending the child—it was thanks to Daniel that her name had been cleared. Rachel had apologised as soon as she'd realised what Cathy had done, and the rest of the staff were back to their usual friendly selves. She couldn't help feeling grateful to Daniel, despite the chaos he'd caused!

'Evidently, he'd gone into the kitchen to make some toast for himself and Tim,' she explained with a smile. 'The pair of them had planned the whole thing like an SAS operation. They waited until the night staff were going for their breaks then Tim kept Madge occupied by pretending to feel sick while Daniel slipped out of the ward. The intention was for Daniel to go out of the building via A and E, which is the one door not locked at night, and find something to take back as proof that his mission had been successful.'

'Only when he reached A and E he spotted you there!' Mark laughed. 'It must have given him a shock but Daniel, being Daniel, wasn't deterred. He took Robbie back upstairs with him and left him to keep watch while he made himself and Tim the toast as a kind of second-best option.'

'Correct. And there wouldn't have been a problem if he hadn't climbed onto a chair to reach the biscuit box. When the chair tipped over, he hit his head and managed to drop the plastic box on top of the toaster, where it caught fire!' Laura sighed. 'What a child! I don't envy his poor mother, do you?'

'She probably thinks the sun shines out of him,' Mark declared, laughing. 'Most parents think their children are rather special. It's only natural. Oh, you get the odd ones, like Lisa Watson, who go against the grain, but it is unusual.'

'I was so pleased when the police traced Katie's father, weren't you?' she declared fervently. 'I believe the courts have awarded him custody and he's taking Katie back to Ireland with him to live.'

'Katie *and* the dog!' Mark laughed. 'Nice chap, and I'm sure that Katie will be well looked after from now on. See, he's another one who believes his child is special. I tell you, it's quite normal.'

'I suppose so.' Laura paused.

'What? You've got that brooding look on your face again. Not having doubts, are you? I mean, if you don't like this place, say so.' He stopped and his face closed up all of a sudden. 'Or if you aren't one hundred per cent sure about us….'

'I'm not!' She put her arms around his neck and kissed him hard. 'I'm one hundred and *fifty* per cent sure about us, Mark. But you have thought this all through, haven't you? What it will mean, sharing responsibility for Robbie?' There was a catch in her voice but she had to make certain that he wouldn't regret taking on such a huge commitment.

'I have. I know what I'm doing, Laura. It's what I want more than anything. Robbie is a *very* special child but, then, he has a very special mother….'

The rest of the sentence didn't get uttered. It didn't need to. Mark's kiss said everything she wanted to hear. As she wound her arms around his neck, Laura knew that things had turned out perfectly for all of them. Her very special child was going to have a very special father!

MILLS & BOON®

Makes any time special™

Mills & Boon publish 29 new titles every month. Select from...

Modern Romance™   Tender Romance™

Sensual Romance™

Medical Romance™   Historical Romance™

MAT2

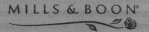

Medical Romance™

DOCTOR ON LOAN by *Marion Lennox*

When Christie saves Dr Hugo Tallent's life, he gives
her the help she badly needs to care for the isolated
Briman islanders. Soon he loves the island and Christie
too, but she won't leave—and there are reasons why
he can't stay...

A NURSE IN CRISIS by *Lilian Darcy*

Dr Marshall Irwin and Practice Nurse Aimee Hilliard
were head over heels in love with each other! But
when she was financially ruined, she couldn't tell Marsh.
How could she keep her independence *and* the man
she loved?

MEDIC ON APPROVAL by *Laura MacDonald*

Dr Aidan Lennox seems to disapprove of everything
about trainee GP Lindsay Henderson. So why is his
approval so important to her? Underneath, she knows
that it's far more than a matter of professional pride!

On sale 2nd March 2001

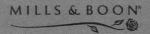

MILLS & BOON®

Medical Romance™

TOUCHED BY ANGELS *by Jennifer Taylor*

Dalverston General Hospital

Meg's healing touch could bring hope to the people of
Oncamba, but she despaired of ever getting through to
Jack Trent. As the image of his flighty ex-wife, she had
enough trouble convincing him she was up to the job in
hand...

PRACTISING PARTNERS *by Joanna Neil*

Helping Ross out at his busy practice suited Jenna, as
her great new job didn't start for several weeks. This
simple arrangement became complicated however
when she realised her feelings for Ross were as strong
as ever...

A FATHER FOR HER CHILD *by Barbara Hart*

Not wanting to spoil their happiness, Nurse Trudi
Younghouse has not told Dan that little Grace was a
surrogate baby. A conversation with Dan suggests he is
against surrogacy and Trudi is in a dilemma—should she
tell him at all?

On sale 2nd March 2001

0201/03b

FREE!

4 Books
and a surprise gift!

We would like to take this opportunity to thank you for reading this Mills & Boon® book by offering you the chance to take FOUR more specially selected titles from the Medical Romance™ series absolutely FREE! We're also making this offer to introduce you to the benefits of the Reader Service™—

- ★ FREE home delivery
- ★ FREE gifts and competitions
- ★ FREE monthly Newsletter
- ★ Books available before they're in the shops
- ★ Exclusive Reader Service discounts

Accepting these FREE books and gift places you under no obligation to buy; you may cancel at any time, even after receiving your free shipment. Simply complete your details below and return the entire page to the address below. *You don't even need a stamp!*

YES! Please send me 4 free Medical Romance books and a surprise gift. I understand that unless you hear from me, I will receive 6 superb new titles every month for just £2.49 each, postage and packing free. I am under no obligation to purchase any books and may cancel my subscription at any time. The free books and gift will be mine to keep in any case.

MIZEB

Ms/Mrs/Miss/Mr ....Initials ....
BLOCK CAPITALS PLEASE

Surname ....

Address ....

....

....Postcode ....

Send this whole page to:
UK: The Reader Service, FREEPOST CN81, Croydon, CR9 3WZ
EIRE: The Reader Service, PO Box 4546, Kilcock, County Kildare (stamp required)